NO SANCTUARY

A Provençal Mystery

Graeme Chambers

 **OzBooks**

An Imprint of Wembley Asset Management, LLC

This is a Pink Title, which means the net proceeds from the sale of this book will be donated to breast cancer research.

For my wonderful wife, Beth, who is the center of my universe, and my children who have each inspired some of the characters I write about. I love you guys. For the folks at Oso Sweet in Chadds Ford, whose friendship and warm aroma of baking and coffee fueled much of this book.

FORWARD

This book would not be possible without the wonderful people in Provence – even the police – who put up with my poor French and are otherwise full of warmth. Apologies to Roussillon which is not the sort of town that would or should see such terrible events. Many heartfelt thanks to Nicola Cassidy and Jules El-more for their plot suggestions, general developmental advice and overall encouragement. Thanks also to my dedicated copy editor Lynne Walker and digital wiz Matthew Revert, both of whom went above and beyond.

1

Mdm. Maxine Borrel entered her apartment and kicked the heavy door closed behind her. She threw her tennis bag down in the corner and snapped the deadbolt into place. She wasn't an attractive woman. Middle-aged with a severe, blocky face above a stocky torso and a large bosom that strained the white sleeveless tennis top, she had muscular, mannish arms with a dark bush of hair in the armpits. She strode to the bedroom, stripped and took a quick shower. As she toweled her short-cropped auburn hair dry she thought that, overall, it had been a satisfying day—taxing, but enjoyable and productive Perhaps she shouldn't have gone back to the office, but there had been things to do before tomorrow. She went out onto the patio and lit a Gauloises while she gazed into the darkness, going over in her mind the follow-up. Yes, it was time to call in the chit that had recently come into her possession. Who would have thought? And such a powerful man, soon to be a powerful ally. Then there were the brothers who were late with their payment. Her smile twisted as she contemplated her prize. She almost wished she had summoned that little Arab shit to the Cassis apartment. She could do with some release, but it had been late, tennis had been tiring. It was time to go to bed.

She stubbed out her cigarette and headed for the bedroom, not bothering to shut the patio door. There was a pleasant breeze bringing the scent of the Provençal terroir into the apartment. She slipped into bed and was drifting off when she started. She cocked her head briefly and then shook it. Probably a noise from outside coming through the open patio door. She plumped the pillow and froze. There it was again. Just a whisper of something, but in a prior life Maxine Borrel had become attuned to the sounds of stealth. She eased out of bed, opened the drawer in her nightstand and withdrew a large, clumsy-looking pistol. Then she crept silently to her bedroom door and listened. Nothing now. Perhaps it had been the wind in the drapes. Cautiously she edged out into the living room. Immediately something heavy chopped down on her wrist and the gun clattered to the floor where it exploded, the shot deafening in the close confines. Then she was thrust violently against the wall with a knife at her throat. She couldn't make out her assailant in the dark, but they were strong and Maxine Borrel could feel rage emanating from them. She was suddenly terrified. Could this be the Russians? She never thought they would go this far.

Long moments passed as they stood silently poised in a savage encounter. It was as if the attacker was waiting for something. Maxine Borrell felt her knees giving way. She made a sudden lunge to free herself, but this person was stronger. The knife sliced into her neck just a little and she gave a whimper and stopped struggling.

"Who are you? What do you want?" she whispered.

The reply sounded as though forced out through clenched teeth. "You don't know who I am, but I know you."

"Look, don't hurt me." Maxine Borrel could barely croak it out. She took several panicked breaths. "Did the Russians send you? I will do what they want. I have money."

Was that a guttural laugh?

Then her assailant leaned in close and whispered in her ear. Maxine Borrel's jaw went slack and her eyes widened in horror.

She gasped out, "Please, it wasn't me. I had no control... There were others. Please. I'm begging you."

When the knife eased away from her neck, she breathed a half sigh of relief. Then the blade entered her abdomen and was ripped violently upward. The pain was obscene. Her tortured scream pierced the night and she dropped into the puddle of her own blood that was already pooling on the floor. She tried feebly to cup her hands to her stomach in a vain attempt to staunch the bleeding, staring numbly down at the bloody gash in her silk pajamas. As her mind strained to grasp what had happened, and why, she vaguely registered her attacker go to the open patio doors and, standing in the shadows, look out. A babble of voices welled up outside. She tried to call for help, but she had no voice. Just a gurgling sensation in her throat. Her hands fell away limply. Things were getting dimmer. She was panting in short sharp breaths as the agony expanded inside her. In the long moments before she died, when the disbelief had receded, she had the time, but not the remorse, for deepest regret.

2

Max's eyes blinked open, confused in the gloom, trying to process the noise that had woken him. Could have been his recurring nightmare in which the sound was always the same—a bang, followed by the rending of tortured metal folding in on itself. As he explained it later to the police, roused from sleep, he couldn't be sure what the noise was, or whether it had even been real. Possibly someone getting an early jump on Bastille Day? He sat up, disgruntled. Without Emma beside him, he slept fitfully these days and often lay awake for hours in the night. So, he resented any disturbance.

He squinted at his phone and saw it was close to one a.m. With a sigh of resignation, he shuffled down the hall and up the half flight of stone steps to check on Luke. Fast asleep, curled in the fetal position around their new Viszla puppy, Dickens. All was quiet again, apart from the raucous, maraca-like sound of countless cicadas from the vegetation outside. Dickens looked up lazily, yawned and burrowed back down into Luke, his snout disappearing under the folds of the coverlet. Max leaned momentarily against the door frame to watch Luke sleep—something he had done often in his son's twelve years, but did more often since... That was when the scream pierced the night—a shriek that carried in its quaver terror, but to Max's ear, something else.

Max was used to listening to people plead, quarrel, lie, appease, and bully, paying attention to the timbre of a voice as much as what was said. He wasn't sure about the scream, but if he had to put a finger on it, he would have said shock or disbelief.

Luke's breathing hitched and he rolled over. Reluctantly alert now, Max hurried to the balcony and looked out into darkness. Here in the French countryside, away from the ambient luminescence of a city, the only light was a wedge of moon and a myriad of pinprick stars in the black canopy overhead. He strained his eyes for a sign of movement, anything. Only the cicada chorus broke the still night air. Then the hum of voices began to swell around the central courtyard, and figures backlit by yellow light appeared on the surrounding balconies. Three floors below, the swimming pool reflected the crescent moon. But other than these neighbors, hastily gathered in their nightclothes, there was nothing out of the ordinary to see. Max breathed in the heavy, warm air, redolent with lavender and wild thyme. It grew everywhere in this part of Provence, clinging in crevices and flowing down ancient stone walls. It was a smell that reminded him of times here with her. He could almost feel her arms around him from behind, her head leaning into the nape of his neck. Reflexively his eyes screwed shut—a bitter-sweet pain. Would it ever go away? Did he even want it to?

A scuffling sound from next door broke the moment, and he turned toward it, a soft sigh escaping his lips. Hans Beeker stood on the next balcony, bathed in moonlight, dressed only in a ribbon of pale Speedos that left little to the imagination and wearing a disheveled sleepiness. In a way, it was a welcome sight, the ridiculousness arresting Max's slide into self-pity. Hans leaned his considerable gut into the railing of the balcony, peering, as Max had done, all around the apartment complex. He turned, caught Max's eye, and tilted his head enquiringly. Max raised his hands, palm up. His gaze swept around the courtyard again, sensing what he couldn't see—trouble. It was the same sixth sense that had made him an exceptional lawyer. Something was not quite right.

Hans grunted and tossed his head towards his right where an elderly woman had emerged onto her balcony topless, her torso bathed in moonlight and her ample breasts sagging. Hans grimaced, rolling his eyes, and Max thought that was pretty rich coming from a fat Dutchman in a thong. He turned away, closed his eyes and breathed deeply again, trying to dispel the vision of both the half-naked Dutchman and the topless old woman from his mind. And then, a thought. Catty-corner on the top floor was an apartment in darkness—the only apartment not brought to life by that primal scream. At this time of the year, the town of Roussillon was very popular, and the twelve apartments in the Old Gendarmerie were in high demand. Max had been lucky to get a lease for the entire summer. Still, he did not know who was staying in the dark apartment, and they could, of course, be away for a night, or out very late, or deaf.

From the corner of his eye, Max saw Hans reach inside his Speedos and begin to scratch languidly. With a shake of his head, Max quickly focused elsewhere. Another image he didn't need haunting him.

His neighbors were starting to drift back inside, and lights winked off. A soft, sleep-laden woman's voice called in Dutch from behind Hans. *"Wat gebeurt er, Liefste?"* Something of a smattering polyglot, Max just about understood: *What's going on, dear?*

Hans threw his arms in the air and yawned. *"Niets."* Then he said something in Dutch that sounded a lot like go back to sleep, and with another grunt in Max's direction, he disappeared inside, and his light went out. Max checked on Luke again before sliding wearily back into his own bed. A sense of unease persisted and sleep evaded him. Perhaps it had been a mistake to come back here? There were too many memories of lazy breakfasts of coffee and pain au chocolat on the terrace in the fresh tranquility of the morning, reminders of long lunches sipping chilled wine while looking out over vineyards, and dinners of wine-fueled debates and laughter. But there were countless memories at home, too, and the cloying sympathy and pity there had only made things worse.

He finally drifted off only to be woken in the pre-dawn by Luke tapping him on the head.

He groaned. "Can't you get in the other side?"

"Your side is warmer."

Max hugged the pillow closer. "Go warm your own side."

Luke giggled, flashing a toothy grin. "I like your warm."

Max groaned again and rolled over, desperately clinging to the sleep he felt he had only just found. Luke clambered into his place bunched up against him like a backpack.

"Go back to sleep," Max pleaded.

Dickens bounced up and crowded his legs. He groaned again. "You too," he muttered, shoving the puppy over with his feet.

The sky was a strip of cornflower blue between the half-open white shutters when he woke again. Luke was snoring gently next to him. *How like his mother.* A lump formed in his throat. He rubbed grainy eyes and headed for the shower, and as he turned on the water, he suddenly recalled the sound of that scream in the night. Who had screamed like that? And why? The shower had a large window thrown open to the elements. He could admire a vista of ochre canyons cutting down to the flat farmland. It was his favorite thing about the apartment, almost like showering outside surrounded by the intoxicating smell of pine, lavender, and thyme. He lingered with his forehead against the warm terracotta wall, cool water sluicing over his bowed head as he breathed deeply and considered what to do with the day. It was tough filling his time now with no work and Luke in day camp. There were only so many times he could wander a street market or photograph chateaus and countryside. Perhaps he should get a bike and join a cycling club. But there was all that gear and those spandex tights in garish colors. Not him at all. Maybe he could take up horse riding again. If they were still here in the autumn, he would do that—not in the heat of summer. He remembered his stint in Texas and the dubious pleasure of sitting under the burning sun astride a sweating horse that attracted flying, biting insects. Could he take a wine-tasting course, or cheesemaking? Both would likely be in caves, a much more temperate environment. It was worth looking into. Or he could continue writing the book he had supposedly been working on since their last trip to Provence two years ago. None of it appealed, he had to admit. In truth, he was adrift in a sea of self-pity, not interested in much beyond Luke—a dangerous state of affairs.

Leaving Luke sleeping, he went to fetch breakfast from the local *boulangerie*. The elevator was new, part of the high-end renovation when the old police station had been turned into luxury apartments. The lobby, however, was original, with a high ceiling and a smooth flagstone floor carved into an undulant patina by the foot traffic of several centuries. The entrance, comprising floor-to-ceiling, arched wooden double doors that swung ponderously on huge iron hinges, evoked thoughts of battles and Knights Templar.

Max felt the morning sun on his skin as he stepped out onto the steps leading down to the cobbled street. He strolled along Rue des Bourgades, swinging his arms long, limbering, like a gymnast warming up, luxuriating in the slight chill radiating from the ancient, heavy stone and stucco walls that lined the street. Hues of ochre and rose spread before him beneath a cloudless sky. How he loved this feeling. It had been right to come here, to get away to a place with only good memories. He passed by the local cheese shop housed in a cave cut into the bedrock of the hill on which Roussillon sat. The swarthy young shopkeeper nodded at him. They saw each other most mornings around this time.

"Ça va?" asked Max.

"*Oui, ça va!*" The shopkeeper grinned, showing crooked, nicotine-stained teeth. "*Et vous?*"

Now that he was awake and outside, Max felt the glory of the morning. "*Pas mal, merci,*" he answered, smiling. Not bad at all.

The young man nodded again in good humor as he situated his chalkboard with today's offerings at the edge of the street. Max had never even heard of most of the cheeses it listed.

The simple exchange gave Max a feeling of belonging, of not being a tourist. It left him humming, brimming with the thought that, yes, if they wanted to, they could live here. He passed by Belle Vue Café perched on the very edge of a cliff. Opposite Belle Vue were the soaring ivy-clad walls of Restaurant Bernard, accessed by a steep tunnel of time-worn stone steps. Both restaurants had stunning views of the surrounding valley. Thinking ahead to dinner, he perused the daily specials at Bernard before turning right to cut across the adjacent parking lot.

Hans Beeker and his wife Angela were coming out of *la boulangerie* as he approached, their arms laden with more baguettes and pastries in paper bags than any two people could eat.

"Ah, Max." Hans held his arms wide as if to block or embrace. "How about last night?"

"Goedemorgen, Hans," replied Max, again calling upon the smattering of Dutch he had picked up while his brother had been living in Holland and trying not to notice that Angela's considerable assets were unrestrained beneath a thin white chemise. In truth, she didn't look at her best this morning—a little drawn. With the broken sleep from last night, he felt sure he didn't either.

"Hi, Angela," he said, staring purposefully into her green eyes and noting the shadows around them. She summoned a mischievous grin, showing dazzling white teeth. He felt sure she knew the effect she had on men.

"I wonder where that noise came from last night," Max mused.

Angela squinted at him. "Noise? Is that what you call that terrific scream?"

"I think you mean terrifying, *liefste*," offered Hans.

Angela wrinkled her nose. "Terrific, terrifying. The same meaning, no?"

Hans laughed, a barrel-chested beer hall gurgle. He had business in the UK, and his English was excellent, although heavily accented.

"Not really." He sounded apologetic. "Terrific means fantastic."

"Angela, you are right. Technically they mean the same," Max said. "But Hans is also right."

Hans swept his long blond hair back and scratched his scalp as Max continued. "Terrific used to mean terrifying, but these days it generally means something enormous, or something really good."

"Well," said Angela, "it was an enormous scream... and frightening."

They all laughed at that.

"And how about the bang before that?" asked Max.

Hans looked puzzled. "I only heard the scream."

"Hah!" cried Angela. "I heard the bang, but Hans sleeps like a bear in winter."

Max smiled. Hans did look like a bear—all hair and muscles. More like a Viking than a Dutchman.

"But she wouldn't get out of bed to investigate," Hans grumbled.

Angela pouted. "Well, I was tired, and I wasn't wearing any clothes."

Max had a sudden vision of Angela arriving on the next balcony in the nude—a far different vision than the old lady last night. His face felt suddenly warm.

"Got to go," he said quickly. "I must get coffee and get Luke to the academy."

"Ah, yes," Hans said, nodding.

Angela made a sympathetic face. "How is he doing?"

"He's good. The academy takes his mind off things, you know…"

Angela's hand settled gently on Max's bare arm. "We know." Then she brightened. "Come for dinner tonight! Luke and Hans can argue over football."

"Thanks," Max replied. "I'll see what he says and text you."

Angela patted his arm as he turned and stepped into the bakery. Madame Duclos rushed forward to serve him, almost elbowing her teenage daughter Claudine aside. Madame Duclos was a widow, a handsome woman in her mid-forties. She reminded Max of Juliette Binoche in the movie *Chocolat*.

"*Bonjour, Max.* Ça va?"

"*Oui, ça va, merci, Madame Duclos. Et vous?*" He had teetered on the brink of using the *tu* form of *you*, reserved for family, friends and children, but at the last moment had baulked. Normally blind to such things, even he was aware that Madame Duclos had taken a liking to him. She had invited him to dinner more than once, offering to have Claudine babysit Luke. As if Luke would allow such a thing… although Claudine's pale, pretty face framed in auburn hair would make Luke moon over her in a couple more years.

Disappointment stirred on the shopkeeper's face. "Please, call me Sophie," she said, and her daughter Claudine coughed, grinning slyly.

"Merci, Sophie," Max smiled. Then quickly turning to her daughter, he asked, "And you, Claudine, how are you?"

Claudine was learning English in school and liked to practice.

"I am good, thank you, Mr. Dempsey."

So cute. Made him wish he had a daughter, something he didn't often feel. Today's world for teenage girls seemed fraught with danger.

"Quatre croissants, s'il te plaît," he said, holding up four fingers, *"...Sophie."*

Sophie Duclos beamed at him as if she had won a prize. *"Au beurre ou nature,"* she asked, knowing full well that he always took butter croissants rather than plain.

"Au beurre," he said and watched as she took five croissants from a basket and placed them in a bag.

Seeing her slip in the extra croissant, Max said quickly, *"Non, Sophie, seulement quatre."*

"Mais non, Max. Luke must have much food for the football, *n'est-ce pas?* My, uh..." she frowned for a moment.

"Treat," Claudine finished for her.

"Oui, my treat."

Max gave in. *"Merci,* Sophie, you are very kind. *Très gentile."*

Sophie Duclos flapped her hands at him, coloring slightly. *"De rien, de rien."*

Someone coughed loudly behind him. The kind of cough that signaled impatience, and he turned to see a stern-faced old lady dressed in black staring coldly at them. Behind her, a line had formed out the door of the tiny bakery. Madame Duclos scowled at her.

Max grabbed his bag and deposited four euros on the counter, and Claudine scooped them up with a grin.

"Pardon," he said to the impatient old lady, sidling past. As he exited the door, he heard the old woman complain in French.

"I have been coming here for years and you don't give me free croissants."

Madame Duclos' reply was brusque. "Are you teaching my daughter English?"

The door shut behind him and Max chuckled. He loved freshly baked croissants but might have to start buying breakfast from the supermarket to avoid the fuss. As he walked back across the parking lot, past the pharmacy with its glowing sign in the shape of a green cross, he stared out across the valley where the abandoned red and gold ochre quarries gave way to vineyards and farmland. In the distance, shimmering in the sunlight, he could see the pale walls of the village of Goult, with its 12th-century castle. He had seen many sights in his lifetime, from the islands dotting the Caribbean to the Alps of Switzerland, but this was his favorite. He couldn't even say why. History of summers here during high school and college, memories of his honeymoon with Emma. Here, for him, was sanctuary from an otherwise hectic life. It offered peace, albeit sometimes transient. He glanced around the empty square which in another hour would be teeming with Asian tourists by the busload.

Three minutes later he was sitting on his balcony enjoying a different vista of gray-green hills clad in olive groves and scrub pine, when Luke slumped into the chair opposite. Dressed in his Mata jersey, shorts and football boots, he yawned as he reached for a croissant. "Ummm," he mumbled as he stuffed half of it into his mouth. Max perused him casually, looking for signs. All seemed well.

"Morning, sunshine."

"Hey, Dad. These croissants are terrific."

Max smiled, thinking back to his earlier conversation. "Are they enormous or terrifying?"

"Huh?"

"Just a joke. Glad you like them." Few things could compare with the buttery goodness of fresh croissants, apricot preserves and *café crème* while overlooking the Luberon. "Of course, you won't remember that I couldn't pay you to eat a croissant back at home…"

Max's voice tailed off, and he glanced anxiously at his son. He usually tried to avoid the subject of home.

"Never happened," said Luke, smearing apricot jam onto another pastry.

"And you wouldn't eat jam."

Luke looked at him skeptically. "Really Dad! Your memory is getting worse. Besides, that jam was just sad."

"That jam, that you didn't touch, was French. And you didn't drink juice," Max added as Luke drained the last of his orange juice.

Luke just rolled his eyes in that mocking way teenagers do. "Come on, Dad. We don't want to be late."

"Could I just finish my coffee and enjoy the view?"

A sudden loud splash announced the arrival of the elderly flasher from last night for her morning laps. She was a seventy-two-year-old Swedish woman and liked to swim au naturelle and then dry off in the sun.

Luke smirked. "Enjoy the view." He whistled, and Dickens bounded out from under the table where he had been snuffling up errant flakes of croissant.

Max jumped up, hastily draining his coffee. "She's early," he grumbled. Then he glanced speculatively across at the apartment that had remained in darkness the night before. Still no sign of life there, but the Englishman, Nash, was out on his balcony next door to it, watching the old woman swim. He saluted Max with his cup. *What's his story?* For a reason he couldn't explain, a sense of foreboding persisted and somehow Nash was involved, he felt sure of it.

"Come on, Dad."

Max shook himself. He just didn't like the man, that was all.

3

As they crossed the lobby, Hassan came out of the elevator wheeling a mop in a bucket and pushing a small floor polisher. He's early today, Max thought. Hassan paused uncertainly when he saw them, then smiled. He was a handsome young man with lustrous black hair and a smooth olive-skinned complexion. Max thought he was a little too stylish for a janitor. But Max liked him, because he always took the time to speak with them, often practicing his English. This morning, he appeared sweaty and out of sorts.

"Je comprend que vous avez de l'animation hier soir," the young man said, leaning on his machine and nodding at them.

Max wasn't surprised that Hassan had heard about the previous night's events. Everyone must have been discussing it by now.

"What excitement does he think we had, Dad?" Luke demanded in a tone that carried *Why didn't you tell me earlier?*

"Oh, there were some loud noises last night, which of course you slept right through."

"What kind of noises?" said Luke.

"Well, some kind of a bang and…" he flipped his palms up.

"Un hurlement de terreur, n'est-ce pas?" Hassan said in a melodramatic stage whisper.

Max grimaced. Luke gazed at Hassan excitedly, then back to his father.

"A scream of terror in the night and you didn't tell me?"

"You were asleep, and we haven't had time this morning. Your French is clearly improving. How do you know the word for scream?"

"*Hurlement de douleur.* Scream of pain. I've heard it at camp."

Max frowned at his son. "Do a lot of boys scream in pain at the academy?"

"Enough," Luke said, laughing. "They're French. They like to exaggerate." Max couldn't suppress a smile.

"And no one heard anything this morning, nothing strange?" Max said to Hassan.

Hassan shook his head. *"Rien."*

Max and Luke pushed through the heavy doors and onto the street before a thought struck Max.

"Wait a moment," he said, palming Luke to stay. He turned and went back in. Hassan was already buffing the floor. "The apartment on the top, on the southwest corner. Is it empty?"

Hassan held up a finger and switched the machine off. Max repeated his question. Hassan's eyes narrowed before he replied, "Apartment 4A? *Non, monsieur.*"

Max nodded. "Do you know who is staying there?"

"Oui, Monsieur Dempsey." Hassan sounded reluctant, as though he shouldn't be sharing this information. *"C'est Madame Borrell."*

"Do you know if she was home last night?"

Hassan shrugged.

Of course, thought Max. He leaves at six. "Okay, *d'accord.* If the police come here, I suggest you have them check it out."

Hassan stared at him for a moment then nodded.

As Max walked away, he noted that the buffing machine had not picked up again and felt Hassan's eyes follow him. Something is going on with that young man. His body language had seemed defensive, his voice a little too high and tight.

"So, about that scream," Luke said as soon as he hit the street, half-dragged by the straining dog.

"Patience, my son."

They retraced Max's short walk earlier to get to the car, which, unfortunately, was parked by the dumpsters containing the trash from the whole village.

"Phew," Luke said, pinching his nose and jerking Dickens' leash to keep him away from the decaying food scraps littering the ground. "It's almost as bad as the cheese you keep trying to get me to eat."

"I know, I know," said Max. "You hate the food here. Didn't stop you wolfing down the croissants though."

"Well, yes, but the meat is terrible."

"Sorry they don't have a Freddy's burger joint here. Your mother and I obviously spoiled you, eating out back in the States."

At the mention of his mother a cloud passed over Luke's face. Max cursed internally. He had to stop doing that. But it was so hard not to speak of home, of their life before. It, she, kept intruding, and he half hoped she always would.

"You and Mom raised me fine," said Luke. His scrunched-up

face examined Max's face, and in that moment, Max realized that Luke was as worried about him as he was about Luke. Max smiled wanly and cupped the back of his son's neck, drawing him close.

"I do try with the food," murmured Luke.

"Once you crack pâté, you'll be eating like a local," said Max.

Luke grimaced. "Yuk. You don't even know what's in that."

"I don't want to know. It's delicious!"

"I'd sooner poke my eye out with a burnt stick," said Luke.

Max laughed. "Of course you would. All I can say is, jam."

"Never happened."

Their car was not your average rental but an iconic 1964 Citroën 2CV6 that had been fully restored and sprayed neon green. Emma would have hated the color. After years of driving luxury cars, the 2CV6's remorseless simplicity had appealed to Max. It felt very French. The fold-down windows, roll-up canvas top and dashboard umbrella gearshift, were, for Max, the quintessential Provençal car. He had bought it at a dealer the day after they landed, and he planned to take it back to the U.S. if and when they ever returned there. It reminded him of simpler times, bowling along through the south of France as a student. Times when he had no money and few responsibilities.

As they drove out of the village toward the soccer camp at Cavaillon, Max filled Luke in on the night's mystery noises.

"That's all I know," he said finally. "No immediate explanation."

"Probably one of the jerk Italian kids in apartment 2B," Luke said scathingly.

"Oh? What makes them jerks?"

"Their general behavior. They act like they are the princes of this place. They were probably just goofing around."

Max blew a sardonic puff from the side of his mouth. "This coming from Prince Luke!" He just stopped himself from adding, "As your mother called you."

"They support Juventus, which is pretty sad," said Luke. "Worse than Hans."

Max made his *Really?* face and then turned on their audiobook, *Gregor the Overlander.* He was glad that Luke seemed unperturbed by last night's disturbance. They settled into the comfortable silence of a driving routine they had established through years of school drop-offs and after-school activities while Emma was working. Dickens lay curled into a tight ball on the back seat.

Their route took them up the winding road that encircled the hilltop village of Gordes. It was a sight Max never tired of, the gray stone walls rising impossibly from the steep rock face in a series of terraces dotted with pencil-thin cypresses, the plains stretching out on all sides beneath the cerulean sky. The road was a steep, narrow incline clinging to the cliff face, made dangerous, or at least stressful to drive, by the reckless French drivers who thought nothing of taking the hairpin bends at seventy miles an hour, or overtaking when the road ahead was obscured. In fact, Max had learned the word *putain*, or whore, exactly in this connection, a word he tried not to use when Luke was in the car.

Today he had no appreciation for the marvelous view. He was stuck behind a tour bus that seemed too big for these roads, lumbering along the narrow incline. Behind him a red BMW sports car was riding his bumper, just waiting, he knew, for the merest glimpse of an opportunity to overtake him and squeeze into the stopping distance between him and the bus. Not for the first time he thought about forcing the *putain* to stop, getting out and giving them a piece of his mind. He had a lot of repressed anger, and they were putting the life of his son in danger. He knew first-hand what dangerous driving could do. It had already shattered their lives.

Fortunately, the bus turned right at the top of the hill, presumably headed towards the castle at the summit, or to Sénanque Abbey. Max turned left, accelerating down towards the flat agricultural land far below. It took only a minute before the BMW caught up on a straightaway and roared past into the face of oncoming traffic, causing horns to blare and Max to brake. As the car flashed by, he caught a glimpse of a young woman in designer shades and a business suit. Parisian probably. His lip curled and his middle finger itched.

"Speaking of food," said Max as he pulled into the football camp, "Mr. and Mrs. Beeker have invited us to dinner tonight."

"Ask Angela to make schnitzel, would you?"

Max frowned at his son. "You don't tell people what to cook when they invite you to dinner."

Luke gave him a pitying look. "Of course, you don't. But you can tell her I love her schnitzel and then she will make it. Honestly, Dad, call yourself a lawyer. There's Paul, got to go." And then he was gone.

They had only been here three weeks, but somehow everyone seemed to know their tragic story. People had taken to Luke, who was always popular back home. Max's fears that Luke would be shunned, or worse, bullied, as a foreigner, and an American at that, proved unfounded. Luke's skill with a soccer ball and his normally sunny disposition and ready grin had everyone, especially Angela, eating out of his hand.

Max massaged his unshaven face as he stared after his son, jostling among the group of young soccer players. He knew that underneath Luke's casual demeanor lurked the darkness they were trying to escape. He still wasn't sure that taking Luke away from family and friends in the U.S. had been the right move. At times, he was afraid he had put his own needs ahead of his son's. But right now, it seemed to be paying off. Without the presence of constant reminders of his mother, Luke appeared to be recovering as only children could.

Max leaned his head against his arm on the steering wheel. Ironically, the better Luke did, the lonelier Max felt in his pain, and not showing it to Luke took all his strength. Dickens jumped into the front seat and stood up to nuzzle his face. Max ruffled the puppy's ears and pushed him down into the passenger seat. He rubbed his forehead vigorously. Today would not be one of the days when he felt he couldn't go on.

The temperature had already climbed into the nineties. The old steamhorse, or *deux chevaux*, as the 2CV6 was popularly known on account of its lawnmower-like engine, had no air conditioning. Max rolled back the canvas top and folded down the windows. The one upgrade he had installed in the car was a set of excellent speakers and a USB port. Now he connected his phone and queued up Fleetwood Mac's *Rumours*.

Instead of returning west, he headed north to L'Isle-sur-la-Sorgue where he and Emma had found the antique filigree light that now hung in the hallway at home. They had spent a happy afternoon there poking around in the many antique and bric-a-brac shops. It was a bittersweet memory. As he drove, the air rushed through the car like a tepid hair dryer, bringing with it the sharp scent of the pine scrub that bordered the winding road and intermittently the fragrance of thyme or lavender, or the sweet smell of bordering peach orchards.

It was market day, and L'Isle-sur-la-Sorgue had a large, bustling outdoor market. Almost every town in the Luberon had a market day, but some, like Roussillon, had only a handful of stalls. This town had scores that lined the quayside along the Sorgue River and overflowed into the surrounding streets. It was a kaleidoscope of color. Stalls piled high with local melons and other colorful fruits vied with stalls displaying soaps of every hue and scent and stalls stacked with linens in bright Provençal colors. Max weaved a path along the first line of stalls, trying hard to stop Dickens from tangling his leash in his efforts to greet everyone they passed. Around him Max heard conversations in English, German, Italian and Dutch as well as languages he couldn't even recognize. His sense of smell was assailed first by the mingled citrusy and earthy odors of fresh produce, then the confused perfume of myriad colorful soaps, then the pungent aroma of the cheese stall, followed by the stench of the fish market and then his mother's Sunday afternoon smell of roasting chicken, each displacing the other as he came level.

It occurred to him that if he closed his eyes, he could have easily recognized the sequence of stalls, all except the seller of kitchen goods which added only the visual and tactile beauty of olive wood bowls and the Laguiole knives he coveted. Attracted by the seventy-eight Euro price placard, he stopped to look at them, admiring their slim, sinuous curves resembling, some would say, a lady's leg. There were stainless steel and bone handles of varying colors, but he was only interested in authentic olive wood. He picked one up and hefted it, feeling the balance. The typical honeybee was embossed at the end of the tang and the handle had the customary cross formed by small metal pins which, according to legend, had once been used by shepherds to pray to God. Disappointed, he laid the knife back down in its velvet-lined box. These knives were from a no-name fabricator, Laguiole just the region famous for these elegant knives. Even the cheap Asian manufacturers had co-opted the name. He wanted the authentic version, handcrafted through a one-hundred-and-nine-step process. One day he would treat himself to the original by Forge de Laguiole as a birthday present.

He took a table under an umbrella at the Café de France on the river and ordered *un grand café crème* from the young waitress who came over. Dickens slumped down in the shade under the table, his tongue lolling. Max's coffee arrived with a bowl of water for Dickens who alternated between lapping at the water and at the giggling young waitress's face as she bent down to rub him behind the ears.

To one side of the bistro, against a bright blue door set in a sun-drenched apricot wall, sat a middle-aged Romany woman strumming a battered Spanish guitar that seemed too big for her. She wore a broad-brimmed red felt hat festooned with ribbons, a long purple skirt with narrow yellow bands at the hem and an embroidered golden vest over a cream blouse. Her lined face was burnished by the sun and wind to the color of whiskey. She was singing "*C'est Si Bon*," one of Max's favorite French classics, in a voice that carried the smoky rasp of a bad Gauloises habit and an accent that wasn't local. Max smiled appreciatively at her, and she nodded and winked. He took out his Peter Mayle novel and with a contented sigh, sat back to enjoy the morning.

Ninety minutes and two *grand crèmes* later, Max rose and stretched. The lunch crowd was beginning to gather, and he didn't want to hog a table when he wasn't eating.

"*Si mignon,*" the gypsy said as Max placed a few Euros in her case.

"*Pardon?*" Max said, flustered.

"*Le chiot,*" she said with a throaty chuckle.

"Oh, the puppy. Yes, he is cute," Max said, relieved she was talking about the dog. "*Oui, très mignon, mais...*" Max searched his memory for the word mischievous.

"*Mais espiègle,*" she said, laughing again as she watched Dickens climbing into her guitar case and bent down to ruffle his head.

"*Oui,*" Max agreed. "*Très espiègle.* Come on, you." He jerked the leash and Dickens reluctantly left the attentions of the Romany lady.

An hour later Max pulled into a parking space opposite the dumpsters in Roussillon center. He was just in time to buy some local tomatoes before the adjacent cooperative farm store closed for lunch.

The woman behind the counter smiled when he walked through the door. *"Ah, salut, Max."*

"Bonjour, Beatrice. Tout va bien?"

Beatrice raised her arms above her head and stretched her lithe body like a cat basking in the sun. "I am great. How about you?"

She really did seem pretty great. Another attractive French woman—friendly, funny, intelligent and classy—just his type once upon a time.

Max smiled and lied. *"Moi aussi,* or at least I will be great when I have eaten some of these with a good pâté de campagne, cheese and a nice, chilled rosé."

He grabbed a paper bag and loaded it with vine-ripened tomatoes and picked up one of the honeydew melons that nearby Cavaillon was famous for.

"What cheese were you thinking?"

"I thought I would stop at *la fromagerie* for some Banon."

Beatrice made an appreciative face. *"Pas mal,* but have you tried the Brousse du Rove?"

Max wrinkled his nose. He was pretty sure the morning blackboard at the cheese shop had listed this cheese. *"Non.* What is it like?"

"Not so creamy as the Banon, but very fresh. Made from the milk of a Rove goat."

"A Rove goat?"

Beatrice's laugh tinkled. "They say, after a shipwreck, some Greek goats escaped and mated with local goats, et voilà, a Rove goat. There are not many of them about. The cheese, it can only last two or three days, so you cannot find it anywhere else."

Max grinned. "That sounds really local. *Bien sûr*, I will have to try it."

Beatrice reached to a shelf and placed a small pot on the counter. "I suggest it with some lavender honey."

"That sounds fantastic."

"Your lunch sounds *fantastique*," Beatrice said. Her eyes crinkled in amusement. "Should I close up the shop now? And join you?"

Max smiled wistfully. That was two women today who had openly flirted with him. Their advances brought up a range of emotions in him—disbelief that they were attracted to him, and the awful reminder that he was now single. Beatrice seemed to be testing the water, but she had just reminded him of the picnic lunches he had enjoyed with Emma looking out over the Provençal landscape. He could not, would not, escape the shadow of her loss. And each time another woman smiled at him that way and he was tempted to flirt, the devastating sense of loss, and guilt, bubbled to the surface. He would never be ready for another relationship.

Perhaps Beatrice had picked up on the sadness behind his smile, because before he could respond she said, "But, *malheureusement*, I have a meeting this afternoon. So, we must perhaps wait for another time?"

Feeling grateful, he nodded. "I would like that." And he would like to spend some no strings time with Beatrice. He could certainly use the company of a few more friends, especially when Hans and Angela left. That was going to leave a big hole. But however attractive Beatrice was, he just wasn't capable of fulfilling the promise held in her eyes a moment ago.

As he turned to leave, Beatrice said, "Oh, Max, don't you live in the Old Gendarmerie?"

Max paused in mid-stride and turned back. *"Oui."*

"There are lots of police there. Almost like old times when it housed the gendarmes. Perhaps your lunch won't be as peaceful as you think?"

"Merde," he muttered under his breath.

He knew it.

Something bad had happened last night. Why else would the police have arrived?

4

Capitaine Idrissa Jacques stood over the body of the woman in Apartment 4A, hands clasped in front of him, posed as if in prayer. Louis Dupre, his corpulent lieutenant, stood off to one side scraping his unshaved jawline. The medical examiner, Claude Picard, a tall, lean man with dark, wavy hair, was kneeling next to the corpse finishing his preliminary examination. He stood and rolled his neck and then his wide shoulders. Jacques heard several vertebrae pop.

"*Et?*"

Picard scrunched his nose. He swept his hand around indicating the burgundy blood puddle staining the rug under the body.

"Clearly, she was stabbed here. Looks like the blade entered the abdomen and was then ripped upwards with great force. Death would not have been immediate. If she was conscious, it would have been agonizing."

Jacques' eyebrows drew together. "But the neighbors all say they heard a shot."

The doctor's mouth turned down. "What can I tell you? There is no sign of a bullet wound."

"Time of death?"

The medical examiner took a deep breath and tilted his head as though smelling the air. "The air conditioning is on, so based on lividity and rigor, I would guess sometime in the early hours of this morning."

Voiced as though he was marshalling his thoughts, Dupre said, "So the same time as a gunshot was heard? Perhaps Borrell shot her attacker?"

Jacques glanced at the medical examiner, eyebrows raised.

"We will, of course, check for gunshot residue on the hands, but if she shot at the attacker, it looks like she missed." Picard swept his arms around the room where a cluster of people dressed in disposable white suits were processing the crime scene. "So far, no other blood and no gun."

"Make sure they check the walls and furniture for bullet holes," Capitaine Jacques said to no one in particular, still staring down thoughtfully at the body.

"Bien sûr," Dupre answered.

"Can we check all the residents and that concierge guy for gunshot residue, also?" said Jacques.

He already knew the answer and was irritated when Dupre pointed out the obvious.

"Not unless they agree to cooperate."

"Well, take a tech and see who agrees to cooperate," Jacques said impatiently. "Get written statements from everyone."

As Dupre left the apartment, he grabbed keys from the kitchen counter and flashed the BMW fob at Jacques. The captain was now beginning to get a sense of the victim from the valuables in the apartment, the plush furnishings, and the car.

After Dupre and Picard departed, Capitaine Jacques watched as the corpse was bagged and removed and then began to walk around the apartment. There was no other word for it but sumptuous. The living room walls were covered in burgundy and gold medallioned wallpaper and the furniture was heavy, carved mahogany. The gigantic area rug covering the clay tile floor looked like a Persian antique, now doubtless ruined by the pool of half-congealed blood. The twin couches adorned with tapestry throw pillows were tan leather. He ran his hand along the back of one. Soft as calfskin gloves.

One wall was covered in a floor-to-ceiling bookcase. The opposite wall showcased a large impressionist canvas portraying a Provençal market scene with a trio around a café table in the foreground. Jacques stared at it for a long moment. He could almost smell the aroma of the fruit on the stalls and hear the soft laughter of the woman as she leaned across the bistro table towards her companions, coffee cup almost at her lips. Capitaine Jacques studied the signature on the painting: *Deymonaz*—doubtless an expensive original.

The double doors onto the terrace were open, and he stepped out into the broiling heat. There were no flowers or plants like on other terraces, just a single all-weather wicker chair and a small matching bistro table. The only sign the victim spent any time out there was an ashtray overflowing with the remains of unfiltered cigarettes. He peered closely. They were all the same brand—Gauloises—nothing to suggest visitors. He surveyed the other apartments stacked on three sides around the swimming pool with a view on the fourth side of distant olive groves set into the hillside. It wasn't a big building, and he could see how a gunshot would have roused all the occupants and how, when they came to their balconies, they would all have been in plain sight of each other.

His lip curled. His gut told him this was going to be an unpleasant, difficult case. It always was when rich people were murdered. He wondered who the victim knew. Rich people always knew someone: the mayor, the police commissioner, a well-connected politician. Then the haranguing calls demanding quick results would start.

His eyes shifted to the distant white limestone peak of Mont Ventoux that looked like snow. He inhaled a long slow breath of scented air, sighing as he let it out. He should let the gendarmes handle this one. For a long moment he stood there, his eyes closed, pinching the bridge of his nose. Then, with another deep sigh and a shake of the head he re-entered the cool of the apartment and headed for the master bedroom.

Halting in the doorway, he folded his arms and surveyed the room. Now here was, well, a boudoir. Bright light poured in from a window framed in heavy damask drapes, but it was still a subdued room, made more so by the heavy, carved mahogany wooden bed and nightstands. The rumpled silk sheets on the unmade bed were ruby red and the coverlet was a masculine paisley in purples and greens. A tapestry armchair sat in one corner strewn with disrobed clothes. He paused as he spotted something half-hidden under the chair. With his foot he nudged aside the pile of clothes and saw a shoulder bag leaning against one of the chair legs. With latex-covered fingers he pried apart the lips of the bag and studied the contents. Apart from a sleek laptop that excited him, the rest looked pretty benign: a folded scarf and a small make-up bag. He called out, and when one of the techs entered the room, he thrust the bag into his hands.

"Get this to forensics. And the laptop goes to Arielle."

Jacques turned his attention back to the rest of the room. The closet was well-ordered and full of expensive designer clothing. He opened drawers in a desultory fashion, flicked through contents and hoped for anything to suggest a motive, a clue to the killer.

The adjacent bathroom was luxurious but offered no enlightenment either. There was nothing here as far as he could see. The techs may find something, or perhaps, by some miracle, one of the neighbors could shed some light.

5

As Max rounded the corner, he saw the street blocked by cars with flashing blue lights, seemingly with the entire gendarme complement and police contingent of Provence milling about. It was as if the Old Gendarmerie had reclaimed its past. He paused, taking in the scene. It must be something bad to bring out both divisions of the French dual policing system.

The Police Nationale was the civilian police force responsible for large towns and urban areas. The Gendarmes were under the control of the military and, among other things, had authority in the smaller towns and rural areas. But the two frequently overlapped, sometimes leading to an uncooperative battle for control. The Gendarmes looked more ominous, often dressed in black, military-style uniforms with berets, jackboots and webbing belts. Like movie stars, many wore dark glasses. Unlike movie stars, they were all armed, some carrying automatic weapons. From the body language of the many officers clustered around, it appeared to Max that whatever was going on, this situation might still be up for grabs.

Beyond a police cordon, Max could see Hassan standing in the street with a group of the Old Gendarmerie residents. On this side of the cordon, a crowd of onlookers, including a bus-load of Asian tourists taking photographs with expensive SLRs, blocked Max's way to the building. Max recalled the early days when he and Emma had stumbled upon this quiet hilltop town. Back then, there had been no building-size buses, no swarming tourist groups and no en-masse click, click, click of cameras. His general aversion to rubber-neckers and the demise of his much-savored plans for a quiet lunch brought out an anger that always seemed to be simmering.

Shouldering his way none too gently to the front of the crowd, he informed a young, overly muscled gendarme guarding the cordon that he lived in the building. The gendarme eyed him coolly, either because of his brusque tone or because he didn't think a Brit would, or should, be living in such a luxurious place.

Max gestured with his palms face up. *"Eh, bien?"* He lifted the tape as though to duck under, but the gendarme snapped an arm across him.

"Arrêt!" he barked. Then, in a manner that suggested complete indifference, the gendarme called over to a statuesque black man who was now speaking with a nervous-looking Hassan. *"Capitaine."*

The man turned his head at the summons. The captain reminded Max of an actor though he couldn't place the name. He was handsome with a strong jaw and a bald pate and dressed in an immaculate suit despite the oppressive heat. When Hassan saw Max, he gave a strained smile. To Max he looked like a panicked rabbit caught in a snare. Then Hassan leaned toward the captain and said something. As he spoke, the captain appraised Max from his sideways tilted head and rubbed his chin. Then he strode over, his face drawn into a saturnine frown.

He made no offer to shake hands but spoke peremptorily in heavily accented English.

"*Bonjour.* I am Capitaine Jacques of the Police Nationale."

He held up the tape so Max could duck under it, then flipped open a black notebook like a stenographer about to take dictation. "Your name is Max Dempsey?"

Max nodded.

"I understand you told Monsieur Aamara," the captain said, indicating Hassan with a wave of his hand, "to check apartment 4A."

Max frowned. "That's not exactly what I said. I said if the police came by, they should check the apartment."

"Tell me why you said that?"

Ever the lawyer, Max was reluctant to answer without knowing what was going on, especially to a surly policeman. And frankly, he resented being involved. "Has something happened?"

The captain scrutinized Max for a long moment, tapping his pen on his notebook, apparently struggling to decide how much to say or whether even to answer this foreigner. Max stared back, unconcerned. He had no obligation to tell a discourteous French policeman a thing. Eventually the policeman seemed to come to the same conclusion.

"A woman has been killed in that apartment."

Max winced. That explained the presence of both the gendarmes and the police. Probably a first in this iconic tourist town. He didn't know the victim at all, but she had seemed like a typical Parisian. Distant and superior. Not the sort to get herself murdered. He fleetingly wondered what she had done to deserve that. Did anyone ever deserve that? Thinking of the drunk who killed his wife, very possibly.

The captain's pen tapping became more strident. "So, I ask you again, why did you tell the concierge to have the police check that apartment?"

Max considered this for a moment. For some reason he was surprised Hassan had called the police. "Again, I didn't tell him to call you. I just thought someone might report the gunshot and scream in the middle of the night. And if the police came, they should take a look at 4A."

The policeman's eyes bored into his own. "And you didn't think to report the incident yourself."

Max grimaced. Perhaps he should have done so, but he really didn't want to be involved.

"I wasn't sure what I heard, and I left early to drive my son to Cavaillon."

"Well, monsieur. After you departed this morning, Monsieur Aamara went himself to check the apartment. When he found the door unlocked and when no one answered he let himself in. He says he found Madame Maxine Borrell dead. He called us, and so here we are to investigate. So, once more, why were you concerned about that particular apartment?"

"*Alors*," Max said, nodding. "The bang woke me. It woke everyone in the building. I thought maybe Bastille Day… but then there was a loud scream. We all went out onto our balconies, all except apartment 4A, which remained dark. Hassan said it was occupied so I wondered why they hadn't been woken as well."

"That is very observant of you," the policemen said, but it sounded more skeptical than complimentary.

Max shrugged.

The captain glanced at the open notebook in his hand. "I understand you are *Americain* and a lawyer."

Max smiled thinly. He didn't care for this man and his attitude. He was either Parisian or he had a giant chip on his shoulder. "I am a lawyer in America, but I am English."

Capitaine Jacques sniffed, and Max couldn't tell whether he disdained lawyers, Americans, or the English. Possibly all three.

The captain questioned Max further, but Max had nothing more to add. He had never even spoken to Madame Borrell. As the policeman turned away, Max could see his neighbors Hans and Angela over the man's shoulder. They were talking to the other Brit staying in the Old Gendarmerie, Jeremy Nash. He was a tall, slim man a little younger than Max, and Max wasn't a fan. He dressed like a dandy, often with an ascot tie and a cream panama, and between his drawling accent and the way he tilted his head back when he spoke, he always gave the impression he was looking down his long aquiline nose at you. Jeremy had been a former MP in England and had regularly featured in the newspapers for the outlandish things he said in parliament. He clearly thought a lot of himself.

"When do you plan to leave?" Capitaine Jacques asked, pausing in afterthought.

"I have the apartment until the middle of September," Max replied, "Then I will see."

"D'accord," the policeman said with another sniff. Then, abruptly, he walked away.

When they saw the captain moving away, Hans and Angela came over to Max.

"Can you believe it?" said Angela. "A murder in the apartments!"

"In a place like this, it's a bit of a shock," Max agreed.

"Scary," said Hans.

They stared at the policemen and gendarmes buzzing around.

"Any idea when we will get in?" Max asked.

Hans grunted. "You know how lazy and inefficient the French are," he said. "Could be hours."

Angela laughed. "Spoken like a true Nederlander."

"What?" Hans said defensively. "It's true. Besides, you are Nederlandse now."

Now? Max had always assumed Angela was Dutch. She spoke with a Dutch accent, and her large build was like most of the Dutch women he had encountered.

Angela must have seen his puzzled look and quickly explained, "I'm German, but I took Dutch nationality when I married Hans."

"Lucky you," Hans said, barking a laugh.

Angela scowled at him.

"Well, I guess that means my lunch plans have crapped out," said Max. "If we can't access the building."

"Crapped out?" Angela asked.

"Sorry, it's an American expression meaning to go to shit, to fail. I believe it has something to do with the casino game craps."

Angela clapped her hands. "I like it. Crapped out. I must remember. Crapped out." It sounded charming in her enthusiastic Dutch accent.

"Did your lunch plans involve wine?" Hans asked.

"Bien sûr."

"Well then it is a good thing that there is a pizzeria around the corner. Come, let's go eat. All this excitement is making me hungry."

It wouldn't be quite the peaceful meal Max had been looking forward to. He liked this couple, but with Hans' boisterous Bavarian biergarten personality and Angela's insatiable quizzing of all things English, they could be a little too full-on. And pizza wasn't up to pâté and cheese with fresh produce.

"Okay," he said with a sigh. "Let's do it."

Sitting under the green and white striped awning on the top terrace of Café de L'Ocrier, they watched the Asian tourists with much amusement and no little degree of annoyance. Bussed in by the thousands in monster luxury coaches that blocked traffic as they struggled around the tight bends and through the narrow streets, their arrival was met with derision by the locals too.

Despite the oppressive heat, the male tourists toted twenty pounds of expensive camera equipment while the women, dressed like runway models, posed vampishly for multiple pictures by every old doorway, fountain and set of stone steps. Angela laughed as they watched one tourist recline in a backbreaking position on a low stone wall that looked out on the backdrop of ochre canyons.

"She should be careful she doesn't fall backwards!" she said with a snicker that suggested she would find that highly entertaining.

"I saw you talking to Jeremy Nash," Max said.

"Hah!" Angela sniffed, turning away from the tourist watching. "That man. I think he came over just for a closer look at my boobs. He stared at them the whole time we were talking."

Hans laughed. "But darling. You go topless on the beach. Lots of men have stared at your breasts. They are, after all," he swept one meaty hand across in front of her, "magnificent. Eh, Max?"

Max's eyes automatically drifted to the subject of discussion before he jerked them up into Angela's face and tried to forgive himself for thinking he would like to have seen her at the beach. "Ah, well," he faltered, reddening. He had never complimented a woman on her breasts to her face. "They are *incroyable*," he finally said, deciding that, in French, he could be forgiven.

"Why, thank you, Max," Angela said and blew him a kiss.

"You see," said Hans.

Angela gave him a sideways glance. "It's not the same. That other Englishman is..." she scrunched her face and finally gave up, tossing out her hands, "*slonzig*."

Max flicked his eyebrows at Hans.

"Sleazy," Hans said.

"Yes, sleazy," agreed Angela. "There is something… ach," she tossed her hands out again, "sinister."

She looked at Hans.

"It's the same," Hans and Max said in unison. "Sinister."

Angela clapped her hands. "Well, there is something sinister about him."

"What did he want?" asked Max.

"Just to bluster about the incompetence of the French police and how he had friends in high places if they caused him any problems," Hans said.

Max frowned. "And the English wonder why the rest of Europe don't much like them."

Angela laughed. "But you are English, Max, no?"

Max looked down his nose at her. "By birth only. Shame on you. Remember I was raised in Australia."

She reached across the table and put a cool hand on his bare arm. It reminded him of Emma's touch. "Never mind," she said, winking at Hans. "We can't all be Nederlanders."

"True," said Max with a smile. "So, friends in high places, huh? Not surprising, considering his political background."

"Apparently his friend owns a bastide near Ménerbes, and Jeremy comes every year for two weeks' rock climbing," said Angela.

"Rock climbing!" Hans and Max blurted in unison.

"Yes. You wouldn't know it to look at him, would you?"

"That's an understatement. He looks like he couldn't claw his way out of a wet paper bag," Max said.

Hans' face creased in a sardonic grin. "Do you think he still wears the hat and cravat when he climbs?"

"How do you English say?" Angela said, pausing to think. "Ah, yes, don't judge a book by its cover. I have seen him at the pool, and he seems pretty fit."

Hans peered at his wife over his nose. She laughed and put her hand on his shoulder. "Don't worry, my love, he is not my kind. I prefer a little more meat on my men."

She patted his belly and he laughed and kissed her hand.

"Anyway," she continued, "he complained that this year the bastide was occupied so he had to rent this place."

"How fortunate for us," Max said drily. He thought for a moment. "But why would he need friends in high places? Could it be that he has done something wrong? I did have the odd feeling last night that he was somehow involved."

"That would not surprise me," Angela said darkly.

"Ah, but you're forgetting that he was on his balcony like the rest of us," Hans said. "We were all there, so it must have been an outsider, no?"

Max considered that for a moment, casting his mind back trying to recall when Nash had appeared on his balcony. He couldn't remember, but it wasn't immediately.

"He does live next door to the victim, and it would take less than a minute to shoot her and run back into his own apartment and appear on the balcony."

Hans rolled this thought around in his mouth. "Maybe." But he looked doubtful.

They stayed until three, when Max had to leave to fetch Luke. He liked to catch the last half hour of practice when they played a match. By quickly picking up his glass and pretending to sip when Hans was plying the wine, he managed to drink less than half a bottle. It was more than he would have drunk before driving in the States or in the U.K., but here it seemed perfectly normal behavior. Anyway, spreading the wine over a couple of hours and a pizza, he felt excused.

"Don't forget you are coming over for dinner tonight," Angela said as he stood up from the table.

"Not forgotten." Then he remembered what Luke had said. Feeling very tongue in cheek, he added, "Luke was wondering if we were having schnitzel?"

Angela laughed. "We are now."

Max grinned. "What time?"

"Seven?"

"*Bedankt*, Angela, Hans."

Angela shooed him away from the table. "See you later."

6

Jeremy Nash watched the Dutch couple go off with the American lawyer. He sniffed, irked that they had not invited him to lunch; he would like to get to know her better. He would have to strike up more conversations, get closer to them, like that lawyer had. He'd probably gotten to know them because he stayed right next door. Jeremy didn't have that advantage.

He could very much have enjoyed a long, boozy lunch looking at Angela's magnificent breasts today. He thought about what she would look like naked. Yes, she was a bit old for him, but still, he would. Yes, he definitely would. Despite trying to hold the picture of Angela in his mind, other, more pressing thoughts intruded, making him perspire under his Turnbull and Asser collar.

He stiffened at the blare of a police siren as another squad car pulled into the street. That bloody Borrell woman. All he had wanted was what she had taken from him. Now look at the mess he was in. He sucked in a deep breath, not even registering the wonderful amalgam of smells around him, and squared his shoulders. He just had to hold his nerve. He glanced at the police swarming the scene and settled on the large, well-dressed black man. He looked vaguely familiar. The policeman met his eyes with penetrating suspicion. Just then the tinny bars of "Pomp and Circumstance March #1" sounded. Reaching into the inside pocket of his striped boating blazer, Jeremy withdrew his phone and quickly silenced it. He glanced at the number.

"What is it?" he hissed, cupping the phone to his face while turning away from the crowd. Surely the man hadn't already heard of Borrell's death. His heart ticked up a notch as he listened for a moment. No, it seemed his friend had not yet heard of the murder. Just as well, it would give him a little time to clear up this mess before the shit truly hit the fan.

"I told you the bitch wasn't going to give it up."

As he listened he tugged a forefinger around the inside of his collar.

"No, I don't know what she wants. She wouldn't say. She just gave me a scathing look and said it might be useful to have friends in high places. I…"

He listened again, the apprehension on his face reflecting the tirade coming from the other end of the phone. Finally, exasperated, he said, "Yes, I searched the place and didn't find it."

He pulled the phone slightly away from his ear as his caller's voice blasted from the speaker.

"No, I didn't have time to search the whole place," answered Jeremy. "She came back early. I couldn't very well hang around."

Another pause.

"I don't know where it is. How would I?" His voice dropped into a plaintive bleating. "Look, I may have arranged the girls, but you didn't object. How was I to know we were being filmed? Jesus!"

He took off his Panama and ran a sleeve across his forehead. "You don't think I know that?" he snapped, a sense of outrage reasserting itself. "I'm the one who should be pissed. From her comments, you're the friend in high places Borrell is interested in. She couldn't give a shit about me."

He closed his eyes and listened to the continued ranting at the other end of the phone. He did not want to think what would happen when his acquaintance found out the woman was dead—which would most likely be tomorrow. "Yes, alright. I'll work on it. Do you think I want this to get out?"

He glanced furtively around and saw with a jolt that the black policeman was still watching him and had now started moving in his direction.

"Look, I've got to go now, Henri," he said aloud. "Thanks for letting me know."

The policeman stopped a foot away. They were of even height, but the solid bulk of the police officer imposed itself on the confrontation. He stared blandly into Jeremy's face.

"Monsieur. Vous-êtes?"

Jeremy had drawn his arms tight across his chest, leaning back slightly as if he expected to be struck.

"Look here, I don't speak French. Don't you have someone here who speaks bloody English?"

The policeman favored him with a thin smile. *"Bien sûr.* I speak some English, monsieur, but it is not bloody. I am Capitaine Jacques of the Police Nationale." He flashed his credentials in Jeremy's face, making him shrink back. "Might I know your name?"

"Why? Why do you want to know?"

The captain's eyebrows shot up before coming together in a frown. The moment lengthened as he scrutinized the Englishman through narrowed eyes.

"There has been a fatality in your building, so we are interviewing all the residents. Is that a problem?"

"No. I suppose not."

The captain tapped his notebook impatiently.

Jeremy cleared his throat. "It's Nash. Jeremy Nash." He rubbed his sweaty hands together, working the thumb of one over the knuckles of the other. "Former MP."

"Thank you," Capitaine Jacques said in a voice so honeyed that it bordered on sarcasm.

"Sorry. It's just… it's just that I'm well known in London. You know. The tabloids."

"I completely understand," the captain said, in a way that made clear to Jeremy he didn't give a damn about Jeremey's notoriety, or the tabloids.

"Which apartment are you in?"

"Uh, 4B."

"How long have you been here?"

Jeremy placed his index finger against his lips as if the answer required great thought. "About a week."

The policeman nodded. "Did you know Madame Borrell?"

Jeremy cleared his throat and peered quizzically at Jacques. "Who?"

Jacques huffed, closing his eyes momentarily before saying in a voice of thinly veiled impatience. "The French woman that lived next door to you."

"No! Is that who was killed?"

The detective's eyes roved over the knots of chattering residents in silent skepticism.

"I didn't know what was going on as I don't speak anything but English," Jeremy protested.

"I thought I saw you talking to…" the policeman consulted his notebook, "Mr. and Mrs. Beeker."

Jeremy coughed into his closed fist. "Well, yes, but they speak English."

"And they didn't mention the death of Madame Borrell?"

"Well, they mentioned a murder, but not who was involved. We had other things to talk about."

From the expression on the policeman's face, he didn't believe a word of this. Jeremy's mind was racing. He couldn't afford to be tied to that bitch and her illegal activities in any way. He would have to brazen it out. He smiled ingratiatingly.

"Look, what I meant was that I didn't know her—the woman that died. I know who she was. We bumped into each other a few times going in or out." He paused as if searching his memory. "And we might have exchanged a few words in passing," he added hesitantly. "But I didn't know her," he finished emphatically, looking at the policeman hopefully. "Am I explaining myself well? Do you understand my English?"

"Oh yes. I understand you very well. So, you have had no dealings with her?"

What had he heard, wondered Jeremy frantically, as he struggled to keep his face impassive. Surely they couldn't know about that yet?

"No, of course not."

The detective eyed him shrewdly. "Why, of course not?"

Jeremy had the distinct feeling that he had somehow been trapped but didn't know how. Had the police found something to connect him to Borrell? Was this a setup to let him dig himself a hole? His mind whirled.

"No, well. I just meant to say…" His voice tailed off. He cleared his throat again and tried a thin, condescending smile. "Well, I wouldn't have said I didn't know her if we had had dealings together, would I?"

Jacques looked him over, a cat watching a mouse. "I would certainly hope not."

Then he made a few notes in his little black book, popped the page with the point of his pen and snapped the book shut.

Jeremy felt sweat trickling down his back. "Look, can I go back in now? It's terribly hot outside."

The captain's lips pursed as he considered Nash under a lowered brow. "No, monsieur. We are still processing the scene." Then, as an afterthought, he added with a derisory smile. "I thought you English came here for the warm weather?"

Bloody power trip, Jeremy thought, as the captain strolled away. Typical Frog inefficiency. He glanced around. Now that the Dutch couple were gone with that lawyer, he didn't know anyone. Perhaps a spot of lunch at the Bistrot de Lavandières on the village square was in order? The food was average, but wine was wine and there was that very cute, very young, waitress.

As a man stepped aside in the crowd, he spied Hassan standing alone and his anger soared.

"You little swine," he muttered, sidling up to the concierge while keeping a sharp eye on the police.

Hassan looked at him fearfully. *"Comment?"*

"Don't give me that French shit." Jeremy poked the young man in the chest. "You spoke English fine the other day."

The concierge's face was screwed in concentration. "Sorry, monsieur. I understand some English, but you talk so quick. What is *swine*?"

Jeremy remembered a word from several years of adolescent French at private school. *"Cochon!"* he snapped. "Now, I want a word with you."

Hassan seemed to shrink into himself. "Yes, monsieur?"

Jeremy scanned the area again. The police were too close for comfort. "Not here. Follow me."

They trudged around the corner and up a narrow alley leading to the church at the pinnacle of the hill on which Roussillon sat. Jeremy stopped halfway along the passage where he could see anyone coming from either direction.

"Where's the video?" he demanded.

"Video, monsieur? What video?"

"Listen, you little parasite …" Flecks of spittle flew from Jeremy's mouth. "I have friends in Avignon. Very powerful friends you and your partner are messing with. It will go very badly for you if you don't hand over the video."

Hassan was backed up against the ancient stone wall. "What video? What partner? I don't understand."

"That Borrell woman," Jeremy hissed. "You told me she could get me girls."

"I did, monsieur. But I don't know anything about them. I only know she has some connections in Marseille that can…" His voice tailed off and he winced.

"I bet."

"*Vraiment*. Truly, I know nothing about any girls."

Jeremy's skepticism showed. "And I'm sure you didn't know we were being filmed."

Hassan's eyes almost widened out of their sockets and a small gasp escaped. *"Non!"* He shook his head vigorously. *"Non, monsieur. Jamais*. Never. "

Jeremy's eyes narrowed. "What connections in Marseille?"

"Oh, monsieur, you do not want to go there. They are very bad men."

Jeremy snorted derisively. "Bad men!" His voice rang with bravado. "My friends can be pretty bad too."

"Not like this, monsieur." Hassan lowered his voice to a whisper as though the very name was dangerous. *"La Brise de Sang*. The mafia from Corsica."

Jeremy stepped back like he'd been slapped, and his face went pale. His hand went to his face, touching as though searching for comfort.

"I must go now, monsieur. In case the police are looking for me."

Jeremy nodded numbly. He and his friend were in the hands of one of the most notorious gangs in France. How was he going to get out of this now?

"Wait," he said in desperation as Hassan turned away. "I need to get back into Borrell's apartment."

The young man looked at him as you would a madman. "Impossible. The police are crowded into it."

"What about when they leave?"

Hassan flinched. "I don't know, monsieur."

Hassan moved to leave, but Jeremy grabbed his arm with steel fingers. Menacingly, he leaned close and spoke. "I need you to get me in there when they've gone."

Suddenly he relented and dropped Hassan's arm. "Look, perhaps I was wrong, and you're not involved. But I need your help. I will make it worth your while." He rubbed the tips of his fingers together in the universal sign for money. "In the meantime, tell me, is there anywhere else Borrell might have hidden something?"

"I don't know, *monsieur*." The concierge rubbed the back of his neck. "Perhaps in her office?"

Jeremy's spirits soared, clutching at straws. He grabbed Hassan's sleeve. "Yes, yes. Her office. Where is it?"

They paused, and Jeremy let go as two Japanese tourists approached and then sidled by, the young woman dressed like a porcelain doll and her companion toting a camera with enough attachments to film anything from an amoeba to a football game. When they were gone, Jeremy reached out again to grab Hassan's sleeve.

"Where? Please."

"In Cassis, above a restaurant. The restaurant is called Le Bateau Ivre."

"You have keys?"

"Of course not." Hassan pulled away sullenly. "I must go."

Jeremy watched him disappear back down the alley. He must get to her office. If the Brise gang got their hands on that film, it would be a blackmail nightmare. If word got out, his friend would be completely discredited, and he himself would be ruined in London, like that Epstein scandal, not to mention the very real possibility of jail time in France.

Mind awhirl, he continued up the passage, turned left onto the town square and took an outside table at the Bistrot de Lavandieres to think the problem through. How would he get into her office? He could hardly break in in broad daylight above a restaurant. What if the police beat him there? Hah! Inefficient as the French were, it would take them days. No, it should be safe, at least until tomorrow—no more mistakes. As the teenage waitress approached, he smiled. Now there was a sight for sore eyes. Of course, it was girls like her that had got him into this mess in the first place. Still, he couldn't help himself. *Look at her. Just look at her.*

7

When Max arrived at the soccer complex, Luke was still in the middle of a game. The sun was fierce, and as he trudged across the dusty ground to the far field, he wondered, not for the first time, whether this was the best learning environment for Luke. Max believed in a team game. As far as he could tell, the coaches here believed in greedy ball-hogging by the midfielders and forwards. Even from a distance he could see a lot of aimless dribbling going on and several wasted opportunities at both ends to supply a goal-scoring pass. As he approached, Luke rounded a bigger opponent heading for goal and was immediately scythed down from behind by the older boy.

"What the hell?" Max yelled.

Luke climbed slowly to his feet and limped around in a circle. The coach refereeing the game glanced coolly in Max's direction and waved—*play on*. Half running and half skipping, Luke chased back.

"They are trying to teach the boys to be tough," the man next to him on the sideline said in heavily accented English.

Max turned to face Eric Cantona, the famous former French international and Manchester United striker, whose son was also out on the field.

"Teaching them to be cheap and dirty, I think," said Max.

The great man snorted. "*Peut-être*. But dealing with cheap and dirty is necessary if they want to be professionals."

"Sadly, I think you are right," said Max. "But I just want Luke to survive the experience. I don't expect him to play professionally."

At that moment, Luke wrecked the boy who had just fouled him, and taking the ball from him, slid a perfect through-ball to a teammate who scored at the far post.

"Bravo," said Cantona with a grin, clapping his hands together just once. "*Voilà*. You may be surprised. He may have what it takes."

Afterwards, they made their way to the car, Luke still limping. They didn't talk about training on the way home—it was their rule. Instead, Max told his son about the news of the murder, how he had spent the day pushing his way through the melee at their apartment complex and how he had somehow still managed to ask Angela to prepare schnitzel later that evening for him.

"So, I guess you didn't get a lot of writing in," Luke said sardonically.

"Ha," said Max.

Out of the corner of his eye, Max watched Luke's face for his reaction to news of the murder.

Luke stared straight ahead, quiet.

"Are you okay?" asked Max.

Luke shrugged.

"Whatever happened, the police will get to the bottom of it," said Max, trying to reassure his son.

Since Emma, Max had been hyper-sensitive to the subject of death around Luke, especially where it involved a woman. The less Luke saw or heard about death, the better. Changing the subject, Max ruffled his son's hair.

"Seems you impressed the big man out there today!"

Luke turned to look at him. "What do you mean?"

"Eric Cantona told me you might have what it takes to play professionally."

"Really?" Luke's eyes widened. "Wait, you spoke to Eric Cantona?"

Max cocked an eyebrow. "Why is that so surprising?"

"Well, it's not surprising that you wanted to talk to him. Everybody does. That's why he usually stands alone on the far side of the field. I'm just surprised he talked back."

"Hmm. Well, if you must know, he started the conversation. Must be my natural charm."

Luke grinned showing teeth half hidden by silver braces with blue spacers. "Keep telling yourself that, Dad."

Max pretended to smack his son's head. *"Coup bas!"*

Luke's forehead furrowed.

"Oh, you don't know that yet?" said Max. "It means *low blow*."

Luke tossed his head, filing it away. "So, he really said that about me?"

"Sort of."

"Good thing Mom wasn't there to hear that."

They both fell silent for a moment.

"Yes, she wouldn't necessarily have appreciated that," Max said with a faint attempt at a smile. "She wanted you to succeed with your brains, not your feet."

"I miss her," Luke said, his eyes glistening.

Max reached across and stroked the back of his head. "Me too. Me too." They lapsed into silence again, and after a moment, Max turned on the audiobook to re-occupy their minds.

They parked, as usual, by the dumpsters, now mercifully empty but still reeking of melted kitchen waste. The three-ring police circus had dissipated, but a policeman still blocked the entrance to the apartment building. Max realized he didn't have anything that proved he lived there, but Hassan was still loitering in the lobby and hustled over.

"Any news?" Max asked.

Hassan stopped chewing his bottom lip. "*Rien, monsieur. They tell us nothing. Putain!*" He flicked his eyes at Luke. "*Desolée Monsieur.* I am, how you say, *un peu bouleversé.*"

A little upset? Max thought it odd that Hassan was taking this so hard. It seemed he was more than a little upset.

Luke grinned. "Don't worry, Hassan, I hear that language all day at camp."

Max frowned him down before turning back to Hassan. "Did you know Madame Borrell well?"

"*N-non, monsieur,*" stuttered Hassan. He cleared his throat nervously. "She was just another occupant, but she was permanent. I see her often since I came to work here. We talked sometimes."

Max knew Hassan was lying in the same way he could tell when a witness was lying. The few times he had seen Madame Borrell, she had swanned through the lobby with barely a glance at Hassan and just the very Parisian and supercilious nod to other guests. But now that he thought about it more, he *had* seen her deep in conversation with Hassan once when he had suddenly entered the lobby, their heads bent close. He recalled they were whispering vehemently, and she had straightened up at the sound of his approach. Then she had all but commanded Hassan to change a light bulb in her apartment "immediately" and had stalked off. Max remembered wondering what they had really been discussing. *Un petit mystère*, now it seemed.

Max saw that Hassan was staring at him in earnest, watching him closely to see if his story was being believed. Max kept his expression neutral, as he had practiced hundreds of times in court and in client interviews. Shrugging slightly, Max turned to the elevator.

"*D'accord*, let us know if you hear anything interesting."

Max and Luke changed back at their apartment and headed to the pool. A middle-aged German couple who had arrived two days before were stretched out on loungers in the sun. Luke went straight for the springboard and launched into a somersault. After a day in the hot sun at the soccer academy, he wanted to cool down and mess about. The German couple stared, pointedly annoyed by the childish intrusion. The man was already beginning to resemble a boiled lobster. That was going to hurt tonight, Max thought with mean satisfaction.

Max slid into the pool and started his forty laps. He hated the boring repetitiveness of it, but it was good exercise, and he was keen to keep his fitness up. Ever since Emma's death, he had been left with an enormous sense of responsibility as Luke's only parent. The murder of Borrell in such a peaceful haven had unsettled him.

Could it have been a robbery gone wrong? What if the culprits had broken into their apartment instead? He could not shake the nagging suspicion left by his conversation with Hassan. That Hassan was a killer seemed highly unlikely—he seemed too soft. But Max's profession taught him that you could never assume. Anyone was capable of anything under the right circumstances.

He pondered their earlier exchange while he cut through the water in long, fluid strokes. What had Hassan and Madame Borrell been discussing that day he'd seen them whispering in the lobby? There had to be some hidden connection between them. The usual motives flitted through his mind crowding out the monotony of the laps—blackmail, robbery, sex? Whatever the reason for the murder, if Hassan was the killer, his only motive to attack the two of them would have to be robbery, and they had brought nothing valuable with them.

"Throw the football for me," Luke called as Max finally pulled himself from the water. He only just raised his hands in time to protect his face from the spiraling football.

"Thanks for that."

"Sorry," said Luke, giggling as he bounced on the springboard. "Just checking to see if your reactions have slowed down, old man."

Max glanced at the Germans who were now sitting up, watching. From their uniform expressions it was easy to discern what they were thinking: *verdammt* loud Americans! Oh well, Max wasn't all that wild about German tourists.

"Let's see your reactions when I wing this at your head while you are in midair," called Max.

"Go for it," Luke laughed as he sprang far out over the pool.

Max's throw caught the airborne Luke squarely on the chest, tipping him backwards into the water. Luke came up spluttering but holding the ball aloft.

"Dempsey leaps and comes up with the spectacular touchdown!"

The German couple rose from their loungers and pulled on matching robes. The woman stared coldly. Max exchanged a look with his son and shrugged. Not many Europeans were fond of Americans. After the couple left, Luke tossed the ball back to Max.

"Made a new friend today," he said before disappearing with a splash under the water.

"Oh yeah, who?" asked Max when his son resurfaced.

"Some kid from Morocco. Yousef."

"Is he any good?"

"He's okay—no Riyadh Mahrez. Some French kids were picking on him."

"Why?" asked Max.

"Cos he's Muslim, I guess, from the names they were calling him. In the end I had to wreck one of them. I told him to cut it out, or there would be more of the same coming his direction."

Luke laughed.

Max marveled at the change that had come over his son. In the U.S. he had been a player whose chief drawback was his reluctance to get physical. Perhaps Cantona was right, or a more troubling thought: was Luke bottling the same simmering rage Max felt? God, he hoped not. He eyed Luke closely, pride at his son's kindness warring with unease.

"You know, you need to be careful," he said. "You don't want to hurt anyone."

"He was a bully. He deserved it."

"Maybe. But you don't want to get in trouble either."

Luke shrugged.

"Perhaps Yousef could come over after camp one day," said Max.

"That would be good," said Luke, before taking the ball and drop-kicking it with a splash, back into the sparkling pool.

8

It was late in the day when Jacques finally sat down with Dupre in his office at the commissariat in Aix. His office was on the third floor: serious crimes. As anticipated, the police captain had experienced a trying afternoon fielding calls from the mayor's office and the police commissioner, not to mention the press. Fortunately, the victim seemed not to have been friends with anyone important, but the callers were still apprehensive about the effect this killing in one of the most acclaimed villages in the Luberon would have on tourism. Jacques didn't think they had much to worry about. Tourists being what they were, a murder might make Roussillon even more popular, if that was possible.

Together they went over what they had. It wasn't much. When Hassan checked that morning, Borrell's apartment door had been unlocked. Significantly, the apartments all had deadbolts as an extra security measure.

"Well," Dupre said ruminatively, scraping away at his stubble, "either the victim let the killer in, or they had a key? I doubt she made a habit of leaving her door unlocked."

"I agree," Jacques said.

Dupre continued his thought train. "But who would she have let in? So far as we can tell, she has no friends or relatives. We have found no business associates. *Personne!* And the concierge says she never entertained anyone there."

"Ah, but he leaves at six. Perhaps she entertained after dark, a lover perhaps?"

Dupre cleared his throat. "You were in autopsy. What do you think?" His own face said he thought it was very unlikely. "Any signs of sexual activity or assault?"

Jacques' face twisted in distaste, clearly remembering the naked corpse of an unattractive woman. "The examiner couldn't see anything obvious. But we'll know more once the kit comes back." He rubbed one hand across his bald pate, gathering his thoughts, then nodded. "So, who had keys?"

"I picked up the victim's keys inside the apartment," Dupre replied. "Supposedly, the only other people with keys were the concierge and the cleaning woman."

"According to... ah, let me guess. The concierge."

"Well, yes."

The captain looked doubtful. "There's something funny with that guy. I want to know everything there is to know about him."

Dupre nodded. "Already on it."

"So, if we assume she locked her door and didn't let the killer in, and we believe the Moroccan concierge, Hassan Aamara, we have just two suspects. The cleaning woman... and him."

"If he killed her, why would he admit that only two people had a key and tell us that she never entertained at home? If it were me, I would say I'd seen many people going up there and for all I knew there were keys everywhere."

"Ah, but you are assuming that these people are smarter than they are," Jacques said.

For a brief moment Dupre looked troubled, wondering who 'these people' might be, before he picked up the thread of their conversation. "Remember we have a smudge of blood on the patio and the patio door was also open."

"I assume the blood did not belong to the victim or either of our suspects?"

"We are awaiting the results of the lab work."

Jacques flicked his head towards the balcony. "Did you go out there? You would have to be a mountain goat to get on and off that balcony from outside."

Dupre ruminated for a moment before nodding. "All the occupants of the building have given almost identical statements. Some were woken by a shot, and some by a scream. They hurried out onto their balcony but saw nothing except their neighbors doing the same thing. Every one of the occupants can alibi another occupant, so they all have alibis that place them on a terrace within moments of the scream."

Jacques nodded reluctantly. "So, an outsider, which still places the cleaning woman and Aamara in the frame."

"An outsider couldn't have left via the balcony. Even if they waited for the fuss to die down, they would have to go through an occupied adjacent apartment."

"That leaves the front door, which might explain why it was not locked the next morning."

They both pondered the implications.

Jacques sighed. "But if the killer had a key, why not lock the door after them to delay discovery of the crime."

Dupre sat forward. "Because that would limit the crime to those people who had keys. By leaving the door unlocked it could be anyone. And don't forget, the victim did not have any visitors. But for the *Americain* this crime may well not have been discovered as quickly, locked door or not."

Jacques silently counted to ten. "So, we are back to either someone she admitted or one of two people with a key."

"Unless..." Dupre paused, seemingly hesitant to voice what was on his mind.

Jacques drummed on his desk with a pen. "Unless?"

"Unless the stabbing took place and then the perpetrator hurried back to their own apartment, fired the shot and screamed before appearing on their balcony to establish an alibi. That would explain why we didn't find any evidence of a gunshot in her apartment."

"Sounds like a lame murder mystery," said Jacques, his lip curled in a sneer. "If so, they must think we are stupid. Sounds like *un rosbif*."

Dupre hunched his shoulders, looking uncomfortable at the derogatory term for British people. "But of course, that is unlikely."

"But possible. It would only take a few minutes to stab Borrell and get back to their apartment."

Dupre nodded. "True. Less for Nash as he was next door." Again, he hesitated, looking like a man who thought he was pushing his luck. "It could be that two people are involved, giving each other alibis."

That had not occurred to Jacques. He stared at Dupre before saying somewhat resentfully, as though the seemingly endless possibilities were his subordinate's fault. "Well, if that is the case, then, in fact, we are nowhere." He paused in thought then suddenly threw down his pen. "But what are the chances that two strangers came together to murder this woman? Check to see if any of the residents are connected." He glanced down at his notebook. "What's the story on GSR?"

"None of the occupants tested positive for gunshot residue, but of course that doesn't mean much. It's easily washed off and only lasts four to six hours."

"And you did not test the American lawyer?"

"*Non*," Dupre acceded. "He was picking up his son from Stages Bousquier. The kid must be a good football player."

"Hmmm. By the time we see him again it will be a pointless exercise." Jacques pinched his lower lip, frowning. "From the way she was gutted, the killer would have been covered in blood."

"It would have been over their hands and arms, certainly," Dupre agreed.

"And yet there is no obvious sign of a blood trail leaving the apartment. It's like the killer disappeared into thin air." The captain rubbed his bald head as if polishing it, then squeezed his thick neck before cracking his broad shoulders. "Make sure they check all the hallways, the stairs and the elevator. Evacuate the building again if necessary."

Dupre nodded.

"Anything in Borrell's car?" Jacques asked, hopefully.

"Three expensive tennis rackets and a receipt from yesterday evening for Le Saint Amour."

Jacques shook his bald head, shrugged his shoulders and opened his hands palm up. Dupre smiled in a manner that spoke volumes. His boss didn't get out enough.

"It's the high-end restaurant at Les Lodges Mont Victoire outside Le Thonet." Dupre paused, clearly enjoying a memory, doubtless food related. "The food is out of this world."

Jacques' expression soured. "How much on the receipt?"

"Two hundred Euros. Give or take."

Jacques rubbed his jawline. "So, dinner for two?"

"Or one of their very expensive bottles of wine."

"Find out."

Dupre looked at his watch, and Jacques knew he was thinking about a carafe of wine at his own favorite bar. *"Bien sûr,"* Dupre answered in a resigned voice.

"What about the phone?"

They had found the victim's phone charging on the kitchen counter.

"Still locked. With Arielle."

Arielle was the technical expert on their team, doubtless in the process of cracking both the phone and the laptop. Obviously, she had nothing yet.

Jacques heaved a sigh and waved the lieutenant away. "Send someone around the tennis clubs this evening. Perhaps that will bring some answers."

He sounded more despondent than optimistic. At the door, Dupre paused momentarily.

"Any idea why the *juge d'instruction* gave this to us rather than the Gendarmerie? After all, it is more their territory."

To Jacques, the question sounded like the disgruntled complaint of someone who didn't want the inconvenience of working the case. Certainly, Dupre had no appreciation of the politics. Still, he couldn't blame him. He had himself half-hoped that the gendarmes would get this one. He had nothing to prove or gain except a whole lot of aggravation.

His thoughts flicked to the local Gendarmerie commander, Pierre Fournier, and his gung-ho, macho, militaristic style. "Perhaps she doesn't like dealing with those hard-arses."

Dupre grimaced. "Who does?" Then as the penny dropped, he turned back. "She?"

Jacques' face was studiously impassive. "*Oui, L'Anglaise*. She is on her way here."

Dupre whistled. "Bon chance."

Suddenly Jacques felt tired. "You can leave the restaurant until tomorrow if you want."

Dupre nodded. "Thanks, boss."

After Dupre left, Jacques remained at his desk lost in thought, waiting for the foreign judge to arrive. He had never worked with this examining magistrate before, but her late arrival validated his expectation that, as an English person, she would doubtless disrespect him.

He was coming up on twenty years in the force, the first fifteen at national headquarters in Paris, before the run-in with that politician and his posting to this backwater that signaled the stagnation of his career. He had learned the hard way that men in powerful positions could wriggle out of trouble, even when all the evidence was stacked against them. The politician he had justly pursued had been a rising star in a governing party that could not afford a scandal. The assault charges were swept under the rug, and when Jacques refused to play ball, he was demoted and shipped out to Provence.

His gaze shifted to the framed commendations on the wall, none recent, and the picture of a much younger him sharing a high moment with the Ministre de la Justice—heady times now well behind him. What did he have to look forward to? His wife, Marie, had hated the South. She had left him six months ago, taking their teenage son, when their daughter had gone to study at the Sorbonne. They were all now back in Paris with the rest of the extended family.

This close to retirement, he was stuck here in this artificial environment populated by tourists and foreigners, his job meaningless, a career that had once seemed so promising in ashes all around him. And now he had to deal with this English judge. Still, he supposed, it could be worse. After Paris, he had first been transferred to the drug squad in Marseille, that suppurating sore on the *cul* of France. That had truly been a nightmare. Squalid *quartiers* gathered in the gritty center, populated by drug dealers, prostitutes and impoverished immigrants who fought their own eternal gang wars, all over-looked by the haughty heights of the wealthy enclave of Carré d'Or. Not even judges were safe from the gangs that vied violently for control of the city. He lasted two years before he called in the last favor he had in Paris, and here he was, waiting out retirement, alone in Aix. He had no friends in the force and generally considered his colleagues as blunt instruments, little better than traffic cops. But there were a few exceptions.

Dupre was a good officer despite his slovenly appearance and habits. Jacques was under no delusions that his lieutenant was the better detective. But he was a terrible administrator and, despite his impressive results, would climb no higher up the ladder, and he didn't seem to care. Jacques felt towards Dupre as a parent towards a recalcitrant teenager. Still, in a weird way Jacques envied him his blasé capitulation.

Then there was Arielle—a breath of fresh air, who made him heartsick for his daughter, Elouise. Never mind the experts in Paris; if anyone could crack Borrell's encryptions, it was her. She had attended the prominent École Polytechnic in Lausanne and earned a master's degree in computer science from MIT in the United States. God knows what she was doing working for the national police when she could write her lucrative ticket in the tech industry.

As if on cue, there was a brief rap at his door which cracked open, and Arielle's disembodied head appeared. He leaned toward her, hoping for some good news.

"A few of us are going to Café des Artistes for a drink. Do you want to come?" she asked, an insouciant smile playing across her lips.

Jacques knew the others did not really want him to tag along, but he appreciated the gesture. He returned a regretful smile.

"Sadly, I await the pleasure of the judge, who should have been here an hour ago."

"Ah," Arielle said, giving him a sympathetic frown. "We should be there for an hour or so. If she doesn't keep you too long you know where to find us."

"Bien sûr. Merci."

The door closed, and Jacques groaned, pushing back into his chair, stretching until he heard his vertebrae crack. He had slept poorly the night before, beset by visions of the appalling scenes he had witnessed in a lifetime of violent crime investigation. Madame Borrell was just the latest in a long line of corpses and not even close to the worst. That kind of filth changed a person. No, it hadn't been a surprise when Marie left him. And the constant battles with his daughter, Elouise. The way she dressed. If she had only seen what he had seen. But thank God she hadn't.

With a measured knock, a uniformed officer pushed open the door. "The examining magistrate is here for you, *Capitaine.*"

"Enfin!" Jacques sucked in his cheeks while he considered how long he could safely keep her waiting. The officer looked at him expectantly.

Jacques' shoulders slumped. "Show her in," he said.

Judge Claire Lejeune was very bright in all senses of the word. She wore a sunny smile as she reached out a slim, lightly tanned hand to shake only the fingers of Jacques' large palm. She wore a patterned red silk chemise that reminded him of a tablecloth his mother once prized, and voguish white capris. Her carry-all was a canary yellow Tory Burch, a brand he only knew because of Elouise.

"I saw you play against England at the Parc des Princes many years ago," gushed the judge in a Celtic burr, staring into his face with evident pleasure. "You were fantastic. Reminded me of Jonah Lomu. And, of course, I really enjoyed you defeating the English."

The captain stared at her in surprise.

Her smile broadened as she read his expression. "I love rugby. It's the only sport we Scots are occasionally good at. Let's face it, our football team is always terrible."

Jacques finally found his voice. "That was a long time ago, and your rugby team is not much better."

She mocked being offended. "Oh, I think we have beaten France more than a few times."

He gave her a sardonic smile. "Must have been before or after my time."

She chuckled. "Probably. Anyway, I am sorry to be late. I got a call from the justice minister as I was leaving the house. *Merde*, but that man can go on."

Jacques' eyes narrowed. Was she telling him this so he would know she had friends in high places?

She placed one hand over her mouth in fake horror. "I think I may have hung up on him. Oh well." She waved her hand as if swatting the thought away. "Anyway, let's talk. I don't want to keep you here late." She checked her watch. Was she really concerned about him, or did she have a dinner date, he mused?

She was not what he had expected. So casual. He couldn't read her, and that made him uncomfortable. More disconcertingly, he found he quite liked her. She knew about his international rugby career and had likened him to the sensational All Blacks winger Jonah Lomu. Grudgingly, he told himself that she might be okay. She wasn't even *une Anglaise* but *une Ecossaise*—much better. The French and the Scots went back as far as the Battle of Bannockburn in the fourteenth century, a crisis which united France and Scotland in fast friendship together in their hatred of the English—or perhaps even further back to the days when Emperor Charlemagne sought governmental advice from the Scots.

"*Capitaine?*"

Jacques jerked his attention back to the judge. She looked amused.

"Ah, *oui*. Let me bring you up to speed."

Over the next half an hour he went through what they knew, but mostly, as he pointed out, what they didn't know. She murmured her empathy at all the right places and at the end she summed up his progress in very unflattering terms.

"So, we have a woman who was stabbed, but all the witnesses say was shot," she said. "We have no bullet, gun or knife. We have her laptop and her phone but have not cracked either one so far. We believe she was a real estate investor in and around Cassis but haven't located her business and don't yet know what real estate she put her money into or whether she had partners or employees. She never had people over to her apartment, but someone got in to kill her, either invited, which could be anyone, or using a key, which appears to limit our suspects to two, neither of whom appears to have a motive. Fantastically, we have no idea who this woman is, but we think she came from up North many years ago. We have not tracked down any friends or relatives. *Un énigme, n'est-ce pas?*"

Jacques squirmed. "*Oui.* Perhaps tomorrow will shed some light on the matter."

"Let's hope so. I have to be in Avignon tomorrow morning, so shall we meet at the scene at one o'clock? That should give you time to answer some questions."

"Bien sûr, Madame le juge."

He showed her to the front doors and then returned to his office. The pressure was on. He needed a drink and for a fleeting moment gave thought to joining his colleagues at the café. A grim smile touched his lips. It might be worth it just to discommode Dupre, whom he was sure had taken him at his word and skipped inquiries for the evening.

There was nothing to go home to in his empty house outside Le Thor. He thought of Marie in Paris, of what she might be doing right now. He thought of his son sitting over his homework, his daughter Elouise, in college, at a lecture, or heading to relax at some student café. A sense of loneliness swept through him. No, even in his rugby days he had never been much of a bar drinker. He huffed as he grabbed his car keys. At home, there was Debussy, a good book and a bottle of Glenfiddich sitting on his sideboard with his name on it. He felt sure the judge would approve. A good whisky might be just the thing to lubricate his review of this case.

9

At seven p.m., Max knocked on the door of the next apartment, and he and Luke were admitted by a grinning Hans dressed in overly tight black shorts and a loose Ajax jersey. He opened his arms wide. "Eh?"

Luke shook his head slowly, an expression of pity. "Keep dreaming," he said.

Like his father, Luke was a committed Manchester United fan.

"Oh, Hans!" called Angela, with a laugh, watching them from the living room. Max was relieved to see that she was dressed in an opaque turquoise shift.

"It's not my fault if Hans has delusional dreams of Champions League success," Luke said.

"What do you mean?" asked Hans. "We are at the top of the Eredivisie."

"That's like being the tallest pigmy," Luke scoffed.

Hans looked mortally offended. "We were in the semi-finals of the Champions League not so long ago. We beat Real Madrid. Since then, all the big clubs are raiding our players?"

His voice receded as he and Luke went out onto the balcony. Max accepted a slightly chilled red wine from Château Pibarnon that Angela proffered. Max was no wine snob, but his face broke into a delighted smile. Not many knew the immaculate wines from the neighboring Bandol region. He sniffed the wine as he followed her into the kitchen, and then sipped. "*Délicieux.* Hans really knows his reds."

Angela's laugh tinkled and she cocked her head. "Max! I never thought you a sexist. I chose the wine."

Max colored. "I'm so sorry. You're right."

"You know I had dreams of being a sommelier."

"Really?" said Max. "Come to think of it, I've never seen a female sommelier in a restaurant."

Angela sniffed. "No, it is uncommon, but I grew up around red wine." A cloud seemed to pass over her face, so Max changed the subject just as Hans joined them.

"Did you hear anything more on the murder?"

Angela paused while pulling on oven mitts, but Hans plowed right in. "Oh yes," he said. "My wife is a busybody."

Angela shot him a penetrating look before explaining. "We talked to Sylvia."

Max looked at her enquiringly, and Angela chuckled.

"You know the old woman who swims naked, Madame Hojberg."

"Oh, her. I've never spoken to her. In fact, I've never seen her with clothes on." He remembered the quite disturbing sight of her last night, peering over her balcony.

"I wish we only saw her with clothes on," grumbled Hans.

Angela flicked him with a dishtowel.

Max smiled and nodded, now thinking of Hans in his Speedos the night before. He coughed. "Speaking of which, have you seen the new German couple?"

"*Ja*, another couple in point. She was down there with her top off." He shivered theatrically.

"You two are bad," Angela said, hiding a smile as she turned to pull a pan from the oven. "Let's eat."

"So, what did the naked swimmer have to say?" asked Max when they were seated at the table on the patio. The sun was sinking towards the olive-clad hills, and there was a pleasant breeze. Luke poked Max in the arm and pointed his fork at the generous portion of *jaeger schnitzel* and *spaetzle* on his plate.

"Yes, you are a spoiled brat," Max said. "Have you thanked Angela for pandering to your demands?"

"Thank you, Angela," Luke mumbled through a mouth packed to capacity with food.

Angela smiled. "I'm glad you like it. This is one of Hans' favorites too, although he could use a little more salad and less *spaetzle*."

"Tell him about Madame Borrell," said Hans, ignoring his wife's remarks.

"Ah, *ja*. Sylvia has lived here for many years. She knows everyone and everything. I just happened to be at the pool when she came for her afternoon swim."

"Hmph! For sure you were," her husband said.

She brushed his comment away with one hand. "She even has a contact in the police. They know very little except that Madame Borrell was stabbed."

She glanced at Luke, who was eating as though he had been starved for a week, and then at Max.

"Are you sure you want to discuss this now?"

"Heck yes," came Luke's muffled voice. He swallowed and added, "What do you think I am going to talk about tomorrow at camp? I'm going to be the most popular kid."

Max shrugged. Despite his misgivings about Luke and death, his son seemed to have come to terms with the death of their neighbor. "He will pester me anyway, so go ahead. He has watched too many murder mysteries on TV with us." He stopped. And the word *us* seemed to swell and hang in the air. After a searching glance at Luke he continued as a thought occurred to him. "You said stabbed. But what about the shot we heard?"

Scrunching her face, Angela replied. "They cannot explain it."

"Where was she stabbed?" asked Luke.

Angela paused briefly, staring into space and then said grimly. "In the abdomen. It would have taken her some time to die in much pain."

The adults sat silently contemplating that thought.

"That sucks," said Luke with a twelve-year-old's complete lack of empathy.

Max shook off the mood. "Any idea about motive?"

Angela furrowed her brow. "The police do not think it was a robbery. The place seemed to have been searched, but many expensive things were left behind. It is as if someone was looking for something in particular."

"So, who was she?" Max asked.

Hans grunted. "Apparently, Borrell was a successful real estate investor. Sylvia said she arrived about twenty years ago from somewhere in the North, possibly Alsace. She owns business properties in Cassis."

Max whistled softly. "That's high-end real estate," Max said, thinking of the small fishing village turned hipster hang-out and tourist mecca. Cassis had a small harbor lined with three- and four-story buildings in peach and apricot tones with blue shutters, the ground floors of which were restaurants or fashion boutiques. Dozens of luxury yachts, interspersed with small, white fishing boats banded with vibrant colors, lined the crowded wharves, bobbing on the tranquil water—a picture postcard scene.

"Anyone who owned real estate there before the transformation would be very wealthy indeed," said Max. "Anyone buying now would already have to be very wealthy—mainly Russians, from what I've heard. Luke and I were there two weeks ago for the beach."

Luke paused in the act of wiping his plate with a hunk of bread to say, "Yeah, the beach is terrible. All rocks and muddy water."

Hans squinted at Max.

"Spoiled brat used to the Caribbean," Max said apologetically.

"Huh," said Hans, sniffing in the way people do when talking about dumb tourists. "You should have taken the boat to the Ca-lanques. There, the water is crystal clear and the sand beautiful."

He was referring to the fjord-like inlets just along the coast from the town. Max nodded.

"Yes, we saw them, but only from a sight-seeing boat. The fer-ries were all booked up. Luke said his legs were sore from soccer, and he didn't want to take the long walk from the cliff parking."

Hans gave Luke a *poor baby* look down his nose.

"Well, they were sore," Luke said defensively. "You try playing six days straight in the baking hot sun." He peeked at Angela. "What's for dessert?"

"Luke!" his father exclaimed.

"It's okay," Angela beamed. "He is a growing boy."

Hans rubbed his hands together, "*Krafne!* Stuffed with chocolate. Angela's specialty."

"*Krafne?*" repeated Luke.

"Little donuts," said Angela. "Hans has, what is it you say… ah, yes, a sweet tooth!"

She reached over and patted his belly. "It is not so good for him."

They all laughed.

"But *mijn lieverd,*" Hans expostulated, "all the more of me for you to love."

His wife seemed singularly unimpressed. "Hmm."

Luke gave a *Yikes!* sideways glance at his father. "Okay then, let's bring on the *Krafne,*" he said, grinning.

10

Dupre drove through black double wrought iron gates and along the gravel drive flanked by plane trees, pulling his personal Renault to a stop next to the stone fountain in front of the main entrance to Les Lodges Mont Victoire. He had been sorely tempted to join Arielle and the others, but the lack of progress on this case bothered him. The sooner they had some answers, the better, and there was little point in visiting a restaurant in the morning when it was closed.

Through the passenger window he noted the disdain on the uniformed valet's face. He looked around his dashboard and passenger seat and had to admit that it looked a lot like he lived in his car, with food wrappers, papers and discarded clothing strewn around. He passed a meaty palm across his ample belly in a vain attempt to smooth his shirt. He hitched up his pants as he clambered out of the car. His dusty, scuffed shoes caught his eye as he straightened up, and he quickly scrubbed the uppers on the back of his pant legs. Clearing his throat, Dupre tried to summon some dignity. He flashed his warrant card at the insolent-looking youth.

"Police," he snapped and immediately felt better as the valet all but jumped to attention.

"Yes, monsieur. How can I help?"

"You can turn out your pockets for a start." He felt even better at the sudden stricken expression on the valet's face. He probably had a few joints hidden away for later, Dupre thought.

"I'm just kidding. I need to see the maître d' at the restaurant." He tossed his keys. "Park it somewhere close. I don't expect I will be here for long."

Dupre said this with an overpowering feeling of regret. He loved this place. He had eaten at Le Saint Amour enough times that he was known to the maître d', Gustav, a tall, thin man with a polished exterior and a superior attitude. But for the slight Baltic accent, he could have been Parisian. There was no question of the customer always being right. With him, the customer was lucky to be eating there. Dupre agreed. Normally, he dressed up to visit the restaurant and felt ashamed to be seen in his present condition. This visit was going to blow his cover.

"Ah, Monsieur Dupre." Gustav passed his eyes up and down Dupre several times with an expression of thinly veiled displeasure. "I almost didn't recognize you." He sniffed in a practiced superior way before going on emphatically, "and I don't recall having a reservation for you this evening."

Dupre coughed gently into his fist. *"Non, mon ami.* I regret that I am not here to dine. As you may see, I have come directly from work on a matter of business."

Gustav frowned, pinching his nostrils so that he looked like a bird of prey. "I don't believe you have previously confided your line of business to me."

With a sinking feeling Dupre displayed his warrant card. This time, Gustav maintained his usual poker face.

"And what may we do for the *Sûreté*?" Gustav asked, using the old, not very flattering term for the police.

Dupre handed him the credit card receipt he had retrieved from Borrell's car. "I'd like you to tell me what you can about the woman who dined here last evening, particularly who she dined with."

Gustav let out a breath of long-suffering while looking at the receipt. "I will have to check," he said, beckoning Dupre to follow. At his desk, Gustav reviewed his computer and matched the receipt with the booking. "Ah, *oui*, Madame Borrell. She is a regular. She dined at 8.30 with one guest."

"What do you know about Madame Borrell?" asked Dupre.

"Pfft. Nothing." Gustav looked Dupre up and down again. "Except that she is clearly wealthy. I do not normally chit-chat with guests." Tilting his head back to look down his long aquiline nose at Dupre, he added, "As we now comprehend, they do not normally confide their business to me."

Dupre cleared his throat again. "Of course. Perhaps then you could tell me something about her companion?"

"A man." Again, Gustav appraised the policeman's clothes. "Well-dressed, of course."

A designer-clad couple entered the restaurant behind Dupre and approached the maître d'. Dupre could feel their eyes on him from behind. "Height, age, hair?"

"I think perhaps you should talk to Madeleine," Gustav said, hastily edging round to block Dupre from view. "She waited on them." As he ushered Dupre into the dining room, he gave the new arrivals an ingratiating smile. *"Un moment, s'il vous plait."*

Dupre followed Gustav across the interior dining room to the terrace.

"Ah, she is waiting on a table of eight. It could be some time." He turned back into the dining room and indicated a table in a dim corner. "Perhaps you would care to wait here. I will tell her to speak to you when she has a moment."

Dupre knew he was already out of favor, and it might be some time before Gustav allowed him back into the restaurant. With nothing to lose, he said in a debonair manner, "Actually, it's a lovely evening. I will wait on the terrace. Perhaps a glass of wine?"

Gustav's tight smile never reached his eyes. "*Bien sûr.* What would you like?"

"Perhaps a Château de Fontcreuse?"

It was a Cassis *blanc*, a luscious, fruity mouthful and one of his favorites when he was fine dining. Without waiting for a response, Dupre turned and ambled to a table on the fringe of the patio. He did not want to unsettle the other guests with police talk.

The wine arrived surprisingly quickly—probably to make him blend in with the other diners as much as possible. As he sipped, Dupre felt himself unwind. It had been a stressful day and it truly was a magnificent evening, with a cooling breeze coming in from the sea. The restaurant patio perched on the edge of a steep drop into the hotel gardens, with a panoramic view across the surrounding tree tops to the hazy summit of Mont Saint-Victoire visible in the distance. Planters of white hibiscus intermingled with the round white-clad tables with their flanking red wicker chairs. Their scent and that of the oleander rising up from the gardens below permeated the air. In another hour or so, when darkness fell, this terrace would glow like an amber gem hidden away in the dark forest. It was calmness itself, broken only by the gentle scrapings and clinks of cutlery on fine china and the low murmur of conversation.

Now Gustav would probably deny him any future reservations. It seemed inconceivable that he would not be able to come here again. He lived a modest life and generally didn't care for the expensive comforts his family's wealth could afford. But good food was his weakness. At the mere thought, his stomach growled, and, as if to taunt him, a waiter passed by carrying a tray laden with the most heavenly aromas.

He had finished the glass and was contemplating another when Madeleine came over. She had waited on him before and now treated him to the kind of smile that exuded inner warmth and kindness.

"Dressed down this evening, did we?" she quipped, giving him a wink.

"It would seem so," he replied ruefully.

"Are you not eating tonight?"

Dupre groaned. "I would love to, but…" He indicated his state of dress with a motion of his hands. "And I don't have a reservation. You see, I wasn't anticipating coming here this evening, and to tell you the truth, I'm mortified to be seen like this. I don't think Gustav—"

"Nonsense," Madeleine cut in. "Contrary to popular belief, the clothes do not make the man." She nodded in Gustav's direction. "You leave Gustav to me." She slid a menu onto the table. "First, let me get you another glass while you take a look at tonight's offerings."

She bustled away, and Dupre grinned to himself. Perhaps all was not lost, and perhaps this investigation wasn't so inconvenient.

By the time Madeleine returned with his favored wine, Dupre had chosen the line-caught sea bass with bouillabaisse, fennel confit with whipped saffron potatoes and fresh asparagus hollandaise.

Madeleine didn't return until his food arrived and then inquired, "So, Gustav said you wanted to talk to me about Madame Borrell?"

"I'm afraid so."

"Is she in trouble? Oh, do tell me she's secretly some terrible criminal. She really is an unpleasant woman!" Madeleine joked.

Dupre raised an eyebrow. "Oh? Unpleasant? In what way?"

"She is always very curt. No, peremptory, like she is dealing with servants. I can't stand waiting on her." Madeleine snorted. "And her tips are insulting."

Dupre nodded. "So, what can you tell me about last night?"

Madeleine pensively tapped one forefinger against her lips before saying, "She came in around nine-thirty. From her damp hair I would say she had been playing tennis."

"Tennis?"

"Yes, she has been here several times for lunch wearing tennis whites."

Dupre was impressed. "I don't suppose you know what club."

She smiled down at him as if the question insulted her. "She wears the tracksuit top for La Rocque."

She doesn't miss a thing, Dupre thought. That would save them a lot of legwork tomorrow.

"And what about her companion? Her tennis partner?"

"Doubt it. He didn't look the type. Besides, she was already seated when he arrived."

"Ah, so they arrived separately."

Madeleine nodded, then continued, "He was thirtyish, dressed sharply, but…" Her mouth performed a lemon-sucking pucker. "Not tastefully. Too loud and too much bling. He kept checking his giant Patek Philippe watch, more, I think, to show it off than to actually check the time."

Dupre paused, a forkful of fish on its way to his mouth, and grinned. "I wonder how you will describe me after tonight?"

She laughed gaily. "You forget I have seen you before. You are always a very classy dresser. Last time I believe you wore tan slacks with a pressed blue shirt and an elegant black blazer."

Dupre whistled. "Very impressive. Have you ever thought of joining the police force?"

Madeleine laughed again.

"Oh, I have always had a good memory, particularly for people I like."

Dupre felt himself blush, but she went on with just a fractional pause. "I can understand dressing down for your kind of work. Can you tell me why you are so interested in her? Is she under criminal investigation?"

Her eyes sparkled as if this would be an unexpected gift. At that moment there was a loud crash and Dupre ducked his head. He noticed that Madeleine hadn't even flinched. He turned around and saw a young waiter on his knees picking up shattered crockery. Madeleine was smiling grimly and shaking her head. Then she fixed her gaze back on him. Taking advantage of the cover afforded by the commotion, Dupre lowered his voice.

"You will doubtless see it in the papers tomorrow, so no harm in telling you that she was found murdered in her apartment this morning."

Madeleine gasped and her face fell. "*Vraiment?* Now I feel terrible for the things I have said about her."

"Don't be," Dupre said drily. "I am getting the impression that she didn't make many friends. But now you can see why I am trying to piece together her last hours. Anything else you can tell me about her companion?"

"He had a tan, and they spoke in a foreign language."

"Which was?"

"I'm not sure, but we get Russians in here from time to time, and it seemed pretty much the same. Now I think about it, he looked and dressed like those nouveau riche Russians. No sense of style."

Dupre had now cleared his plate. The portions weren't generous, but the taste was to die for. He dabbed his mouth with the white linen napkin.

"What was their attitude? Did they seem like friends?"

The waitress shook her head emphatically, setting her blond curls bobbing. "*Non,* I don't think so. In fact, towards the end of the meal they seemed to be arguing. As soon as she paid the check, she got up to leave, and he grabbed her arm."

She paused, clearly replaying the scene inside her head. Dupre leaned forward across the table in interest.

"And?"

Madeleine uttered a short, humorless laugh. "She nearly broke his fingers as she peeled them off her arm. Then she stared down at him like you might at a turd on your shoe, said something and stalked out."

"And what did he do?"

She gave a slight gasp, eyes wide. "He said something I didn't understand, but he looked like he wanted to kill her."

"Really," said Dupre, nodding thoughtfully.

"After she'd gone, he finished his wine while talking on his phone. He seemed quite agitated. After a while he left."

Dupre scratched his jaw. "You didn't happen to see the car he drove, by any chance?"

Madeleine shook her head. "Sorry, but I'm sure Tristan did."

"The valet?"

"*Oui.*"

"Thank you, Madeleine. You have been most helpful. With that memory and those observation skills, if you ever need a new job."

Her laugh rippled. "And take a pay cut?"

He smiled wryly. "Can I send a sketch artist over tomorrow?"

She nodded. "*Bien sûr*. But perhaps at two after the lunch crowd."

"Of course. And thank you for this," he added, pointing to his clean plate and then patting his belly. "Are you sure things will be okay with Gustav?"

She nodded slowly and her mouth pinched a little. "Oh, I am quite sure. You see, the general manager of Les Lodges Mont Victoire is my uncle. Come back anytime." She winked. "But perhaps with a dinner jacket, yes? If you have a problem, ask for me. Now, how about some chocolate mousse with raspberry coulis and an expresso to finish?"

Dupre was overcome with warm feelings for this woman. "That would be amazing."

"*Bon.* This meal was on the house. And now I must see to my tables. Have a good evening, Monsieur Dupre. Now I know you are a policeman, when I wait on you, I will expect some juicy gossip." She chortled as she walked away.

Outside the restaurant, Dupre walked to his car in a daze of gastronomic pleasure. The valet hustled over with his keys, looking distinctly nervous.

"Ah, Tristan," said Dupre.

"*Oui, monsieur?*"

"I understand that you were on duty last night."

The valet paused for a moment before answering cautiously, "*Oui, monsieur?*"

"Do you perhaps remember a man, thirtyish, dressed loudly with a lot of bling and a fancy watch?"

Tristan held his palms open wide. "That could be many of our guests, monsieur."

"I'm guessing he had a fancy car as well. He was foreign, perhaps Russian?"

Tristan looked relieved. "Ah, yes. There was a man with a Porsche 911."

"Any chance you got the registration number?"

"*Mais oui*," Tristan blurted excitedly. "I am required to note all cars for insurance." He reached for a blue ledger under the valet stand. "Here, in this book." He opened it and leafed rapidly through the pages. Then he handed the book to Dupre and pointed to an entry.

"That's the one."

Tristan stood back and puffed up proudly.

Dupre noted the license plate in his notebook. "Now we are getting somewhere," he muttered to himself. Who would this belong to? One of the residents of the Old Gendarmerie, perhaps. He was willing to bet it wouldn't be the American. He didn't seem the sort to drive a Porsche.

"Well done, Tristan." He slipped the valet a twenty-euro tip. As he started to walk to his car, he turned back momentarily.

"And Tristan..."

"*Oui, monsieur?*"

Dupre adopted a mock stern voice. "Keep those pockets clean, eh? Getting high while driving expensive cars will end in disaster."

Climbing into his cluttered Renault, Dupre couldn't help but chuckle at the stunned expression on the young man's face.

11

It was not a bang that woke him this time, but a scream that galvanized Max into immediate, frantic action—an automatic parental response. The scream was not of terror, but of anguish, and it came from just down the hall. By the time he reached Luke's room, Luke was sitting up, only half awake, rocking back and forth with his knees pulled tightly to his chest and crimped by his thin arms. He had the aspect of a little boy again with tears streaming down his face. Max flung himself down next to his son and held him with strong arms and a shoulder to lean into. He stroked his son's hair.

"I miss Mom," was the boy's plaintive whimper.

Max took a deep breath and squeezed a little tighter. "I know." He sniffed heavily, grabbing a deep lungful of air to hold back his own tears. "I wish I could make the hurt go away," he whispered, his lips kissing the top of Luke's head.

He meant the hurt for Luke only, because the hurt he himself held was something he wanted to cling onto, in the same way a person wallows in songs of lost love at the unhappy end of an affair. That hurt, that gaping emptiness, the painful blessed memories, was where the ghost of his darling wife still lived. He was afraid that when it was gone, he would lose the last of her forever.

It had been a while since Luke had one of these episodes. Max did not want Luke to forget his mother, but he did want him to move on in a way that, if he was honest, he doubted he could ever do himself. He wanted him to live without the deep pit of aching grief that racked his own dreams, without the cloud that overcast all his waking moments.

Eventually the boy's tear-hitched breathing calmed, and Max felt the weight of his son gather against his chest. He laid him back down and scooched Dickens up next to him, satisfied when he saw Luke's arm nestle across the puppy in his sleep.

He went out onto the balcony and slumped into a chair, staring into the profuse darkness that only rural towns could achieve. It took him a few moments before he registered an ephemeral white shape standing motionless to the side of his balcony. He turned and saw Angela clad in a diaphanous white robe watching him, like a ghost in the moonlight. For once he did not register her state of undress. His thinking eye was turned inward, grieving over memories of Emma.

"Is he alright?" Angela whispered.

Dreamlike, Max nodded hesitantly. "For now."

"Bad dream?"

Max's sigh was deep and melancholic. It drew his attention back to reality. "I don't know. Something made him need his mother."

Angela seemed on the verge of tears. "I wanted to come and hold him."

Her compassion drew a weak smile from him. "Hold that thought until the morning. He may need one of your hugs then."

"Do you want to talk?"

"Thank you, Angela. You are very kind, but I think I will try and get some sleep. Tomorrow might be a difficult day if he's very tired."

Back in bed, Max did not sleep but dozed fitfully. Just before daybreak, Luke slid in beside him, bunching his back into Max's front, summoning a cocoon. The arrival of Dickens on his legs chased away any remaining possibility of sleep for Max, but he stayed, nestling his son until rhythmic breathing indicated that Luke had fallen back to sleep. Then Max eased out of bed and went out to watch the sunrise.

As he looked at the melon-colored bands breaking across the gray-blue horizon, he wondered if he could wait long enough to visit the patisserie for breakfast. No, he needed coffee now. He would have to take his chances with whatever edibles Luke's voracious teenage appetite had left in the cupboards.

As he walked back inside, he heard the buzz of his mobile phone. He dashed into the bedroom to lift it, thankful it was on silent. He looked at the number. *Bridget*—Emma's mother.

He took the phone outside and answered it quietly.

"Hello?"

"Max?" came Bridget's voice, tremulous.

Usually she spoke in a matter-of-fact, confident voice. She had the fortitude of ten women, having made her way alone at eighteen from Ireland to Philadelphia where she met and married Phil, a big bluff American. All through the aftermath of Emma's death, she had remained stoic and quiet in her grief, her strength a rock to which they all clung. Now, she sounded frightened, and Max's heart sank. What now?

"It's Phil," said Bridget, the brogue still strong. "He's been rushed into hospital. They think it's a heart attack."

"Oh no," said Max.

"I'm sorry," said Bridget, her voice faltering. "I didn't know if I should even call you, but I…" A small sob escaped her. "I just didn't know what else to do."

Max felt guilt course through him. His mother-in-law sounded so bereft, a feeling he was all too familiar with. She had not intended to guilt him, but he knew that had they been in America, they would have been at her side in half an hour. The family needed to rally, and he, usually the stable one in command, was not there. Worse, if Luke's beloved Pop-Pop died so soon after his mother… well, that didn't bear thinking about.

"Oh, Bridget. I'm so sorry we're not there," said Max.

He knew his mother-in-law would not want empty platitudes, so he let her talk and listened while Bridget relayed how she'd summoned an ambulance after Phil had suddenly experienced dreadful chest pains. She was still at the hospital waiting for news. They'd managed to stabilize him in the emergency room but were now prepping him for heart surgery. The talking seemed to help and gradually her breathing calmed, and her voice lost its desperate edge. Then Emma's sister Amy and her husband arrived.

Max wondered whether he should tell Bridget they'd catch a flight back. But was that really the best thing to do? To put Luke through a trauma like that again? What would be the point? Even if he could get a flight, whatever was going to happen would be over by the time they got there. And that would expose both of them to that cloud of pity that would only serve to refresh their loss. He had his doubts, but he didn't think he was wrong. They both needed time to grieve alone and put Emma's death behind them. Maybe then, when family and friends could see they had moved on, things would get back to normal at home. Was he being selfish? He just didn't know. But if the worst happened to Phil… Well, he would cross that bridge when, if, they came to it.

"Please, let me know as soon as you have any news," Max said before they hung up. Max had already decided he wouldn't tell Luke about his grandmother's phone call. Nothing would be served by scaring him. He would have to wait and see what happened. He looked to the orange morning sky and concentrated his thoughts on the hope that Phil would pull through. Life, as he knew so well, could turn, in an instant.

When Luke got up, his hair was awry, and the shadows under his eyes indicated a night of uneasy sleep. They had a subdued breakfast of toast and orange juice on the terrace.

"No naked swimmers this morning, Dad," said Luke, trying to lighten the dark mood.

Max, who had been trying to think of something humorous to say, smiled. "Small mercies."

He thought about keeping Luke from camp and doing something fun with him for the day but doubted that just the two of them, alone with their thoughts and shared grief, would help matters. No, he would stay the course he had embarked upon. Luke was better off with kids his own age, his mind occupied by the strenuous demands of soccer. But how would he, himself, handle the day?

True to her nature, Angela came out of the apartment next door as they left and caught Luke in a coddling embrace, kissing him fiercely on the forehead. With any other woman—even his mother—this would have been embarrassing for pre-teen Luke, but he melted into Angela's arms and stayed there til she pushed him away to wipe her eyes.

"I'm sorry if I woke you last night," he mumbled, his eyes downcast.

She chucked his chin up and looked at him with feigned surprise. "I don't know what you're talking about. I just needed a hug this morning, that's all." She shoved him gently away. "Now you better get going or you'll be late."

He gave her a quick squeeze again and then was gone, whistling for Dickens to follow. Max blew Angela a kiss and went after them.

He drove Luke to Stages Bousquier and watched as he caught up with some friends and walked through the archway into the camp. Now Max had to fill a whole day by himself. He did not want to go back to the apartment. The place seemed less tranquil after Bridget's call and with the ghost of Luke's nightmare still lingering. Added to that was the murder victim's apartment in view from their balcony. An unpleasant reality had disturbed his sanctuary. Trouble was he had nowhere to go, so he drove aimlessly when he pulled away from the camp. That's what he and Emma had done everywhere they had gone together: at home, in the Caribbean, in England and of course here, just for the pleasure of rolling through the landscape talking or enjoying their togetherness listening to a book or music.

Max felt the clouds of black grief closing in, brought on, as usual, by a number of factors—this time, a bad night's sleep, the guilt of being absent in a family crisis, and the fear of having to break some really bad news to Luke. He drove on, locked in dark thoughts that oppressed him, barely noticing the landscape as it swirled by. At what couldn't have been a worse moment, Chris Stapleton's "Starting Over" popped up on his playlist. He put his hand over to his phone to change the song immediately, knowing the pain it would bring, but then drew in a breath and stopped himself. *Let it play,* he thought. He had a masochistic desire to wallow. The song, about a couple reaching for a new lease on life, had been one of their favorites.

"That'll be you and me," he had told Emma. "Once Luke goes to college, we'll start over. You can quit your job, and we can go wherever we want for weeks or even months at a time!"

He had imagined spending three months each year here in Provence with her. Now that could never happen. Suddenly he was blinded by tears. He pulled over to the side of the road and lurched out, leaving the door open.

There was a low, stacked stone wall bordering a field of lavender and he leaned on it, his head in his hands. He closed his eyes, and in a sharp slice of clarity, the sight of her battered body on a stainless-steel table in the New Castle County morgue cut into him deep, leaving him struggling to catch his breath. He felt the darkness swirling over him, a disorienting fog. He hadn't cried or moaned or railed then. He had been uncomprehending. He had looked at his beloved's face, cleaned of blood but still gashed and misshapen, and his mind went blank, the voices around him sounding as in an echo chamber. Behind him, Stapleton's whis-ky-rich voice beat on him, singing about not knowing where he was going, only knowing he had to go. *That's what he was doing,* Max realized. He was running, trying to leave his loss behind. He didn't know where he was going, but the pain was always there. It would always be there, carried with him inside like a cancer.

He dry retched, and his legs buckled under him. He slid down the rough stones onto the hard-baked clay. Sitting with his back to the wall he pulled in his knees and wept, despair wrench-ing great wracking sobs from him. Mercilessly, Stapleton sang on about the strength of his sweetheart's love. Emma had been his rock, his *raison d'être*, and now he was a shell, a hollowed-out husk. He sucked in a great calming breath and knuckled his eyes. No, he had Luke. He had to pull himself together.

When Coldplay's "Viva La Vida" followed, he almost laughed at the bitter irony of a song about living life.

He was hauling himself to his feet when a phalanx of cyclists came level with the car. The leader braked to a halt, his pink outfit clashing horribly with the neon green of the 2CV6. He was a tall man with a handsome masculine face and long, tanned limbs partially sheathed in skintight spandex. Brave man, Max thought to himself, the incongruous sight bringing a spark of light relief to his mood.

"*Tout va bien?*" the man asked, concern in his voice.

Max cast his eyes over the rest of the multi-colored troop who were all staring expectantly at him. He managed a weak smile and nodded gratefully. He would be okay now.

"Oui, maintenant ça va. Vous êtes très gentil." It had been kind of them to stop. *"Merci."*

"You are British," the man said in heavily accented English.

"Actually, mostly Australian." Max always denied his English heritage. True, he had been born in England, but his parents moved when he was a baby and only moved back when he was in his teens. Even though he had told the police captain he was English, he scarcely considered that he shared any attributes with the English.

The cyclist nodded, clearly amused. "Ah, but that explains it." He glanced back at his companions and spread his arms. *"Un Australien, voilà,"* he said, as though they had been betting on something, and the cyclists to a man grinned and gave a thumbs up.

Confused, Max asked, "Explains what?"

"The car." He grinned. "Way too cool for *un rosbif.*"

The derogatory term for the British dispelled the last traces of Max's black mood, and he laughed.

"Bien sûr. Enjoy the cycling." He swept his arm across the arc of the blue sky. "It's a great day for it."

"Absolument." The man gave Max a penetrating look, the bridge of his nose furrowed in an expression of concern, before smiling once more. "You should join us one day. It lifts the spirits. We leave from Ménerbes at seven a.m. on Mondays and Thursdays. That is, when I'm not on call."

For a brief, hilarious moment, Max wondered how he would look in pink spandex too. *"Merci. J'y penserai."* He would think about it. He put out a hand. *"Je m'appelle Max Dempsey."*

The cyclist grasped his hand in a firm grip. "Claude Picard."

Max had taken an instant liking to this man. This was a man he sensed he could be friends with.

"A bientôt," Claude said as he mounted his pedals and, with a double-checking backward glance, began to move away.

Max watched the pack stream down the road like a lurid Chinese dragon eddying in the wind and envied their camaraderie. He let out a long breath, stretched and gazed up at the cliff towering over this section of road. He closed his eyes, feeling the sun warming the nape of his neck. After a few steadying breaths he came to a decision. Today was not a good day to be aimless.

He climbed back into the car, put it into gear, and, with a squeal of tires, hung a U-turn. Out of sheer obduracy he hit play on Chris Stapleton's "Starting Over" and sang along. Yes, he and Luke were starting over without Emma, but they would not be overcome. His mood lightened and on impulse he cued up Jesse Cook's "Nomad." He had never been to the Middle East, but the whirling, soul-strumming music on this album seemed full of joy and hope.

An hour later he was walking into the Carrières des Lumières outside Saint-Remy-de-Provence. The vast, dark caverns formed from limestone quarries dating back to Roman occupation were lit solely by giant projected works of Van Gogh on every available stone canvas, some carved into huge monoliths from the ancient rock. The images revolved and interchanged in time to the sweeping, resonant music of Debussy. It was breathtakingly beautiful and exerted a magical, calming persuasion on Max.

He sat down on a rock ledge before a soaring image of *Café Terrace at Night* and let the cherished memories of Emma flow.

A cheap poster of this painting had hung on Emma's kitchen wall when they met in DC so long ago now; it was all she could afford. They had come a long way since, collecting original art. Just last year he commissioned an original oil reproduction of this painting, and he remembered her face when she unwrapped it on her birthday. Tears had filled her eyes. That painting was still hanging in their bedroom at home.

Here in this rocky cathedral, his thoughts gradually morphed from desolation to sad resignation. He accepted that he had been lucky to have Emma for as long as he had, and she had left him with the gift of Luke, a gift, he thought wryly, that would keep on giving.

He moved slowly through the network of subterranean chambers as *Starry Night*, *Field with Poppies*, *Sunflowers*, and other masterpieces slid and flew around him, projected and freed from the physical constraints of a frame. Van Gogh would have loved this, he thought.

When he finally left the caverns and had reception, his phone pinged. There was a text from Bridget.

He opened it with trepidation.

Phil out of surgery. Doctors say things went well. He's awake and talking to me. He's not in pain. Am relieved.

Max felt a weight lift off his shoulders. He tapped out a quick but thrilled reply and resolved to come clean with Luke that evening. He had felt bad keeping Bridget's phone call from Luke that morning. Now that it was just the two of them, they shared almost everything, good and bad.

By the time he made it back to Roussillon, Max was feeling inspired. He promised himself that he would get out the laptop after a glass of Chablis over the rustic lunch he had missed yesterday and work on his novel. First, he stopped by the co-op to pick up a fresh melon and found Beatrice looking as sunny as ever, sunny enough to lighten his load still further.

"Ah, Max, you have news?" she said as she totted up his purchases.

He tutted. "You tell me. I know how these small villages work, and I bet you know more than me!"

She smiled, adopting a coy expression.

"Did you know Madame Borrell?" he asked.

Immediately her expression soured. "She came in here sometimes, *oui*. Very shocking. For a small place like this?" She lowered her voice and leaned in. "A most unpleasant woman. Truly, she was not liked."

Max thought back to his lunchtime discussion about Nash with Hans and Angela. He still had some uneasiness about the idea that a murderer was perhaps living among them. "Did you ever see her with anyone else?"

"*Non*." She shook her head. "She was always alone." Then her brow contracted. "No, I am wrong. She never came in here with anyone, but I do remember *seeing* her with another person."

"Oh? Who?"

Again, Beatrice's expression darkened momentarily. "Tall, narrow Englishman with a small beard. I do not know his name, but he wears *un chapeau crème*."

She put her hand to her head reflexively as though donning a hat.

"A cream-colored hat?" asked Max.

She nodded.

"I think I know the man you mean, but from the look on your face, you don't seem to like him either."

"He is a pig." Beatrice's eyes flashed angrily. "He made some suggestions to me that were not nice."

Max's lips tightened. "Yes, I have heard this about him. I'm sorry."

She snorted. "Why should you be sorry?" She closed one eye as she peered at him. "From you, those suggestions would not be bad," she said with a glimmer of a smile. "Pah! But from him." She puckered her mouth as if she'd tasted something bitter.

"So, you saw him with Madame Borrell?"

"*Oui*, out there," she waved her hand towards the parking lot. "Next to *la pharmacie*. They were arguing. He looked very angry, but she was laughing at him."

"Maybe he made those same suggestions to her and she turned him down."

She snorted again. "That I would find very hard to believe on both sides, but since they were both ugly, unpleasant people, perhaps they were a good match. *Non?*"

"Perhaps," he said with a wry smile. He really liked Beatrice. Twenty years ago, in another lifetime…

12

Capitaine Jacques stood almost at attention, hands clasped behind his back, looking out of his window at a fender-bender in the crossroads below. He was in a sour mood. Someone had stabbed a wealthy French woman to death in her luxury apartment, and as yet, he had nothing—no evidence and no leads, just a growing list of suspects. He glanced at the clock on his wall again. Nearly eleven a.m., Dupre had still not arrived, and they were meeting the judge at the victim's apartment in two hours without anything additional to offer.

True, they had the victim's phone and laptop which should account for something, but so far neither of them had been cracked. How hard could it be for someone as good as Arielle?

He was counting on the hope they would contain some clue about what was going on with Borrell that got her killed.

Borrell's cleaning woman had also been brought in to be questioned and to examine the apartment. She didn't think anything obvious had been taken, but things seemed disturbed; Madame Borrell usually kept strict order. So, had the killer been searching for something? If so, and if not valuables, then what? Then there were the injuries. They spoke of a *crime passionnel.* But there were no signs of such a struggle. Capitaine Jacques grunted to himself. Truthfully, the victim didn't look like the sort to incite passion, although, to his surprise, the search of her apartment had revealed birth control pills. This threw into question the whole idea that she never entertained anyone at the apartment.

No one had seen anyone coming or going from the building that night. Forensics had discovered traces of only three other people in the apartment. The concierge was one, but Hassan had admitted to being in the apartment from time to time in the course of his duties and more recently when he had discovered the body. His fingerprints were few, and nowhere one would not expect. Traces of the cleaning woman had obviously been found all over the apartment. Their fingerprints had been taken for elimination. A third set of prints had yet to be identified, but thanks to a new forensic test—something to do with the concentration of amino acids—they knew it was a male. His fingerprints had been found in almost as many places as the victim's, so he was either a frequent visitor or someone who had searched the apartment. Then there was the spot of blood on the patio. In all events, they would have to have DNA or fingerprints to match.

Capitaine Jacques dropped into his chair, reaching out to tap the file on his desk. He wanted to take a DNA sample and fingerprints from every male in the apartment complex, but he knew Judge Claire Lejeune was unlikely to grant a warrant when all the occupants had alibis. Of course, they could put out the request for volunteers and narrow their search that way, but experience told him a group of wealthy residents like that would club together and cite their civil right to privacy. His lip curled.

And then there was the American lawyer. He had an uneasy feeling about Monsieur Dempsey, and his gut was hardly ever wrong. Lawyers were always a problem.

Jacques had performed a background check on Dempsey. The man was in his late forties and a very accomplished trial lawyer in the United States. According to a magazine article he had found online—the fact that he was even the subject of a magazine article was a red flag—he had moved to the U.S. from England as a young lawyer. He had become a litigation partner in a multinational law firm based in New York, a lucrative partnership he had left behind to spend more time with his son Luke. The heading read: "Leaving the High Life Behind" and discussed Dempsey's decision to walk away to ensure a better work life balance.

Thinking of his own estranged family and how nice it would have been to be able to afford to quit his job before they left him, the article did nothing to warm Jacques toward the man. From other more recent news articles, Jacques discovered that the man's wife, Emma, had died in a road traffic accident only six months ago. So that was why he was in France, thought Jacques, a shade of sympathy creeping in. Dempsey had come with his son to escape his own trauma. With difficulty, he collected his thoughts. The American lawyer had no obvious motive to kill Madame Borrell. Still, Jacques couldn't shake the feeling that this man was going to be *un emmerdeur*—how did the English call it? Ah *oui*, a pain in the neck.

What bothered him most about this case was what little they knew about the victim. They had spoken to everyone in the building, but no one knew Madame Borrell. She came and went. She was supposed to be a real estate investor but they had found no trace of any business records. Possibly she had work colleagues, a partner even, but no one had yet surfaced following the reports of her death in the press this morning. An old Swedish woman, Madame Hojberg, who had lived in the building since it was converted, guessed she had come from up north by her accent but so far police enquiries had found no relatives. And there were two glaring anomalies in this case. First, her one and only credit card was issued by a Swiss bank that had refused to share any information. What sort of person had a Swiss bank account? Second, her national identity card and driving license were in her wallet, but beyond that, they found no identifying papers in the apartment.

Strangely, he thought, they had not discovered a passport. Of course, not everyone had a passport, but a woman as wealthy as the victim obviously could be expected to travel on vacation, no? Her car was registered to Madame Maxine Borrell at the apartment address. He tugged on one earlobe. The restaurant receipt Dupre had found could be something. Who had she dined with the night before her death?

He checked the clock again, drumming his fingers on his desk. He growled softly to himself.

The phone rang and he picked it up. "Jacques."

He caught his breath when he heard the voice on the other end. She had caught him totally unawares.

"*Madame le juge.*"

He had to admit to being grudgingly assuaged by their meeting yesterday, but he was still not convinced she could supervise a murder investigation. He listened for a moment and confirmed that he could meet at the murder scene at two o'clock. Hanging up the phone, he sat back, putting his feet up on the desk and rocked his swivel chair backward, almost to the point of tipping over. He liked to think of himself as a fair-minded person. Why should he dislike Madame Lejeune? Just because she was British? Was he not also a foreigner, from Senegal? But then, as a Senegalese, he had been born a French citizen.

Was she even a French citizen, or was she working here because the UK had been part of the EU? If that was the case, shouldn't she have lost her position now that the UK had left with Brexit? She had a law degree from England, but he had a law degree from France. Was he not more qualified? Her husband, a junior minister, was most assuredly French and had powerful connections. That had certainly obtained her appointment as a judge. He pondered these thoughts. Ah well, she was the judge and he was not. Besides, he admitted to himself, he had never wanted to be a lawyer or a judge anyway—too much politics. *C'est la vie.* He smoothed down his nonexistent hair and swung his long legs down. Time to get some more answers and maybe grab some lunch before he met the judge.

Jacques took the stairs and made his way down to the second floor. He found Arielle at her desk.

The young woman looked up as he approached, as if some sixth sense had alerted her. *"Ah, Capitaine, quoi de neuf?"*

Jacques flinched.

"I'll tell you what's new," he said gruffly, irked by Arielle's hipster and nonchalant greeting. "What's new is that there's nothing new! We have nothing! Please tell me you've got something for me."

Arielle pulled a laptop towards her from the clutter at the back of her desk. Jacques' eyes narrowed. He hated disorder. His own desk was completely regimented. How Arielle got anything done was beyond him.

"I haven't defeated the security yet," she said, rubbing the back of her neck, perplexed. "It is serious security for a regular person. I'd say there is more to our dead woman than you thought."

"You mean you can't access this computer?" Jacques said, incredulous.

"This is a Lenovo ThinkPad X1 Carbon—the best of the best, with a ridiculous level of encryption. Whatever she has on here she didn't want anyone else to see."

The captain's spirits sank. "What about the phone?" he asked glumly, already knowing the answer.

"Same. Fingerprint and password."

"Well, we have her fingerprints—or rather, her fingers." Jacques said with a bleak look.

"Yes, but fingerprints stop working after death. Something to do with the electrical charge. And anyway, we don't have any of her passwords."

"Well, let's get a warrant and go straight to Apple."

Arielle hunched her shoulders apologetically. "I don't think that is going to help much. They generally refuse to help police access phones, even those of known terrorists."

Jacques grimaced and threw his hands in the air. "So, we are nowhere then?"

Arielle stabbed the laptop screen several times with her index finger like she was picking a fight. "Oh, I will get in. It's just going to take a bit longer than I'm used to." She locked eyes with him. "But I will get in," she re-stated with the assurance of one unacquainted with failure. "Of course, it would be easier if you could locate her password at her office."

Jacques threw his hands wide and snorted. "What office?"

Arielle smiled, a little too smugly for Jacques' mood. "The laptop was recently serviced and the IT consultant left a sticker on the bottom. I called them and they told me they billed a company called BRDO Real at this address."

She handed Jacques a scrap of paper with an address in Cassis scrawled almost illegibly. Jacques squinted at the paper. Then he smiled with satisfaction.

"Now we are getting somewhere.," He paused as a thought occurred to him. "So do you think if they serviced it, they might still have access to it?"

"Nice try," Arielle replied with a lop-sided grin, "But I already tried that too. They reluctantly gave me the password they used once I told them we were investigating her murder. She had disabled the fingerprint recognition and apparently the password only got them into the root directory, not the files." She grimaced. "I tried it and it no longer even works for that. From this I conclude she changed her password when she got the laptop back."

Arielle shook her head, setting her rose-streaked hair swinging.

"She was one careful woman," she said, sounding impressed.

"How about BRDO Real? See what you can find out about them?"

"Already ahead of you, *mon Capitaine*. Rien! Zero! Zilch! Except for the address, they have no online presence. And according to company records they have only one officer on the books. Maxine Borrell."

Jacques chewed the inside of his cheek. The location of Borrell's office was at least another lead. "Fine," he said finally. "Good work," he added somewhat grudgingly.

She beamed.

"Go and find me a password there, *mon Capitaine,* and we will see what our guarded victim was hiding."

"But how will you get around the fingerprint?"

Arielle winked at him. "Oh, I have my ways."

So much for lunch, thought Jacques. "Perhaps you should come with us for the search," he suggested. "There may be more computers at the office."

Arielle popped out of her chair like a jack-in-the-box.

"Love to," she clipped.

Her smile was radiant with excitement, and he reflected that she probably didn't get out of the office much and worked long hours. Despite the weird rose-framed glasses and the severe lop-sided haircut with rose gold highlights, she was quite pretty. He glanced at the entwined blue roses tattooed on her left forearm—quite the theme. Lesbian perhaps?

He cleared his throat. "Downstairs in ten."

As Jacques went back upstairs to fetch his jacket, he passed through the bullpen and yelled, "Dupre!" A disheveled head appeared above one of the partitions.

"*Oui?*" the head asked.

"There you are. Finally." Jacques held up his watch arm and waggled it admonishingly. "Where have you been?"

"Visiting Madame Borrell's tennis club."

"*Allons-y*. We are going to Cassis. You can fill me in on the way."

Dupre looked dismayed. "Cassis. *Bien sûr*, but why?" Before Jacques could answer, Dupre added disconsolately: "It is almost lunchtime."

"Yes, I had realized that," Jacques responded brusquely. "Get the car and I will meet you downstairs in ten minutes."

Arielle was waiting outside, smiling broadly, when Jacques got to the front of the building. She had a large pink Hermès bag slung over her shoulder that must have cost a month's salary. It looked quite out of place against the blue detailed tattoos down her arm. As a tech, Arielle was not required to wear the traditional light blue shirt and dark blue skirt of a female police officer. Instead, she was wearing lemon yellow shorts with a sleeveless white blouse. She had a light tan, and to Jacques, she looked like she could be on vacation in Martinique instead of helping them track down a murderer. Well, she was brilliant at her job, Jacques reminded himself.

Dupre took an age to pull the standard white and blue Peugeot 308 hatchback of the Police Nationale up to the curb. Jacques' annoyance mounted when he saw the reason why. His subordinate had stopped in the cafeteria to pick up a sandwich. He appraised his colleague's paunch riding above creased gray pants. His top button was undone, his hideous tie askew and the white shirt that strained across his bulging belly was crumpled as though he had slept in it for the past week. Jacques had never known Dupre to appear any different at work, but he could barely tolerate it. It was not respectful of the job, he felt. If Dupre was not so very good at his job… Unconsciously he fingered his own perfect Windsor knot and glanced down at his crisp white shirt and tailored blue suit, searching for specks to flick away.

As Arielle opened the rear door and climbed in, Dupre looked at her in surprise and, hastily swallowing a packed mouthful of food, managed to croak out, "We're bringing the talent to Cassis?" he asked Jacques, nodding back at Arielle.

"*Salut, Louis,*" said Arielle, smiling.

"Well, we could find more computers," said Jacques. "It is Borrell's office."

Dupre wiped his mouth with the back of his hand causing Jacques to shudder. Jacques glanced at the half-eaten *pan bagnat* on Dupre's lap. There lay a demi-baguette stuffed with tomatoes, black niçoise olives, bell peppers, anchovies and, worst of all, tuna. The smell was overpowering. Jacques wound down the window even though hot air rushed in.

"Are you really going to eat that while you drive?"

"Don't worry, *Capitaine*. I do this all the time," said Dupre as he pulled into traffic. The car's sudden forward movement caused the sandwich to slip sideways, and Dupre slammed the brakes as he clamped his knees together to prevent his lunch from hitting the floor.

"*Merde!*" yelled Jacques.

Behind them came the squeal of tires and the angry sound of car horns. Dupre looked at Jacques sheepishly, the car wobbling as he accelerated again while trying to right his lunch. Arielle stifled an explosive laugh in the back seat.

"*Désolé,*" he said meekly, before lifting the sandwich to his mouth again.

Jacques looked at the new splotch of oil on the gray pants and cast his eyes to the heavens. Then, with an exasperated expulsion of breath, he pulled out his phone and called Judge Lejeune to push back their appointment.

"Something has come up," he explained.

"Something good?" Judge Lejeune asked.

"Possibly. We have located the victim's office. We are on our way to Cassis."

"*Bon. Pas de problem.* Let me know when you can meet."

The rest of the drive was uneventful, the end even pleasant, descending through the winding, pine-clad roads of Cassis Forest with an occasional glimpse of the Mediterranean sparkling under a cobalt sky. Jacques listened but didn't look at Dupre as he spoke through mouthfuls of sandwich.

"An excellent tennis player," Dupre said. "Aggressive and ruthless. The manager said Madame Borrell did not socialize at the club and did not seem to have any friends there, possibly because she seemed to enjoy humiliating other members on the court. She never really talked about herself. There were rumors she had a toyboy, but the manager thought she was a lesbian!" He waved his hand in the air at this, and a black olive plopped onto his lap.

Jacques rolled the window down further and put his head out to suck in some fresh air.

Arielle whistled from the back seat. "*Fantastique*," she crowed.

Jacques twisted in his seat to stare at her, eyebrows raised. "Really?"

"Well, I mean, from a purely academic standpoint, our victim is a complete cipher. Such a challenge, *n'est-ce pas*? A true mystery?"

"Yes, well, we don't really have the luxury of academic exercises with the mayor and commissioner breathing down our necks," Jacques replied coldly. "So, you'll excuse me if I prefer an easy solution."

Arielle caught Dupre's warning glance in the rearview mirror and downcast her eyes. "Yes, *Capitaine*. Of course."

Dupre recounted his conversation with Madeleine at Le Saint Amour the previous evening.

"And the license number of her dining companion's car?" Jacques demanded impatiently. "Have you followed it up?"

Dupre grimaced. "The car is registered to a company in Luxembourg. We are running that lead down now, but..."

"But it is most likely another dead end because it's a company in Luxembourg." Jacques sighed. "Super." Luxembourg was well known as a haven for hiding company ownership and assets.

It was a subdued three who pulled into the crowded town center of Cassis. Jacques scowled at the horde of tourists choking the narrow streets, remembering how peaceful it had been when he first came to the area. The address given to them by the IT company led them to Quai des Baux. On the ground floor was a restaurant called Le Bateau Ivre. Jacques got out of the police car, stared wistfully for a moment around the quaint fishing port in front of the restaurant, and then looked up. On the first floor, maroon shutters sat back from the windows. On the top floor, an intricate wrought-iron balcony jutted from the peach stucco. The maroon shutters were closed.

"Let's see if someone can let us in," said Jacques, turning towards the restaurant.

"Pas de problem." Arielle held up a set of keys, jingling them like she had just been given a Maserati for her birthday. "Louis picked these up in the apartment, and they ended up in the evidence locker."

Dupre whistled. "You think of everything."

Arielle winked.

They found a door in the side alley. Next to it was a brushed nickel plaque for BRDO Real. Dupre ran his fingers across it. "What do you think BRDO stands for?"

"Who knows?" Jacques said dismissively.

"Perhaps Bureau of something Development, or the something Organization," Arielle suggested.

Using the keys, they entered the building and tramped up two flights to the top floor where they found a heavy security door ajar. Jacques gently eased it open. Arielle gasped, and Jacques let out an expletive. In front of them was what looked like the aftermath of the Mistral, the famed cold wind that blew up through Southern France, caught and bottled in one room. Papers littered the floor, and glass from a smashed vase. So, the mysterious searcher had been here too, and not so careful this time. Madame Borrell had something that someone desperately wanted.

"Curious," Jacques murmured. The search of the Gendarmerie apartment had been careful, as though not to alert the occupant. Yet here it was frenzied and undisguised.

"Yes," agreed Dupre, as if he could read his superior's thoughts. "It is as though they knew Borrell would not be coming back."

Examining the open door, Jacques muttered, "Either a professional or someone with a key." He turned to Dupre who was staring pensively at the mess. "Call forensics," he barked before he entered the room, pulling on blue latex gloves and stepping gingerly around the scattered papers.

The offices of BRDO Real consisted of two rooms with a kitchenette and bathroom. In sharp contrast to Borrell's apartment, the interior design was Scandinavian, with blond wooden floors and sleek furnishings. The walls were pale periwinkle, and when Arielle threw open the patio doors and shutters, bright sunlight flooded in. The walls caught the light and reflected it like a luminous sky.

"*Waouw! Quelle vue spectaculaire*," Arielle said, stepping out onto the balcony and surveying the harbor.

Jacques followed her out and leaned on the balustrade, capturing deep, calming breaths of the tangy salt air. From here he had a perfect view of the imposing Château de Cassis, poised at the very edge of the Cap Canaille cliffs that plunged straight into the azure blue of the bay below. But the beauty of the scene provided little balm for his troubled mind. Was anything about this case going to be easy?

"Do you mind if I have a quick bite?" Arielle asked, sitting down at the wrought iron bistro table and pulling a plastic container from her capacious bag.

Jacques glanced at the healthy-looking salad she was open-ing, and his stomach growled. She wasn't likely to compromise the crime scene out here anymore than they had just by walking into the place.

"Sure, why not," he said glumly. "Bringing the keys saved us some time, and we have to wait for forensics anyway. In the meantime, there is enough for Dupre and I to do."

He dragged himself back inside and scanned the room. The desk was a large L-shaped affair of brushed nickel with a Carrera marble top. Notably absent was any sign of a desktop computer, just papers haphazardly strewn across the surface—more signs of an undisguised search. To one side was an Uplift desk that could be raised if you wanted to work standing up. How *chic.* Madame Borrell must have cared about her fitness. The pale gray leather executive chair and matching guest chairs were opulent. A large geometric-patterned rug in faded colors of navy, aqua and rose pooled around the desk like a deep pond. He felt sure that, like its mate in Borrell's apartment, it would be an antique hand-knotted Persian. The whole setup probably cost more than Jacques' entire household of furniture.

The svelte, white filing cabinets ranging along one wall looked as if they had just been unboxed, unlike the abused and battered relics back in his own office. Several drawers hung open. Whoever had been here was looking for something in a hurry. He bent down and picked up several of the scattered pages. They appeared to be nothing more than rent statements and invoices related to addresses in Cassis, the stuff a real estate investor might be expected to have. He skimmed them back onto the floor.

On the wall across from the desk was a large painting of two faces side by side rendered in abstract blocks of vivid color. One face resembled Madame Borrell herself and the other seemed vaguely familiar. He peered at the bottom right corner for the artist. *Yazmin.* He pursed his lips. Unsurprisingly, this name didn't mean a thing to him, and he thought the image gaudy and a little disturbing. Despite the vibrant colors, there was almost a malevolent aspect to the faces.

Dupre's voice floating from the second room summoned him from his reverie. *"Mon Capitaine. Viens ici."*

The second room was similarly decorated in ash wood and pastel colors. The shutters had been opened, and the light from the large window opening onto the alley was captured and transmuted to incandescence by the soft primrose walls. Gauzy filigree curtains wafted in the slight breeze. A bed sat wide against the wall, its sheets crisp white cotton. Another original canvas by Yazmin dominated the wall across from the bed: a line of a half dozen small birds perched on a branch, rendered in the same blocky patches of primary colors. This room showed no signs of the hurricane that had hit the office next door. Everything was neat, like a disused hotel room.

Jacques stood ruminating. Why would a woman who lived in a luxury apartment in Roussillon have this separate apartment? A guest apartment? But for someone so security-conscious, that seemed unlikely. Possibly she worked late and didn't like the tortuous drive home in the dark? That didn't seem likely either. From what little he knew of her, she had been a commanding, forceful woman.

"Capitaine!"

Jacques was roused from his musings and turned to Dupre who was holding a leather-bound Filofax in his surgically gloved hand. He waved it enthusiastically.

"This was in the bedside drawer."

That surprised the captain. It seemed like the sort of thing the searcher might have been looking for.

"What does it contain?"

"Odd notes, appointments and…" he paused for effect, "a list of passwords."

"*Eh bien!* Now we are getting somewhere. Does it say who she was meeting the night she was killed?"

"No, these appointments are years old," said Dupre, flicking through the pages.

"Hah!" exclaimed Arielle, coming in behind them. "No one keeps a diary like this anymore." She took the Filofax from Dupre and looked through the pages, amused. "Very old school. I'm sure she kept her up-to-date calendar, notes and reminders on her phone. Probably her latest passwords as well."

"Of course," Jacques muttered.

"But don't give up hope, *mon Capitaine.*" Arielle waved the Filofax in the air. "These passwords might still work, or at least give us a pattern to follow."

Jacques looked at her resignedly. "Before we touch anything else, let's get the crime scene guys in here. I want every file in those cabinets inspected and every paper on the floor examined. Somewhere in here there is a reason for this break-in. Robbery was not it."

He cast his hand around the room, pointing at the obvious items of value left behind.

"Right," agreed Dupre. "The fact that they searched only the office and not this bedroom would seem to indicate that whatever they were looking for was something to do with her business."

Jacques made a small sound of exasperation. "Then why search her apartment in Roussillon? It's not making any sense."

13

Michel Briancon sat at the bar in Le Bateau Ivre glowering into a glass of milky white pastis. The bottle stood by his elbow. His hand shook as he raised the glass to his lips. His brother Julien stood on the other side of the bar wringing a dishtowel as though it were a chicken's neck. Their eyes met. That had been close. If it wasn't for the fact that Julien had been smoking under the awning out front and saw *les flics* arrive, Michel and his associate Paolo would have been caught red-handed. God knows what would have happened then. Paolo was a psychopath who could shoot police officers as soon as look at them. As it was, Julien had raced to the bottom of the backstairs to warn his brother.

Despite his muscular appearance and reputation, Michel was not a brave man. He had come tumbling out of the bitch's office, hair and eyes wild with exertion and panic, shoving Paolo before him down the stairs and through the access door into the kitchen. Julien had raised his eyebrows hopefully, but Michel shook his head. He had not had time to find what he was looking for.

"Rien."

Julien blew out a breath of disgust, scowling his blame onto his brother. Julien had seen the early report of her death on the television above the bar. He had made no effort to conceal his excitement. The recent pandemic had decimated the tourist trade and the restaurant had struggled. Their savings were almost exhausted. Finally, just two days ago, out of sheer desperation, they had gone to Maxine Borrell for a loan. They knew her reputation around town, with her tenants and borrowers. But because of their landlord-tenant relationship and Michel's connection to the Brise de Sang, they had hoped for more favorable treatment. Since Julien flatly refused to get in bed with the Brise, it was not like they had a lot of choices. None of the banks were lending money to restaurants. As he thought back on their meeting, Michel's anger rose. Far from being sympathetic, *la chienne* had been callous and gloating.

"Why do you think I keep my office here when I own other buildings? I mean, the view is very nice, but I was waiting for this to happen and wanted to be on hand when it did."

They had been forced to secure the loan with a deed to the building they were in—a building that had been in their family of fishing folk for generations—and he knew with absolute certainty that at the slightest hiccup in repayment at the exorbitant rates Borrell charged, she would take the building she had been trying to buy from him for years. As they were leaving, she had snickered.

"I guess you will soon be my tenants, eh?"

Killing the bitch had done the whole world a service, and especially them. If they could just get the deed back before anyone else found it. With the money she had loaned them safely tucked away and no one the wiser, they would be golden. So the moment the news broke, Michel had gone to look for the documents in her office. Then that *putain* Paolo showed up, sent by Battistu, the local Brise chief, to find a laptop and destroy anything that could link them to Borrell. Alone, Michel could have conducted a discreet search, but Paolo just ransacked the place. The laptop wasn't even there and *les flics* arrived before he finished searching.

"Perhaps they won't find it before they leave," Michel suggested sullenly.

"*Pas de chance,*" Julien murmured, picking up a glass. "Now that it's obvious the place has been searched, *les flics* will go through it with a fine tooth comb. If it's there, *les flics* will find it." He slapped the dish towel on the bar angrily. "We could lose everything."

Michel had no idea who would take over her business, but he knew the Brise were not the only people she partnered with. None of them were people you wanted to owe money to. He poured himself another drink.

"When they leave, I will look again."

Julien suddenly froze, staring past Michel. Hearing a soft step, Michel turned to find a tall, bald, black man standing by the side entrance. He glanced back at Julien, who had become suddenly engrossed in cleaning the spotless glass in his hand. How long had the policeman been there before Julien noticed him, and how much had he heard?

The man stepped forward. "*Bonjour. Je suis Capitaine Jacques.*" He flashed a warrant card. "*Et vous* êtes?"

Michel took note of his immaculate suit and handsome tie. This *flic* had style to go with his rugged good looks. Michel had the feeling he had seen this guy somewhere before. Jacques...

Jacques... it was at the edge of his brain but wouldn't come. Scornfully, he watched the nerves descend on his brother, who cleared his throat and introduced them both.

"Julien Briancon. This is my brother, Michel. We own this restaurant."

"Are you also the owners of this building?" said Jacques.

"*Oui.*"

"I wonder what you can tell me about Madame Borrell from upstairs?"

Michel watched Julien's mind work sluggishly through a range of responses. Was he going to tell the policeman they knew her? Or that she was a stranger?

"*Oui, monsieur?* What can I tell you?"

Jacques made an impatient clicking sound and let out a long breath. "How about everything you know."

Julien was back to wringing the chicken's neck. "Ah, *oui.* Well, we didn't know her very well. She was very private, and we were just her landlord."

He smiled anxiously, turning his face towards Michel for confirmation. Michel nodded, scowling.

"She wasn't exactly warm," Michel said, taciturnly. "We stayed away from her, mostly, if we're being honest." He uttered a hollow laugh.

"Oh? You didn't like her?"

"I didn't say that we didn't like her," Michel snapped. "I said we just kept ourselves to ourselves." He noted Julien's warning look. "Of course, we were sorry to hear of her tragic death. Do you know what happened? Who did it?"

Jacques narrowed his eyes on the brothers. His voice was low and measured. "Do you know anyone that might have wanted to harm her? Any rows upstairs? Raised voices?"

"As I said, she wasn't very friendly." Michel tossed back his drink like a saloon cowboy downing two fingers of whisky—a gesture full of embittered impatience. "Ask around. She was not a nice woman." His jaw clenched when he thought about the terms of the loan, and he felt himself flush. "She was a hard businesswoman." As the implication of what he had just said filtered through his brain, he hastily added, "Not that we did any business with her. That's just what we heard around." He watched Julien use the dishrag to wipe his sweaty hands.

At that moment, they were joined by a corpulent man who appeared the antithesis of the captain. His overgrown, graying locks were unkempt, and he had several days' stubble. His wrinkled shirt was loose at the neck, held together by one of the ugliest ties Michel had ever seen.

"Ah, Dupre. These gentlemen were telling me all about Madame Borrell," said Jacques.

"I heard," said Dupre, eyeing both Michel and Julien keenly. In that moment, skewered by Dupre's piercing gaze, Michel grasped that this slovenly, overweight policeman was perhaps more dangerous than his boss. He also realized their conversation had carried into the back corridor and been picked up before Dupre entered the room. He wondered again how much the captain had heard before they noticed his arrival. Julien fidgeted ceaselessly, clearly agitated, his broad forehead beading with sweat. The fact did not seem to be lost on the policemen.

"Can you tell me where you were two nights ago?" asked Jacques.

"*Bien sûr, Capitaine*," said Julien in a rush. "I was here until eleven and then I went home to bed."

The captain's mouth twitched in a fleeting expression of skepticism. He turned to Michel. "And you?"

Michel coughed and glanced at his brother. He turned around to face the police captain again. "I was here with Julien until we closed and then I went home to bed."

"Anyone see either of you after you left here?" Dupre asked, scribbling in a black notebook.

"My wife," said Julien, and Michel saw the relief on his face that he had an alibi despite the certain knowledge that he had done nothing wrong.

"I live alone," Michel muttered, his low voice full of resentment.

"What?" asked the captain. "Speak up, man."

Michel coughed. "I live on my own."

"What do you know of Madame Borrell's business?" asked Jacques.

Michel shook his head. "Only that she owns properties around town. I repeat. She was a hard *chienne.*"

"We got that," Dupre interjected. "Can you be a bit more specific?"

Stung by the policeman's tone and despite Julien's pleading look, Michel replied, "She loaned money at exorbitant rates, took people's property, treated her tenants badly… or so I hear. Maybe that's where you should be looking—at someone who lost their property to her, or someone she evicted?"

The two brothers glared at the policemen.

"What about business associates?" asked Dupre. "Rich-looking businessmen driving fast cars. You ever see anyone like that coming and going?"

Julien looked agitated again. He scratched the back of his head as if searching his memory and Michel knew he was struggling to economize with the truth. Of course they had seen known gang members going up there. Hell, they sometimes stopped downstairs for a drink and to chat with Michel, but neither wanted to be classed as informers. If word got out that they had talked to *les flics* then anything could happen.

"*Oui*," Julien said cautiously. "Sometimes we saw men come, but mostly I guess her visitors went in by the side alley which we cannot see."

The captain blew out a hard breath. "What about the ones you did see. Recognize anyone?"

Julien closed his eyes momentarily as if he was thinking, then set his face in a picture of pensive honesty before throwing up his hands in a gesture of defeat. *"Personne."*

This time it was Dupre who looked skeptical. "No one? You're sure?"

Julien studied the floor. "Business associates? *Non.* They weren't from around here. Perhaps I recognized some of her tenants coming and going, but I don't remember. I don't know any names."

"She ever eat in here?" Dupre asked.

Ah, this Dupre was a sharp one. "Not very often," answered Michel. "To be honest, she didn't like our food." He scowled. "Said it was tourist crap."

"Too stuck up for here," Julien added with a shrug. "She preferred to eat up at the château."

He pointed his chin up towards the cliff top. Members of the Brise didn't often eat in their restaurant, thank God.

A waitress pushed through the swing door from the kitchen and entered the bar. She gave the policemen a short appraising glance and then looked at Julien and Michel.

"What about you, *mademoiselle*?" Jacques said. "What do you know of Madame Borrell?"

She looked up into the face of the policeman, working her mouth like she was sucking something tart. Then she looked askance at Julien.

"They are the police, here about Madame Borrell," Michel said, feeling like he was stating the obvious.

"Ah, *oui,* I heard what happened. *Terrible*," she said, although her face did not register the matching emotion but something more akin to satisfaction.

"So, *mademoiselle*," Dupre said, turning his frank gaze on the waitress.

The waitress held up a plump left hand like she was proffering it for a kiss. *"C'est madame."*

Noting the gold wedding band, Dupre nodded. *"Bien sûr, madame. Et votre nom?"*

"Danielle Foulquier."

"Well, Madame Foulquier," Dupre paused. "What can you tell us about your upstairs neighbor?"

"Pas trop," she replied.

The captain struck his forehead several times with his

fingertips. "Not much, not much. That is all I hear from every-one. Was this woman a ghost?"

Danielle took a half step backwards and glanced at Dupre with a furrowed brow.

He smiled reassuringly at her. "I understand she ate in here occasionally."

"*Oui, c'est vrai,*" Danielle murmured.

He probed gently. "Did you wait on her?"

"*Bien sûr.* Sometimes."

"So, you must have observed some things about her."

Danielle sniffed. "I'm sorry to say it, especially as she is dead, but she was *une chienne.*"

"So your bosses told us," the captain said drily.

"Go on, madame," Dupre said, moving to one side to draw her resentful gaze away from the other policeman. "In what way?"

"She treated us like slaves," Danielle said, a rancorous note creeping into her voice. "Worse. Like dogshit."

Dupre rubbed his stubble. This matched what Madeleine at Le Saint Amour had said.

"Did she dine on her own or with someone?"

The waitress blew out a staccato breath. "Never alone. She complained about the food. We were just a convenience with visitors she didn't care to impress."

"What about the people she dined with? What can you tell us about them?"

"Nothing special. Just suits." She paused, a finger tapping on her lips. "No, wait a minute. They were always foreign. In fact, there was a foreign guy just last week."

Julien scowled at her and cleared his throat.

The captain grunted. "Foreigners, here in the south of France in the summer. *Quelle surprise!*"

Dupre remonstrated, "But what would a foreign tourist be doing having lunch… dinner…?" He looked at Danielle who smiled gratefully at him.

"Lunch," she prompted.

"Lunch with a local businesswoman?" Dupre continued.

"Perhaps he was renting a vacation apartment from her?" said Jacques.

"I believe she only had commercial properties," Julien offered tentatively.

"What did they talk about?" Dupre asked Danielle.

"I don't know because I couldn't understand a word they said," she replied.

Jacques closed his eyes and appeared to be counting under his breath. Then his eyes popped open, and he smiled ingratiatingly. "They were speaking a foreign language?"

Danielle nodded animatedly. *"Oui."*

"Can you say what language?" Dupre coaxed.

Danielle slowly shook her head.

"Can you say what language it wasn't?" Jacques demanded. "English, *par example?*"

The waitress squared up to the captain and put her hands on her wide hips. She stared up into his face, an expression of intense dislike on hers, and said in very clear English, "No, it wasn't English, nor was it Chinese, or Punjabi, or Swedish or Italian, or—"

Dupre put a gentle hand on her arm. "What would be your guess?"

She stepped back from the captain and sniffed. Then she turned to Dupre. "If I had to guess, Russian."

"Ah," he nodded. "Thank you."

"Could be an investor?" Jacques posited. "Damn Russians are buying up half the coast."

With a sympathetic glance at Dupre, Danielle began to turn away and then stopped and put her fingers to her lips. "Oh, and there was a young man who came in a few times."

Jacques jerked like he'd just been stuck with a pin. *"Vraiment?"*

"Oui."

Michel liked where this was going. Putting the attention on the Russians and some random young buck suited him just fine.

"Can you describe him?" prompted Dupre.

"He was perhaps in his late twenties. Dark. I didn't pay too much attention. He was handsome though." She wrinkled her nose and added, "Too handsome for her."

Dupre didn't quite suppress his smile.

"Ah, *oui*," said Julien. "Now I remember him. I have seen him with her a few times. He didn't look rich like the others." His voice suddenly faltered, and his mouth dropped open. His gaze shifted beyond the policemen.

Jacques glanced around. "Ah, Arielle. *Bien.*" He raised his eyebrows. "Success?"

Arielle shook her head as she held the laptop up. At the sight of it, Michel's stomach dropped. This was undoubtedly what that idiot Paolo had been searching for.

"No luck with those old passwords, but forensics have arrived," said Arielle.

Michel saw Julien glance his way but fought hard to keep his face impassive.

"Go and supervise," Jacques told Dupre. "I'll head back with Arielle."

He frowned at the two brothers. "I don't suppose any of you know anything about a break-in upstairs."

Michel's eyes warned his brother to stay cool. He shook his head at the captain. "Break-in?"

"Yes, someone ransacked Madame Borrell's office. Must have made quite a noise. You didn't hear or see anything?"

Michel shook his head again.

The policeman's face curled in a sneer. "Didn't think so." He put his calling card on the bar.

"If you remember anything else, please give us a call." He stared pointedly at Michel. "I will leave a man here until we clear up this mess, in case the intruders decide to return. But if you see anyone you recognize outside the apartment or trying to gain access, call me immediately, *d'accord*?"

"*D'accord,*" said Julien quickly.

Michel glowered and made no response.

They both watched as the captain and his female officer left. Michel had a bad feeling about all this. Earlier he had been elated when he thought he could recover the deed. And now? Everything had gone to shit, as usual. When those policemen look up his record, which they will certainly do now, they'll find he already has form—two years in prison for aggravated assault with a knife. When *les flics* put two and two together, that will doubtless drop him in the shit. And Julien too perhaps, by default. He'd never hear the end of that. He didn't have long to wait.

The moment the police were gone Julien grabbed his brother's sleeve and pulled him across the bar until their heads were bent close.

"Imbecile," he hissed. "I saw that *connard* Paolo sneaking into the kitchen when *les flics* arrived. What the hell is he doing here anyway? Why couldn't you just search her offices on your own?"

Michel tugged his sleeve away. "You don't want to know. I didn't have a choice. He was sent."

"Well, I know you were not with me Tuesday evening," Julien said. "So where were you that you lied to *les flics*?"

The less Julien knew of his business for the Brise, the better. He gazed coolly at his brother. "Nowhere near that *chienne.*"

Julien looked like he wanted to believe him.

"Then it was that *maniaque*, Paolo. She must have done something to piss off the Brise."

Michel shrugged. "*Peut-être.* I don't know, but I do know they wanted that laptop."

"Yes, and now thanks to him ransacking the place, the police will go through every paper in there. There is no chance we will get that deed back."

14

In front of Le Bateau Ivre lay the turquoise Mediterranean, not even separated by a low wall, just a wide swath of gray flagstones and a short drop into the water; a narrow concrete jetty thrust out into a harbor crowded with boats of all types rocking gently in the wakes thrown up by the ferries. Having slipped out through the kitchen, Paolo Negroni stood in a black cigarette boat halfway down the jetty, slouched against the gunwale. He alternated taking deep drags from an unfiltered Camel and biting on the nicotine-stained nails of his left hand as he watched the building from his boat. He cursed under his breath. That had been a narrow escape. Perhaps he should not have left. The boss would not be happy, and when the boss was not happy...

He had been told to recover Borrell's laptop by any means necessary and then torch the office. He checked the gun nestled in the small of his back for the umpteenth time. It was a tic when he was experiencing an adrenaline rush. He contemplated the consequences of shooting *les flics*. There were only three and they appeared unarmed. He felt his blood pumping as he imagined their faces had he waited and hit them as they came through the door. But shooting cops was a bad idea, and, anyway, the shots would have brought people running, leaving him no time to continue the search. And how would he have made his escape back to the boat? *Merde*, with all these tourists around he would likely be filmed.

The laptop didn't even seem to be there. Best thing he could do was sit tight and wait for them to leave, wait for Michel to reappear. Maybe they wouldn't even be able to get into Borrell's office. Paolo was an old hand with the police and knew their limitations. Cops couldn't just break down a door. Then a thought dawned on him. Michel had hustled him out and was the last to leave. Had he closed the door? No. *Merde!* As if to confirm this mistake, the maroon shutters on the second floor opened, and a tall black man who reeked of *flic* stepped out onto the balcony accompanied by a young woman. She then sat down to eat at the bistro table while he leaned on the railing and took in the view. Like they fucking owned the place. Paolo sighted along his index finger and puffed out an imaginary shot as his thumb came down like a hammer.

While he watched and seethed, chain-smoking, a police van pulled up, and several people dressed in plain clothes climbed out and pulled on white suits with booties. Paolo scowled and spat over the side. Now that they had brought in a forensics team it was pointless to hang around. They wouldn't miss a laptop. He was about to start the engine when he saw the two from the balcony coming out the front of the restaurant. He whistled under his breath. Now that he could see her front on, he realized that she was hot. Then he noticed that under one slender, honey-colored arm, she was cradling a laptop. His gut sank. He should have stayed, shot them and taken it. Battistu would not be reasonable or forgiving.

He jumped forward and flicked his cigarette into the water. He could do it now. With the two of them he may not even have to fire a shot. He could club the big guy and threaten the girl. He was willing to bet that if he waved his gun in her face, she would hand over the laptop. He tried to clamber over the side in a hurry, but just at the wrong moment, the boat rocked in the wake of one of those damned tourist ferries, and as it bobbed away from the dock, he almost fell into the water. Frantically he scrambled for a hold and successfully grabbed one of the cleats, hauling himself upright. Cursing, he leapt from the gunwale and started down the jetty, but before he could reach the pavement the pair had climbed into the police car. He paused uncertainly at the edge of the street staring at them, flexing his fists. He started forward and stopped, plans spinning through his mind. He could do this. It would be just like a carjacking. He would jerk the door open, thrust a gun in the black guy's face, and if the girl didn't hand over the laptop he would blow his fucking head off. But then she could describe him, and his face would be all over the news. He would have to kill them both. He had just started forward again when Michel appeared. Crossing the street in quick strides, Michel came up and grabbed Paolo's arm.

"What the fuck are you still doing here?"

Paolo's eyes narrowed. "She has the laptop," he hissed, jerking his head toward the police car.

"I know."

Paolo wrenched his arm away, a mad gleam in his eyes. "Well, I'm going to get it."

He started forward again, but Michel's fingers clawed at his arm again.

"Are you fucking insane?" Michel glanced around the crowded waterfront. "You can't shoot two cops here in broad daylight. He shook Paolo and stared down his crazy expression. "Think, *mon ami*. There would be a massive manhunt with your face all over the news. And," he added as a clincher, "Battistu will have to kill you. He won't risk having you taken."

The light of madness dimmed, and Paolo pushed Michel roughly away as the police car started moving away down the quayside. Paolo closed his eyes and cursed Michel, himself, his luck, Battistu, the whole world. For a brief moment he considered jacking a car and following them, but opening his eyes, he saw there wasn't another vehicle in this pedestrian part of town. He kicked the bench in front of him and stalked back to the boat, running through a litany of excuses.

"Do you want me to come with you?" Michel called after him.

"What the fuck do you think?"

Scowling, Paolo punched the starter and the engine sprang to life with a deep, throaty roar, creating a whirlpool of white foam. Michel leapt nimbly into the well of the boat and they eased out into the harbor.

Less than an hour later, the two walked into the Bar du Telephone where they found Battistu watching France play Portugal on a giant LCD screen that seemed out of place in the shabby bar. Battistu was a big man with the look of a brawler. He had a fat scar down the left side of his face and the ugly weal of a large burn on his right forearm. Paolo knew that under the black silk shirt lay a mess of scars and bullet wounds. Battistu turned black eyes on him as he and Michel approached. Paolo coughed nervously, his heart rate increasing and tightness constricting his breathing. He tried to keep the fear off his face, hoping the story they had worked out would sell.

"Sorry, boss. The police were swarming all over the place when I got there. Detectives and forensics. A whole team."

Battistu turned a savage gaze on Michel who nodded slowly. Battistu's penetrating stare returned to Paolo's face and settled there unwavering, one meaty fist repeatedly clenching and un-clenching on the scarred tabletop. Long moments passed and Paolo felt he was being pierced to his very core, leaving his knees weak. Battistu was no one's fool. Eventually the big man spoke in a voice that sounded like a Rottweiler about to attack.

"That's too bad. That laptop had all her business informa-tion—information we need to continue business with her east-ern associates and information that could prove very unpleasant for us should the cops unlock it. If we can't get it, it needs to be destroyed." He scowled at Paolo. "You should have torched the place to make sure there was nothing on paper."

Paolo swallowed hard. "With half the Aix police force in-side?" he croaked.

Battistu stared him down. "Yes!" he snarled. "Do you have any idea of the shitstorm that is going to descend if that *putain's* laptop is cracked?"

Again, Paolo swallowed hard. He caught Michel's scowl at the mention of torching his restaurant. He hadn't told Michel that part.

"I told you to send her a message that we were unhappy about the Russians. Not kill her before we cleared things up."

"Boss. I didn't kill her. I swear it." Paolo felt the percolation of diarrhea. He gave Michel a vicious look.

"You," said Battistu, pointing at Michel. "You have a friend in the local Gendarmerie, yes? I want that computer, or I want it destroyed. I don't care what it costs. And I want to know anything else they found that might tie us to her."

He smashed his fist down on the table. Michel shot Paolo another angry glance. Paolo knew that Michel had an old classmate who was a sergeant in the Gendarmes—an old classmate who happened to have a serious cocaine habit that Michel was only too happy to feed at a price, a habit that gave Michel leverage. He didn't remember telling Battistu, but now Michel would think he had. He was suddenly feeling exposed. Fucking Battistu knew everything. He had to fix this.

"Do you want me to go back and torch the place now?" he asked hopefully.

"Now? *Abruti!*" Battistu screamed at him. "What is the point now? If there is anything to find, *les flics* will have taken it with them." Battistu clenched his fist again, and Paolo flinched backwards. "So go and find out what they know. *Imbeciles!*"

Paolo stumbled backwards, turned and practically ran out of the bar, Michel following after. That could have gone very badly. It still could if Michel's contact couldn't get his hands on the laptop.

"Call him now," demanded Paolo.

"But—"

"NOW! We'll meet at my cousin's place. And put it on speaker. I want to hear what he has to say."

Reluctantly, Michel took out his phone and dialed his contact's number.

"*Quoi?*" Michel's number had obviously been recognized. The voice on the line was brusque.

"Tacos Francais, three o'clock," said Michel.

"What the f—" said the voice before Michel hung up.

Paolo nodded. This was not business you could do over the phone, and any record of such a short call could be a wrong number. The guy would come. He didn't have a choice.

Tacos Francais in Aix was on a back street, sandwiched between a high ancient stone wall and a pink stucco house. The steel shutters on the storefront and the bars on the adjacent windows gave the place an edgy feel, as if anything could kick off at any moment. It was a good, quiet place for a meet. Besides, Paolo loved the tacos, advertised as *Finally an authentic French taco*. That always made him grin.

"Hey, Marc," he greeted the heavy-set, swarthy individual behind the counter.

"Paolo," the man responded guardedly.

"How can a taco be authentically French?"

His cousin stared at him for a moment. "Fuck off." He indicated the door with a thrust of his chin. "Don't you ever get sick of that joke?"

Paolo's grin widened and he winked at Michel.

His cousin lifted heavily from his stool and placed his meaty hands on the counter. "Do you arseholes want something or not?"

"Just messing, Marc," Paolo said. "It's just that the sign always amuses me, is all."

"Yeh. Fucking hilarious."

"Give me two orders of tacos with merguez, goat cheese, and Moroccan sauce and two beers."

Five minutes later Marc slapped plastic trays down on the counter, each with two small square packages wrapped in beige tortilla crisscrossed with grill marks.

Paolo grabbed one and took a huge bite, sausage and cheese spilling from the side of his mouth. He swiped the back of his hand across his lips and choked out, "We're meeting someone, and it's probably best if you're not here. Find something to do in the back for a while. I'll let you know when we're done."

His cousin stared at him resentfully. "Can't you find somewhere else to do your business? I don't want to be involved."

Paolo stared back. He swallowed and ran his tongue around the inside of his mouth for a moment before belching. "So, you don't want any more of those cheap supplies that fall off a truck? Or maybe you want your wife to find out about the *salope* I hooked you up with?" He jutted his chin forward aggressively. "Or I could just tell Battistu that you don't want to be involved."

Marc blanched. "Okay, okay, I'm going." He rounded the counter and locked the front door before disappearing into the back.

Ten minutes later, a uniformed gendarme appeared at the door, and Michel let him in. The officer looked around warily before turning a threatening gaze on Michel.

"What the fuck do you want while I'm at work?"

Michel reached out and gripped the gendarme's shoulder—from a distance, it seemed like a friendly gesture, but his pincer grip, tone of voice and the glint in his eyes were anything but.

"Armand, it's not what we want, *mon ami*. It's what Battistu wants."

Paolo took pleasure in watching the man stiffen at the mention of the boss's name.

"We have a bit of a problem," Michel said. "You see, a tall, bald, black cop and a hot blond female officer took a laptop that didn't belong to them." His head waggled in feigned dismay. "Criminals everywhere." He uttered a half laugh. "Anyway, we need it back, or if that is not possible, destroyed."

"How's that my problem?"

Michel stared hard at him. "Cocaine! Wouldn't go down well at work."

Armand took a step back. "You wouldn't."

Michel shrugged and tilted his head towards Paolo. "It seems I may not have a choice, *mon ami*."

Armand swallowed hard. "If that's who I think it is, then they are not gendarmes. That laptop must be with the Police Nationale in Aix." He looked pleadingly at Paolo. "Surely you have someone inside there?"

Paolo nodded slowly. "We did, but he displeased Battistu. I heard he was badly injured in a bar fight and is still recovering in hospital." He rotated his thick neck. "Sadly, it seems he might not walk again."

Armand swallowed hard once more. "I'll see what I can do," he croaked.

Paolo patted his arm. "Battistu will be very grateful," he said.

15

After the captain left with Arielle, Dupre went through the filing cabinets at Borrell's office with one of the techs. He took the files over to the marble desk and sat in Borrell's chair, marveling at how comfortable it was. He didn't at all mind sitting in a dead woman's chair. Perhaps he could buy this chair from the estate, but then, if he took it to work, no doubt some light-fingered *flic* would take it. Ironically, some of the worst thieves worked in the station house. He'd already had his favorite chair taken from his desk twice this year; the first time he'd found it on the forensics floor and wheeled it back with loud swearing and threats of retribution. The second time, he had not recovered it at all. Certainly, Borrell's chair would disappear within hours.

The files were primarily records of real estate holdings. They hung, regimented, in the cabinets in neatly tabbed folders. Dupre looked just long enough to jot down the addresses and tenants in his notebook. It would take hours to assemble and go through the rest of the scattered files, something he very much wanted someone else to do. There were a few prime properties in the town center, but the rest were spread around the suburbs. There were also some loan records, and he whistled when he saw the interest rates. How many of these loans had turned into real estate holdings? More than a few, he bet, particularly in the pandemic. She didn't seem to be the sort of businesswoman who would cut anyone slack in a depressed economy. Quite the opposite. He sighed heavily. He would have to visit each of her properties and talk to every borrower, and with those interest rates, any one of them could have a motive to see Borrell out of the picture.   As he flicked through a file, his eye fell on a surname: Briancon. He took out the paperwork and saw the two names attached: Julien and Michel. Their friends downstairs. They had just taken out a twenty-five-thousand-euro loan with the victim. The first payment hadn't even been made, but the interest rate was so high the payments would barely make a dent in their debt.

Dupre pursed his lips as he considered this. Interesting that the brothers had not mentioned this. No wonder they didn't like her. Had they been the ones who searched her office looking for these documents? If so, why would they search her apartment at the Old Gendarmerie? Looks like they belong at the top of the suspect list. Still, he would have to talk to her tenants and other debtors. But first, a glass or two of nicely chilled Chablis downstairs. It would give him a chance to observe the Briancon brothers again. And, after all, he had not really had a proper lunch.

"Your boss is not very warm and fuzzy, is he?" Danielle remarked as she brought him his wine.

"No, but that makes a good policeman. He has integrity, which is not always something you find in this job."

Danielle bit her bottom lip. "If you say so. I wouldn't like to work for him."

"I could say the same for the guys you work for."

With a tip of his head, Dupre indicated Julien Briancon staring belligerently at them from the bar area. Danielle glanced around. Julien was far enough away that she couldn't be overheard.

"They're okay. Julien is married and pretty fair and honest." She glanced around again. "Michel... that's a different story."

Dupre peered over the lip of his raised glass. "Oh yes? Where is he anyway?"

The waitress flapped a hand in the direction of the front. "He left right after your boss. I saw him..." she stopped abruptly, biting her lip, clearly not wanting to finish.

Dupre let the moment hang as he took another sip.

"You were saying?"

"I think I've said enough," she said with a furtive glance at Julien.

"We can continue this down at the station if you would like." Dupre leaned forward across the table. "But I won't tell if you don't."

Danielle took a deep breath. "Let's just say he got in with a bad crowd." She lowered her voice even further. "The Brise de Sang." It was a whisper so low that he practically had to read her lips.

Dupre's mouth compressed into a hard line. He wasn't surprised she was afraid to say the name. The Brise de Sang were one of the most notorious criminal gangs in France, a Corsican mafia with fingers in every serious criminal enterprise—drug smuggling, human trafficking, extortion and fraud.

She glanced once again at her boss. "Nothing too serious, I don't think," she hastened to add. "A bit of debt collecting is all."

"So, he can be violent then," said Dupre. "That's serious enough in a murder investigation."

Danielle put her hand to her mouth. "You don't think…" She paused wide-eyed, staring down at him. "Look, I have to get back to work."

Suddenly she seemed to want to put as much distance between him and her as quickly as possible. Dupre drained his glass. The plot was, as they say, thickening. He would pull up Michel Briancon's record as soon as he got back to the station.

In the meantime, he would take a walk to see what else he could learn. So far it had been quite an enlightening day. He left the restaurant and turned left along the quay. On the water, ferries bound for the Calanques plowed through the iridescent green sea.

He stopped at the gelato stand and bought a passionfruit ice which he licked as he strolled past the colorful throng of tourists sitting at tables under multi-colored awnings or wandering between expensive boutiques. The briny air cut sharply through the mélange of cooking smells. He always felt freer when not in company with Jacques.

An hour later he was feeling less jaunty. He had been to three stores and an office building to enquire about Borrell. He was hot and tired. Everywhere the answer was the same: Borrell was a nasty piece of work who would stop at nothing to get what she wanted. The people he had spoken to had been too terrified to talk as they had been visited in the past by her friends from Corsica before they agreed to sell their properties. So, here was another connection between the victim and Michel Briancon. They both had ties to the Brise. It seemed that Borrell kept very bad company between the Russians and the Corsicans. Every-one he spoke to told of crippling loan payments and then being forced to turn over their properties. Had one of these disgruntled businesspeople ordered a hit on Borrell? It didn't seem likely as it would not get them their property back, particularly if it fell into the hands of her unsavory business partners. Could the Corsicans or Russians have had her killed? If so, why? Possibly they did not want to share. There was certainly no shortage of candidates who wished her ill, but they were no nearer to identifying the culprit. He thought the American could be capable of such violence. Dupre could feel his simmering rage, but what was his motive? If her connection to the mafia had somehow threatened his son, perhaps?

Then there was Nash. He didn't look the sort—too effete, and what was his motive? The concierge Hassan was a possibility, but he looked too scared, and again, no motive. No, so far, his money had to be on Michel Briancon. He had ties to the local mafia, he was violent, and the brothers owed the victim a good deal of money. If he was a betting man, he would bet that Michel was the one who ransacked Borrell's offices.

His shoulders began to droop. It was late afternoon and time to get his ride home with the forensics team. He hoped his evening plans would not be ruined again, although yesterday had turned out unexpectedly well with his visit to Le Saint Amour. He hoped he'd see Madeleine again soon. She made him feel good about himself and had cracked open a door he had closed long ago. Perhaps he should make a proper reservation and test Madeleine's power over Gustav if it came to that.

When Dupre arrived back at the station, he was shocked to find the subject of his thoughts was waiting for him in the reception area.

"Madeleine?" he said, surprised.

She was out of her waitress uniform, and he thought she looked charming in tan shorts and a sleeveless floral blouse, her blond curls swept up in a loose chignon. His spirits rose instantly and the surprise and pleasure he felt at seeing her was evident in his voice.

"To what do we owe this honor?"

She smiled impishly. "Waiting for you." She was clutching a Xavier-Marie Bonnot murder mystery.

He caught himself subconsciously sucking in his belly. It was no use. "How can I help you?"

"*Ah, non, monsieur.* It is how I can help you."

Dupre looked at her curiously, inviting her to go on.

"It occurred to me after you left that I saw Madame Borrell's companion leaning on the rail looking out over the gardens while he smoked and talked on his phone."

"*Oui?*"

Madeleine opened her eyes wide in invitation, and suddenly Dupre caught on. "Ah… So, he left his fingerprints on the railing?"

The waitress was delighted. *"Avec certitude."*

"Madeleine, I said you would make a good detective," he beamed. "I could kiss you!"

The truth was, he really could.

Madeleine blushed. "Perhaps another time," she said, glancing around at the other occupants of the room.

Dupre turned and saw the desk sergeant watching them with obvious amusement. He cleared his throat. "Ah yes, perhaps." Then he colored as he realized what her response implied. Flustered, he said, "I should get someone over there immediately before something happens to those prints."

"Don't sweat it. I blocked off that stretch of railing with chairs and warned the staff that it was a crime scene. No one will go near it."

Dupre could not help himself. He clasped her pretty face in his hands and kissed her forehead. "You are *merveilleux!*"

Madeleine stood back and blushed even more.

As soon as she left, Dupre arranged to send a tech to the restaurant. He left work on a high note.

Just after six, Arielle, Dupre, and two colleagues, Benny and Gaston, entered the Café des Amis on Place des Carmes, a local police hangout. It was dark after the glaring sunlight outside and smelled of grease, *pomme frites* and grilling *onglet.* But it was cool inside. The outside tables were for tourists.

Dupre was huffing from their brisk five-minute walk in the still, hot air, adding to the fatigue he was already suffering from canvassing half of Cassis. A sheen of sweat glazed his broad forehead, and his fleshy jowls were flushed. He collapsed onto the nearest chair with a sigh.

"You walk too fast," he complained to the others.

Arielle gave him a look that mingled pity with amusement and said, in a tone of voice that acknowledged she was wasting her breath, "Louis, you really need to get in shape. Eat healthier and cut down on the alcohol."

As she said the last part, she held up a three-fingered salute in the direction of the bar and called out, *"Trois Ricards, Fabien, s'il te plait."*

Dupre grunted at the irony, casting his eyes up and down her lean runner's frame. "Easy for you to say."

The others in the group laughed.

"Leave him be," said Benny. "He will never change now." He pulled a mock, sad face. "And to think you were once on the books at Olympique."

Arielle's head jerked. "You were a professional football player for Marseille? How did I not know that?"

Dupre glowered at Benny who remained unabashed and went on.

"Oh, yes. You are too young to remember, and anyway, he never made the first team. Messed up his knee and then he was done. Can you imagine our fine colleague here," Benny continued as he swept his hand to take in Dupre's girth, "dressed in shorts and a tight football jersey flying down the wing?"

He and Gaston chuckled.

"I was a fullback," Dupre growled.

"Louis, I am so sorry," Arielle said. She reached across the table and placed her slim hand on his hairy paw.

"C'est la vie," he answered with a shrug. "It was a lifetime ago, and I've moved on." He expelled a long breath. "But the knee still gives me problems, particularly if I exercise."

Fabian brought their drinks. For Dupre, he had brought a carafe of chilled vin rosé and a plate of pommes frites. There had been no need for Dupre to order them. Arielle could not keep the disapproval from her face. The others gratefully took the glasses of cloudy pastis Arielle had ordered. Dupre had gulped his first glass before Arielle even took a sip. She pretended not to notice.

After a long silence, Arielle picked up their conversation. "So, you were a professional football player, and the captain was an international rugby player. I feel like an athletic underachiever."

"You and me both," said Gaston with a grimace. He was a plug, short, bald and stout. "The best I manage is a round of golf with Benny here on the weekend."

Benny chortled. "That's because you have twenty children and don't have the time. But with that many children you must be getting your exercise another way, eh?" He winked and nudged Arielle, who grinned.

Gaston looked sheepish but laughed along. "It's only seven kids."

"Wow," said Arielle. "That's quite an athletic endeavor just running after so many kids."

Gaston nodded. *"C'est vrai, bien sûr!"*

Arielle glanced sideways at Dupre. He had lapsed into morose silence, nursing his glass, half the carafe and most of the frites already gone. Had she unwittingly brought some resentment bubbling to the surface? She knew he wasn't married, but she knew little about his private life. In fact, he didn't seem to have a private life as he always seemed to be in the station. A lot like the captain, she thought. A lot like her. They all had much more in common than first met the eye.

"Louis, what will you do this coming weekend?" she asked, knowing the answer but hoping it would be something to do with the woman she'd heard had come to the station looking for him earlier.

Dupre came back to them from wherever his thoughts had drifted. He groaned. "We have a murder to solve. Unless something miraculous happens tomorrow, I don't think you or I will get much of a weekend."

Benny hacked out a short bark of laughter. "Your boss is a real martinet." He winked. "You should switch to our team, Arielle." Benny and Gaston worked in the fraud squad.

"*Oui*," Gaston chimed in enthusiastically. Everyone knew Arielle was the best cyber geek in the division, if not the force. "We don't work weekends. Fraud is very rarely urgent."

"What? And work my way through accounting ledgers for days on end? No thanks," snorted Arielle.

Benny started to object, but Dupre cut him off. "Forget it, you guys. You cannot poach Arielle." He gazed at her like a fond uncle. "She is the main saving grace in our work." He cast his eyes down, embarrassed. Arielle reached out a hand again and rested it lightly on his arm.

"You are too kind, *mon cher* Louis, but I'm not sure our captain sees it that way. I see him giving me that disapproving stare."

Dupre looked up and frowned. "Forget it. He's like that with everyone, but he's okay. Being…" He paused, searching for a politic word before he gave up and made a face, waving one hand in a circular pattern. "You know …" He skipped a beat. "I think he feels that he has to be more than perfect. He's afraid people will think he was promoted because of the race card. Not because he earned it by hard work and acumen."

"Well, wasn't he?" Gaston said, with just a trace of bitterness. "Everyone knows you are the better policeman?"

Dupre shook his unkempt head. "There is more than one type of policeman, *mon ami,* as you well know. I am a hunter. I search for answers."

"And truffles," broke in Benny with a laugh.

A sheepish grin crossed Dupre's face. "Well, that too," he admitted. His face grew serious again. "Jacques is an administrator par excellence. I could not, and would not, want to do his job. *Non, mes amis,* Jacques is a good boss, and I would not want another."

"Even though he treats you the way he does?" Arielle asked.

Dupre shrugged. "He gives me free rein. We are a good team, and you, *chère* Arielle, are integral to that team. Don't listen to these bozos."

She laughed, an effervescent sound. "I'll drink to that," and she raised another three fingers in Fabian's direction. "You never know. We might crack the case tomorrow and our weekend will be free." Realizing that Dupre was not going to offer any information, Arielle winked slyly at him and said, "I did hear a strange rumor about you kissing an attractive woman at the station house."

Dupre ducked his head and quickly took another swig. He felt heat rise up his neck. "I don't know what you're talking about," he said, unable to prevent the ghost of a smile stealing onto his face.

16

Max returned from dropping Luke at camp, planning to work on his novel in the sunshine on the balcony—a project that had been on the back burner too long. He was feeling the vibe. Today was the day when he would make some real progress.

He shouldered past the few journalists still hanging around the Old Gendarmerie waiting for any developments, ignoring their cries for comment and turning his face away from the cameras. He hated publicity at the best of times, and the last thing he needed now was for his and Luke's own tragic story to get mixed up in this.

As he entered the Old Gendarmerie, Dickens scampering beside him, he ran into a small knot of people standing just inside the entrance. It appeared the group had just met up, for they were still shaking hands. Max recognized the police captain from the previous day and assumed the other two were somehow connected to the police. There was something vaguely familiar about the woman though. She didn't look very official, dressed as she was in bright designer clothes and open-toed sandals and carrying a white, crocodile print shoulder bag.

"*Bonjour,*" Max said as he passed, heading for the elevator.

The group followed him with their eyes, suspicion written across the captain's face. But it was the quizzical expression on the woman's face that drew his attention.

"Bonjour, Monsieur Dempsey,*"* replied the scruffy, pudgy man with something like a friendly tone. Max didn't know him but assumed they had his name from the investigation.

"Wait a minute," the woman called.

Max was surprised to hear English spoken with a faint Scots burr. He turned back. *"Oui, madame?"*

"Max Dempsey?"

"Yes?"

"From Leeds University?"

Then it hit him. "Claire MacFarlane. What are you doing here?"

She laughed gaily. "Oh, that is a long story. Well, not so long, but worthy of a glass of wine. It's Claire Lejeune now. Are you living here?"

"For the moment."

The captain watched this interplay with a solemn face and then coughed.

"Ah yes, *Capitaine*, apologies," said the judge, but she smiled at Max. "Work. But can we catch up after? I shouldn't be too long."

"Bien sûr. Do you want to stop by the apartment for that glass of wine?"

The judge shook her head.

"Unfortunately, I must go back to the office after here. But I will do you one better. How about an early dinner, my treat? Say Restaurant Jean Paul at seven o'clock?"

Max whistled. Restaurant Jean Paul was the best restaurant in town, situated in the Auberge des Vignes luxury hotel. "That's some treat!"

Claire was nonchalant. "The owner is an old friend, so we may not even have to pay."

"Sounds bloody marvelous," Max said, playing up his British accent.

Claire grinned back at him and winked as she handed him her business card. "In case your plans change."

Max looked at the card. "*Juge d'instruction*," he read out loud. "Does that mean you're in charge of this case?"

The judge slid a look at Capitaine Jacques. "I'm not sure."

"Hmm," Max said, staring at the police captain with a look that plainly said he thought it would be better if he were not in charge.

Claire noticed the look and her eyes crinkled. "*A bientôt.* Cute puppy, by the way."

She turned back to the police captain who was staring stonily at Max. As Max headed to the elevator, he heard Claire's rapid-fire explosion of French. Her accent was flawless. It was too quick for him to catch all of it, but from what he did, the surly police captain didn't seem too happy with their dinner arrangement. But what was the problem? Could they suspect him?

Max dropped by Hans and Angela's apartment and asked if they wouldn't mind watching Luke that evening.

"You have a date?" grinned Angela.

"Not quite," said Max, smiling back. "Dinner with an old friend."

"I'm so happy you are going out," said Angela. "We will take Luke anytime."

"Just don't let him walk all over you, or you'll be watching rubbish on TV or gaming."

Angela stepped forward and gave him a squeeze. "Don't worry, we will keep him under control," she said in a laughing voice that made it clear she would do no such thing. "Besides, I like gaming. Just go and enjoy your date."

"Not a date," he objected.

The corner of her mouth twitched. "Okay, if you say so. Got it."

"No, seriously. Not a date."

The very thought gave him a hollow feeling in the pit of his stomach. And it was the last idea he wanted her putting in Luke's head.

17

"Well?" Capitaine Jacques demanded.

He looked down at Arielle, sitting at her desk twiddling a pen back and forth through her fingers like a dexterity exercise.

His meeting with the English judge that morning had been of very little help. And she now turned out to be old friends with that irritating American lawyer. Unbelievable.

Twenty-four hours had elapsed since they had investigated the offices of BRDO. Twenty-four crucial hours without any progress whatsoever. He was feeling the pressure. Far from having no suspect, they had too many to properly identify. A second round of interviews with all the residents of the Old Gendarmerie did not produce anything new. The plain truth was that they were all alibis for each other. Everyone had come out onto their balconies following the sound of a shot, which now couldn't be explained, and an agonized scream. Unless one subscribed to Dupre's lame murder mystery theory, none of them could have been in Borrell's apartment sticking a knife into her gut. They had outside suspects aplenty, but could place none of them at the scene. Things were currently at an impasse, and it was driving Jacques mad.

Arielle's face told the story. "*Désolée, mon Capitaine.* It took longer than I thought. She had 2FA, so I had to use her fingerprint."

Jacques frowned enquiringly at her.

She threw up her hands. "Two-factor authentication?" she said as though it should be obvious to everyone. Then she sighed and continued in the kind of patient voice reserved for children. "It means…" she checked her explanation as Jacques' frown deepened.

"Okay, well… "

"How did you use her fingerprint?" Jacques cut her off. "You told me that a dead finger wouldn't work."

Arielle's face scrunched as if at an unpleasant memory. "I called some hacker friends, and it seems that a little wood glue on the victim's finger…"

Noting the stern look her boss was giving her, she paused, and an awkward silence hung between them before Jacques shook his head as you would at a disappointing teenager.

"Hacker friends?"

"Ah, yes. Well, never mind," she said quickly. The pen did a few more tricks between her fingers. "The point is that there is very little stored on the laptop and nothing that I can find that might be of interest to the case. It seems that she stored everything on a remote server. I have tracked that server by its IP address, and it is in Romania. Unless we have that access key, we can recover nothing."

Arielle pushed the laptop away in frustration. Jacques was staring at her in disbelief.

"Can't you just hack in?"

Her strangled laugh gave him a reply before her words. "No chance. It has AES encryption." She shook her head. "This woman had a lot to hide."

"AES? What the hell does that mean?" said Jacques.

Arielle sounded dejected. "It means no hope. Government standard for classified data—virtually uncrackable."

Jacques closed his eyes and squeezed the back of his neck. This case was going nowhere. When he opened his eyes again his face was set in dogged determination. He would hold someone to account for this murder.

At that moment Dupre stuck an excited face around the door. "I think we may have him!"

"Who?" said Jacques. "Who the hell do we have?"

"The concierge Hassan. We have his fingerprints and DNA."

"*Putain!* I know we have that. He was in the apartment." Jacques spoke as if he were addressing an idiot. "He was the one who found the body!"

Dupre had come into the room and was grinning. Jacques felt ready to explode.

"Not in the apartment. In the offices in Cassis." The lieutenant folded his arms triumphantly.

"*Hein?*" Jacques felt momentarily confused. "Where?"

"All over, but mainly in the bedroom and bathroom. Looks like he may have stayed there."

Jacques punched one large fist into the palm of the other and a smile of satisfaction suffused his face. "I knew it," he exclaimed. "Go bring him in!"

"Perhaps he can shed some light that will help with the encryption protocols," Arielle suggested.

The captain nodded and rubbed his jawline. "He knows something alright. I knew there was something off about him."

"There were traces of other people also, but we don't have a match for any of them yet."

"They were business offices so you would expect visitors, but not the doorman of her building and not in the bedroom," said Areille.

"Anyone else's fingerprints or DNA in the bedroom?" asked Jacques.

"Besides the victim, no," Dupre replied.

18

It was early afternoon when Max walked into the apartment building armed with a roast chicken he had picked up in the outdoor market in Gordes. It would pair well with some fresh tomatoes and a glass of rosé. As he pushed open the massive entrance doors, two police cars screeched to a halt on the cobbles in front of the building. Max loitered inside the lobby to see what was going on now. He recognized the unkempt plainclothes detective from that morning and nodded hello. The detective gave him a cursory nod in return and marched up to Hassan who was standing frozen in the lobby, fear written across his face.

"Come with us," the detective commanded.

"What? Why?" The young man was almost bleating.

"You need to answer some questions in connection with the death of Madame Borrell."

Hassan cast around frantically and saw Max watching. "Monsieur, please. You are a lawyer. Can they do this?"

Max momentarily debated the wisdom of getting involved, but the young Moroccan looked terrified, and he hated bullies. "I'm not a French lawyer, Hassan, but even here I think they can only take you if they arrest you."

The detective cocked an eyebrow at Max before turning back to Hassan. "I can arrest you if you would like, or you can come and help us with our inquiries by answering a few questions."

"Please, monsieur?" Hassan held out his arms in supplication to Max.

"You need a local lawyer, Hassan."

The young man's shoulders sagged. "I have no money for lawyers."

"I'm sure they have court-appointed defense lawyers here."

The detective snorted out a derisive laugh, and Max felt an immediate flush of sympathy for Hassan. He was aware that migrants from North Africa were not always treated well in France.

"I will see what I can do, but in the meantime, I advise you not to say anything at all. *Comprenez?* Nothing. *Rien!*"

As Hassan was hustled out of the building the lieutenant paused at the door and gave Max a cautionary glance. Still, Max went to the door and watched as the uniformed officer thrust Hassan none too carefully into the back of one of the police cars. The French police had an unenviable reputation for lacking finesse and empathy. Max sighed and went to his apartment. Another fine lunch down the drain. He pulled out his laptop and started searching. After ten minutes he gave up, frustrated at not being able to find a local criminal defense lawyer in whom he could feel any confidence. He took a deep breath. There was only one thing to do. He picked up his phone and dialed Claire Lejeune. She answered on the second ring.

"Max, *quelle surprise.*"

"I know we've only just caught up. And this is a bit unorthodox, you being the examining magistrate and all, but I need a recommendation for a decent criminal defense lawyer," said Max.

The concern was apparent in her voice. "Oh, Max. What has happened?"

"It's not for me. It's for Hassan. They just arrested him."

"I know. I just got off the phone with Capitaine Jacques." She sounded sympathetic. "Are you sure you want to get involved? It doesn't look good for him."

"Oh?"

"I shouldn't say, but they have found his fingerprints and DNA at the victim's offices in Cassis. He has some explaining to do."

Max digested this information. "I see. All the more reason he needs a good lawyer."

There was a pause at the other end of the phone. "You want Maître Helene Blanc in Avignon. You didn't hear it from me."

"Thanks, Claire."

"I'm on my way to the station now. I'll make sure your guy is treated well."

An hour later, Max was sitting in front of a stern-looking woman in her late thirties. She was dressed all in black—a black chemise, blazer and suit trousers—a sharp contrast to her almost-porcelain skin. Not for the first time, Max wondered how anyone could maintain such a complexion under the burning sun of the south of France. Her shoulder-length dark hair was swept back in a loose knot, and she leaned forward across her crowded desk as she spoke in good English.

"And what is your interest in this young man?"

"Honestly, I don't know. He is the concierge at the apartment building I am living in at the moment. I don't really know him, and to be honest, I thought he might have known something more than he was letting on, but..."

He took a moment to consider his next words.

"But I have a gut feeling that he didn't do it. His terror when he saw the police. Like a little boy. He just doesn't seem capable." He shrugged.

Maître Blanc's lips twisted in a wry smile. "Perhaps it is the defense attorney in you." In response to his surprised look she continued, "Oh yes, I googled you. You are very well known in the US for litigation it seems."

Max let out a despondent sigh. Particularly now, he hated the intrusion of the internet.

"Perhaps," he acceded. "I'm sure you understand that sometimes we get a gut feeling about the truth."

She bent her long neck forward in acquiescence. "*Bien ⊠r.*" She started to shuffle papers into neat piles on her desk. "Well, let's go and see what the accused has to say, shall we?"

"Huh? You want me to come?"

"Why not? Two heads are better than one, and I would like to see such an esteemed American attorney in action. Perhaps I can learn something?"

Max was nonplussed. "*Maître*, from what I hear, you have nothing to learn from me."

She tilted her head and studied him from shrewd eyes as dark as her hair, putting him in mind of a raven. "When I have nothing left to learn, I've been doing the job for too long, and it is time to quit." She paused momentarily. "And you do not want to say how you got my name?"

Max paused. He had promised Claire.

"Bien," said the Maître, sounding slightly irked. She stood up and grabbed a worn attaché case from a chair in the corner.

"Oh, and one more thing I should tell you," Max said warily. "I know the judge on this case. We were in law school together."

He saw an understanding spark in her eyes as she quickly put two and two together. "Of course," she murmured. "Claire Lejeune. I know her well." There was no antipathy in her voice, but neither was there any hint of a friendly connection.

Blanc opened the door and ushered him out. A short while later they entered the office of the *juge d'instruction* in the Aix headquarters of the Police Nationale. Claire was dressed informally in a white lace top and tan capris as though she had just come from lunch. At the thought of lunch, Max pictured the chicken he had left on his kitchen counter and the rosé chilling in the fridge and his stomach growled. At Claire's welcoming smile he half expected to be offered a glass of wine. That would be nice. It quickly became apparent that Capitaine Jacques did not share the judge's warmth for him.

"What is he doing here?" His deep voice was more a growl than speech.

No one spoke for an extended pause while the policeman stared at the judge expectantly. Finally, Claire looked at the Maître questioningly, her slender arms resting on her desk, fingers playing an invisible keyboard, and then ever so discreetly winked at her.

When Jacques realized the judge was not going to lead, he waved his hand impatiently in the air. "He's a potential suspect."

The Maître flashed a predatory smile. "Oh? Aren't you holding a suspect you have arrested in the cells? How many suspects do you want, Monsieur le Capitaine? If Monsieur Dempsey is a suspect, then I guess I can take my client home?"

Max did his best to stifle a grin and look serious. He could see why Claire had recommended this woman.

Jacques scowled. "Well, a witness then."

"But you have his statement. Does it mention my client? How will his being present prejudice your investigation, do you think?"

"It's just not right." He looked to the judge for support and found none.

Helene Blanc dismissed his objections with a wave of her well-manicured hands and a sharp puff of breath that left no doubt that she had no patience for his nonsense.

"If you must know, I have retained Monsieur Dempsey as my assistant in this matter," she said coolly. "That is an end to it."

This brought an unavailingly concealed snigger from Judge Lejeune. She shrugged at the captain. "I see no harm in that. Monsieur Aamara is entitled to whatever representation he chooses. Are you really concerned that *un advocate Americain* will undermine your case?"

Visibly seething, Jacques got up and barked at an officer standing outside the door to take the two to Hassan.

"He really doesn't like you, does he?" the Maître whispered to Max as they left the room.

They followed the officer down a spartan cement block corridor, leaving Jacques and the judge behind in her office.

"What did you do to him?" Blanc asked.

"Rien! He doesn't seem overly fond of the judge either, so perhaps he just dislikes the English. Or Americans. Or lawyers."

In a small room on one side of a steel-topped table bolted to the floor sat Hassan, cowed and nervous. His shoulders were hunched forward as though he was trying to take up as little space as possible.

The Maître leaned across the table conspiratorially, her voice warm and empathetic. "My name is Maître Helene Blanc."

Hassan looked up and nodded slightly before returning to stare at his hands, the thumb of one repeatedly rubbed across the knuckles of the other.

"We are here to try and help you," said the Maître.

Again, the merest nod. Hassan's eyes wouldn't settle; instead, he hunted around the room like he was searching for an escape route.

Maître Blanc's voice became as firm as a slap. "But we can only do that if you tell us the truth. The whole truth. It is private, and the police cannot overhear us. Do you understand?"

Hassan's eyes rested on the lawyer's face for an appraising moment before he glanced at Max.

Max contemplated the concierge for a long moment. "Hassan, I know you are lying, or at least not telling the truth about something." He said it in the same way he might have said it to Luke. "I know this judge and she will be able to tell also. And she will find out what it is you are hiding. So whatever it is, you need to tell us first, however bad it is, before the police find out."

Hassan's hands went to his face, scrubbing at the sudden onset of tears. He was rocking slightly in his chair. Max arched his eyebrows at the lawyer, and she motioned for him to wait.

Finally, Hassan said in a subdued voice, "She paid me."

"She? Madame Borrell?" Helene said softly.

Hassan nodded.

"For what?"

Hassan covered his face more completely and let out a low moan. "For sex."

Maître Helene Blanc looked startled. "You are saying that the dead woman paid you to have sex with her."

The young man's voice trembled. "*Oui*. I know I shouldn't have, but I needed the money when my father became ill. Then, later, she wouldn't let me stop."

Helene's brow furrowed. "What do you mean she wouldn't let you stop?"

Suddenly Hassan's voice exploded in anger. "She said she would have me fired from my job. I need that job!"

The Maître stared at Hassan, the fingers of her left hand tapping against her lips. After a pause, she asked, "How is it that your fingerprints and DNA were found in an apartment in Cassis?"

"That is where we met. She didn't want anyone in the Old Gendarmerie apartments to see us."

"Did you have anything to do with the business conducted at those offices by Madame Borrell?" Max asked.

Hassan shook his head vehemently. "She just told me when to show up. Sometimes I spent the night, and sometimes she kicked me out after…" His voice tailed off.

"Okay," Helene said gently, and she stood up. She jerked her head towards the door, and Max followed her into the empty corridor.

"Hmph," Max said. "I only saw the woman a few times passing through the lobby, but she didn't seem the type."

Helene barked out a small laugh. "And what type would that be?"

"Oh, I don't know. She just seemed so... so Parisian. Not someone who would need to force a young man into prostitution."

The Maître heaved a sigh. "Some people like prostitutes for the anonymity, the lack of any emotional ties. Or maybe it wasn't about the sex, per se. Maybe she just got off on the power and control. Like a rapist." She turned her raven gaze on him. "You realize that this gives Hassan a serious motive?"

"Unfortunately. But only if they knew Hassan wanted to stop. What if Hassan owned it? He could say: sure, he was having sex with her for money, in which case, why kill the golden goose?"

The Maître's head oscillated as she considered his words. "Well, he wouldn't be lying, and we are not obliged to tell them. Do you think he can pull that off?"

"I don't know. He's obviously not very proud of it."

"Come on, let's see." She turned to re-enter the room, and Max put a hand on her arm.

"I noticed you didn't ask whether he had killed her."

"Neither did you," she said.

"No," he admitted. "I don't believe for a minute that he did it. Call it a gut feeling. But I still know better than to ask a question we don't want the answer to."

"Moi aussi."

"He could always refuse to answer any questions," Max suggested.

"He could, but then Claire will definitely charge him. They have his fingerprints at the crime scene, her blood on his clothes and his fingerprints at her apartment in Cassis and in the Old Gendarmerie. He has a key and no alibi. They will pitch this as a *crime passionnel.* I think our best shot is showing that he had no reason to kill her."

"That could backfire."

The Maître huffed. "Quite possibly, but then we will be in no worse position than we are now."

After they had explained all this to Hassan, they were brought to a larger, less intimidating room with a conference table where Judge Lejeune sat next to the dour Jacques.

The Maître surveyed her opposition briefly. "My client has a statement to make, and then he will answer some questions." She over-emphasized the word *some.*

For a moment the judge surveyed them over the top of her reading glasses. Then she pushed the glasses up onto the bridge of her nose with her index finger and focused her attention on Hassan. "Go ahead," she said.

Hassan cleared his throat and glanced at Max. Max nodded encouragingly.

"First, I did not lie about anything I told you, and I didn't kill Maxine." His voice trembled. He coughed again, nervously. "But I didn't tell you the whole truth. I was ashamed, and I didn't want to get into trouble. The truth is that Maxine was paying me to have sex with her."

An exclamation of disbelief erupted from Jacques, drawing a sharp look from the judge. *"Conneries,"* he muttered under his breath.

"No, not bullshit," Hassan went on earnestly. "You can check my bank account. You will see payments from her. That is why I was in the apartment in Cassis. She didn't want to use her apartment in Roussillon in case someone saw us. Besides, she said Roussillon was her private space. I never saw her take anyone there."

He lapsed into silence and stared down at his feet.

"Questions?" asked Maître Blanc.

The judge leaned forward. Her voice and posture were non-threatening. "Hassan, how well did you know Madame Borrell?"

Hassan uttered a short, staccato laugh. "Not at all, except what she liked in bed. We never did anything else together. A couple of times she fed me at that restaurant downstairs before… but she never talked about herself. We barely talked."

As he spoke, he appeared to shrink into himself, and his gaze roved around the room, constantly avoiding eye contact.

"Did she ever discuss her business?"

"Never."

"Do you know if she has any family?"

"No. Like I said. She never discussed herself."

"But perhaps you overheard her on the phone?"

Hassan considered this for a moment. "Sometimes, but it seemed like business and didn't mean anything to me. She always talked in a foreign language."

"Any idea what language?" asked the judge.

Hassan shrugged. "Maybe Russian."

"Any other questions?" the Maître asked.

Max looked at Hassan trying to disappear into his chair. He looked plain guilty of something. But of what?

Claire Lejeune eyed Hassan shrewdly. She was no one's fool, and Max could feel it coming. She could sense something. A prosecutor's intuition, perhaps.

"Were you in love with Maxine Borrell?"

His mumbled reply was barely audible. *"Non."*

"So how did you feel about her?"

Hassan looked desperately from Max to Helene Blanc. Helene assumed a resigned expression. She couldn't countenance a lie. Reluctantly they nodded at him.

"I hated her!" erupted Hassan, his face a picture of revulsion.

"Bon. Je le savais!" exclaimed Jacques, a smile of triumph lighting his face.

Helene's lip curled as she said, "You knew it, did you? Well, it doesn't mean he killed her."

"It's enough to charge him and hold him," the captain snapped. "He had motive and opportunity, and by his own admission, he's a criminal, selling sex."

He looked to the *juge d'instruction*, and with an obvious hesitancy, she acquiesced with a curt nod.

The Maître exchanged an *Oh well* glance with Max. They had both known the risk.

"Where did you put the knife?" Jacques demanded.

"What knife?" Hassan asked.

"Don't play games. The knife you used to kill Madame Borrell, your lover. What did you fight about?"

"That's enough," the Maître said sharply. "My client is done answering questions."

The captain glowered at them and finally summoned a uniformed officer. "Take him back to his cell."

As the cowed young man was led from the room, Max put a hand on his arm. "Try not to worry, Hassan. I will..." He glanced at Helene. "We will get to the bottom of this."

Once Hassan was taken away, Maître Blanc turned to the judge. "Well, if you are going to charge him, I would like access to the forensic reports and the crime scene."

Capitaine Jacques opened his mouth, but before he could utter a response, Claire had agreed. *"D'accord."*

Openly ignoring the scowling policeman, the Maître smiled winningly. "And I want to know everything you discovered at the offices in Cassis and anything else that might be relevant." She used her pointed chin to gesture at a file on the judge's desk. "We can start with a look at the autopsy report. We will see it eventually anyway."

Jacques spluttered out an objection, but the judge was already pushing the file towards the Maître.

"We are here to get to the truth, are we not, *mon Capitaine?* If they can assist us with this... "

Together Max and Helene bent over a set of color photographs of a naked corpse with a long gash almost from abdomen to sternum. It wasn't a pleasant sight. Max felt sorry for Hassan. The woman could have been his mother—not someone he would have wanted to sleep with by any stretch of the imagination. More than that, mused Max, she was not someone he expected Hassan would want a physical confrontation with. Based on the little he now knew, he did not feel sorry for the victim.

They read the report, going back over several sections and exchanging glances with each other. A large red welt was highlighted on Borrell's left arm. She had been gutted, by the looks of the knife wound.

"I don't understand," Max said.

"What don't you understand?" the judge asked.

"I had heard she was stabbed, and the captain asked about a knife, but I heard a shot. There are no gunshot wounds?"

"We thought she must have been shot too," Maître Blanc interposed.

"Apparently not," said the judge.

"So let me see if I understand the situation?" Max said, rubbing his jawline and staring hard into the green eyes of his college friend. "She was stabbed, but not shot?"

"Not just stabbed, eviscerated," the judge said. "The killer ripped upwards." She made a sawing motion as she pulled an imaginary knife upwards. "Designed to inflict pain, don't you think?"

Max winced. "That explains the scream I heard."

"Someone really hated her," mused Helene Blanc.

"*Exactement*," said the captain. "Just like your client."

"Perhaps she shot her assailant?" suggested Max.

Clair shook her head. "There was no gunpowder residue on her hands, and there was no gun found at the scene."

Max spoke slowly as he thought. "So, she didn't fire a gun?" His eyes widened. *"Bien sûr, un mystère."*

Clair nodded pensively. *"Oui, assurément."*

Max stared up at the ceiling as he continued. "So why would someone shoot at her, miss, and then stab her? Unless they only had one bullet, they would fire a second time, no?"

Claire and Helene shook their heads and shrugged in synchronicity. Jacques looked away, his mind already made up.

"Or having missed, the gun was knocked out of their hand, or Borrell was too close, and they started grappling. A knife is much better at close quarters."

Max glanced down again at the autopsy pictures. He ran his fingers along a photo, marking the unusual development of Borrell's musculature. "She looks like a powerful woman," he said. "Not someone you would want to get in a close fight with if you had a gun."

"From the way the wound was inflicted, it was obviously a personal thing," Jacques growled.

"*Obviously* if they intended to inflict pain," Max agreed. "But then why shoot at her in the first place if they wanted to inflict pain—to torture her as such? And here's a question for you." He stared into the captain's eyes. "Who brings both a gun and a knife to his lover's apartment? Sounds more like a professional hit than a crime of passion."

"I assume you have tested my client for gunshot residue?" the Maître posed.

"Of course," said Jacques.

"And?"

"Nothing." The policeman sounded sulky.

"But Maître," interjected the judge, backing Jacques up. "You know GSR typically only lasts for four to six hours. So, if he showered and laundered his clothes…"

The lawyer inclined her head. "*Oui,* I understand that, but it is one less piece of evidence you have against my client."

Max had been going through possibilities in his mind but remained perplexed. "Any bullet holes in the apartment?"

The judge turned to the policeman.

"No," Jacques admitted.

Max threw up his hands. "So, having shot at the victim just once, they grappled, the killer stabbed her viciously, then he left, taking the gun with him, leaving no trace of that shot behind?"

"I have a possible scenario," the judge said.

Helene inclined her head invitingly in the judge's direction.

"How about this? The killer had a gun loaded with blanks, which they used to hold up the victim. They fired a shot to scare her into submission until they could get close enough to stab her."

Max snorted. "Who takes a gun loaded with blanks to kill someone? It just doesn't make sense."

Claire laughed. "People do lots of things that don't make sense. Particularly criminals."

"I assume you already executed a warrant and searched my client's apartment?" the Maître asked.

The judge nodded.

Maître Blanc paused for a beat. "And did you find a gun?"

"No gun," Jacques said. His lip curled. "But I am sure he would have disposed of it."

The Maître smiled thinly. "Still, one more piece of missing evidence. No gun, and from your question to my client you clearly haven't found a knife. And no gunshot residue. Looks like a very circumstantial case."

Max stared pensively at the report and photographs, his fingers drumming the desk. "I feel that there is something here. I just can't put my finger on it. But I'll tell you this. I bet there is no sign of a struggle in that apartment or evidence of one on Hassan's body."

"It's getting late, and I have an appointment," the judge said. "Why don't we all meet in the victim's apartment in the morning? Say, à dix heures?"

"Ten is fine," Max said, "I just have to drop Luke at the football academy."

"Even on Saturday?" Claire asked.

"Oui, even on Saturday, although it is only a half day. We are going zip-lining in the afternoon."

The two women exchanged an amused glance. "I'm glad my children are grown," Claire said. "I plan to sit in the garden by the pool with a good book and *une verre du vin*."

"Actually, a glass of wine sounds marvelous right now," the Maître said. "À dix heures, *demain.*"

"Until ten, then," Claire said to her. "Enjoy the evening."

Claire said nothing to the lawyer about her own dinner plans with Max.

19

Max barely made it to Cavaillon in time. The lime green 2CV6 rocketed along the four-lane D907 Route Touristique des Bords du Rhône. Perhaps *rocked* along would have been more accurate because Max pushed the needle almost to its seventy-mile-per-hour limit, causing the old car's independent kinematic suspension to vibrate wildly. Route Touristique ran alongside the east branch of the Rhône River as it split to encircle the Île de la Barthelasse before coming together again west of Sorgues.

Despite its name, the whole route was very non-scenic, passing such non-Provençal landmarks as the massive blue hulk of the IKEA warehouse at the intersection with the six-lane A7 Autoroute du Soleil. But it was fast. He pulled into the parking lot just as the day campers were exiting the arched wrought iron gate. Luke came out laughing and jostling with a dark-haired youth.

Max got out of the car and leaned against the door. When the two boys came close enough, Luke made introductions, "Yousef, *c'est mon père.* Dad, *voici mon ami,* Yousef."

Max reached out a hand. "*Salut,* Yousef."

The boy looked at him shyly and then took the proffered hand. "*Bonjour, Monsieur Dempsey.*"

From the corner of his eye, Max saw a woman dressed in an abaya sidling uncertainly toward them. He turned to face a plump woman in her mid-thirties, her round face framed by a fringe of wavy jet-black hair. The lack of hijab struck him as odd until he remembered the French ban on wearing them that many thought was discriminatory. Max was struck by her luminous beauty, but her dark eyes ringed with kohl were watchful, and her lips compressed nervously. He put on his warmest smile.

"*Salut.*"

"*Salut,*" she said. He had expected her to talk in French and was surprised when she added in perfect English, "I am Zoya, Yousef's mother. I have heard much of your son, Luke. Yousef speaks of him often."

"*Oui?*"

"Yes. Very much. He says Luke is one of the best football players in the camp and that he is very kind to him."

Max couldn't help feeling a little self-satisfied to hear of Luke's soccer prowess from someone other than Luke, but it was not without a pang of sadness as he knew Emma would have been elated to hear that Luke had been kind. Kindness had been something she valued more than any other sentiment. Zoya must have been watching the conflicting thoughts run across his face.

"You must be very proud of him," she said.

Max roused himself. "Er, yes, I am." His eyes rolled toward the sky as he caught the smug grin on Luke's face. "Most of the time."

"My husband and I own a Moroccan restaurant, Marrakech, in Apt. We would enjoy very much if you could be our guest."

Max glanced at Luke who was nodding vigorously.

"We'd love to. It's been a while since I ate Moroccan food. When would be good?"

Luke quickly jumped in. "We don't have plans for tonight, Dad." His face took on a wheedling look. "And we always eat out on Friday. Pleeeease."

"Sorry, son, but I do actually have plans this evening."

Luke stared at him in surprise. Max had been dreading this moment, trying to explain that he was going out with another woman. Not that he had anything to worry about, thought Max. Claire was a happily married woman, as far as he knew.

"I'll explain later," he said hastily.

"How about tomorrow?" suggested Zoya.

Both boys nodded vigorously.

Max laughed. "Yes, tomorrow should work."

Zoya beamed.

As they drove away from the stadium, Max pondered whether Luke was missing the friends he had left behind at home. Perhaps he needed Yousef as much as Yousef seemed to need him. He turned to Luke.

"What makes you think you will even like Moroccan food? You've never had it."

Luke gave him a cheeky grin. "Broadening my horizons like you always say." He ducked as Max pretended to cuff the back of his head. "Besides, it can't be any worse than some of the places we have eaten." He paused for effect. "Remember the lamb shank we had in Restaurant Bernard? All shank, no lamb. Would have been great if I was a dog."

"Alright," Max conceded. "That was pretty awful. The problem is that you don't like what the locals eat, and that's what's usually best."

"Pâté, stinky cheese and smelly fungus. No thanks!"

"Truffles."

"Whatever. They use pigs to find them, so that should tell you everything you need to know." He sat back and folded his arms. "Anyway, what are you doing tonight?"

"I met an old college friend today and agreed to have dinner and catch up."

"Sounds boring. So what am I doing?"

"Angela has invited you to dinner again."

"*Fantastique!* Do you think she will make schnitzel again?" he asked, wide-eyed with hope.

"Probably," said Max.

"Cool," said Luke. "So did you get any work done on the book today?"

Luke was goading him. "Huh! Chance would be a fine thing." He explained about Hassan's arrest, fudging the prostitution aspect.

Luke looked scandalized. "That's crazy. Hassan's no killer."

"Oh! You have a lot of experience with killers, do you?"

"Come on, Dad, you know he didn't do it."

Max nodded. "You're right. I don't think he did it, but it's really not our business. The investigating judge is an old friend. She will be very fair. We should just let the police get on with it."

"Dad. You always go on about what's fair and what's not. This isn't fair. You have to help him." Max glanced sideways at the earnest face staring at him.

"What do you expect me to do? I'm not a French lawyer. I got him the best criminal defense lawyer around here. I don't even mind paying. But I'm not sure what else I can do."

"I know you, Dad. You're a problem solver. That's why all those clients pay you the big bucks. You'll figure it out."

Max pulled in next to the dumpster, put on the handbrake and turned off the engine. He turned to gaze at his son. He was so proud of him it brought a lump to his throat. First Yousef, now this. He recognized the look on Luke's face. It said his son thought he was invincible, that he could do anything. He would learn soon enough, but for now he so didn't want to let him down.

20

At just past seven o'clock Max met Claire in the lobby of the Auberge des Vignes. In French fashion, they exchanged the *bisous*, three kisses on alternate cheeks. They were shown to a corner table by the window with long views over the valley to the blueish hills in the distance. In the foreground to the right were the towering, serrated cliffs of the canyons on the Sentier des Ocres.

"Have you walked the Ochre Trail?" Claire asked, nodding towards the orange cliffs.

"Of course. Several times. I love how they change color, from yellow to orange to red, at different times of the day."

"Wait 'til the sun starts to set. The view later will be amazing. They seem to blaze with fire."

"Can't wait."

The maître d' brought their drinks order: his a Citadelle gin and tonic, hers a glass of Cassis white.

"Do you know the legend behind the cliffs?" she asked.

He shook his head. "No."

"They say the deep red comes from the blood of Dame Sermonde who jumped to her death to escape her jealous husband."

"Speaking of which, you don't have a jealous husband, do you?" He was looking at the expensive engagement ring and platinum wedding band on her left hand. "He won't mind that you're out to dinner with such a handsome man?" he added jokingly.

Claire laughed, but when she spoke, Max sensed sadness in her voice. "I wish. I'm not sure he notices what I do anymore. He is so busy. It gets like that, doesn't it? When you're married so long, it's like passing ships in the night."

Max thought of Emma. *No*, he wanted to say. It doesn't always get like that. He and Emma spent as much of their spare time together as was possible, and they always missed each other when separated.

He studied Claire as they spoke, casting his mind back over twenty years. She had been one of the few beauties back in law school with her curvy figure and pale, oval face. She still had her thick mass of wavy auburn hair—but now her hair was darker and straighter with a silver streak in the front. Her face was still smilingly youthful, the fine age lines around her eyes expressing wisdom and experience.

"I'm sorry," he said. "That it's like that. For what it's worth he appears to be missing a good deal."

Claire's pale face flushed pink. "Why, Max Dempsey, are you flirting with me? You never bothered back at uni!"

"No. Well." His face went through all kinds of contortions. "Perhaps a little. I was a little slow back then and…" He paused and she leaned forward expectantly. "Let's just say I admired from afar."

She sat back in surprise. "Gosh. I guess you weren't the only one who was a little slow back then. I wish I'd realized."

An awkward silence hung between them for a moment, broken only by a backdrop of low murmuring voices, cutlery scraping on plates and the clink of glasses. Feeling uncomfortable, Max took the opportunity to glance around the restaurant replete with subdued refinement—the picture windows framed with long cream drapes, the gray upholstered chairs, the floor of large, aged flagstones. Very nice. Then Claire's laugh roused him.

"Don't worry. Vincent is in Paris on business until next week, so you are quite safe as far as jealous husbands go." She stared down at the table and fiddled with her place setting. "I'm not sure the same can be said about our police captain. He doesn't seem to like you very much."

Max welcomed the change of subject. He sipped his drink. "I gathered," he said drily. "Although I can't imagine why. I'm generally so likable."

As if by way of confirmation, a waitress approached and addressed him with obvious affection.

"Ah, *Bonsoir*, Max. Or should I say Monsieur Dempsey this evening?"

It was Beatrice, and she was staring at him in her usual alluring way.

Max cleared his throat. "*Bonsoir*, Beatrice. I didn't know you worked here."

She spread her hands. "Co-op produce does not pay so very well and so…" Her shoulders hitched in a gesture of resignation.

Max glanced at Claire. She was grinning like the proverbial Cheshire cat.

"Beatrice, this is an old friend from university, Claire..." he faltered. "I just realized I can't remember your married name."

"Lejeune," Claire said brightly.

Beatrice's face was unreadable. "*Oui,* I know *Madame le juge,*" she said, coolly polite. "*Bonsoir, Madame.* May I take your orders?"

When Beatrice was gone, Claire said, "I see you haven't lost your appeal to the opposite sex."

Max snorted. "What appeal? You wouldn't have given me a second look back then. Or now if you didn't know me."

"I gave you several looks back then. You just didn't pick up on it. And you certainly had Rachel on a string for three years." She gave him a knowing look. "And then there was Sam."

He coughed and took a long sip. "Oh, you heard about that."

She smirked. "Sam was, still is, one of my best friends. Of course, I heard. But don't worry, I don't think Rachel did, so your reputation is intact there."

"I have often wondered what would have happened if I hadn't been such an immature jerk. Sam was, I think, my first soulmate. I see her from time to time when I'm in London. That feeling is still there almost thirty years on."

"Those are the crossroads of life. Where would I be if I hadn't met Vincent? In all probability, not in Provence."

"And I suppose I wouldn't be here right now either if it wasn't for..." his voice trailed off, and he clamped a massaging hand over his mouth, not wanting to start down this conversational path.

Claire put down her wine glass.

"I'm so sorry," she said. "It must have been devastating for you. And you have a son—Luke, isn't it?"

She saw the surprise on his face.

"The police had to do a background check on you," she said by way of explanation.

He took a deep breath, tugging at one ear lobe. "It was, is, devastating. But I'm coping, day by day. Some days are better than others. The nights are the worst. And every little thing, everything, stirs a memory. That's why we came away."

Claire nodded, listening intently.

"I worry for Luke, mostly, about how it will affect him."

Claire reached across and squeezed Max's hand. Her warmth sent an electric current up his arm. It had been so long since he'd felt affection like that, from a woman. Angela's motherly hugs didn't count. This felt different.

She dropped his hand, and he took a large gulp of wine.

"He is lucky he has you," said Claire. "Even though I know what a pressure it must be on you. You must be very close?"

"We are," Max replied contentedly, regaining some of his composure.

Beatrice came back with a breadbasket, and Max coughed, dabbing at his eyes.

"So, *Madame le juge?* How did that all come about?" he asked, emphatically changing the subject.

Claire toyed with one earring. "Hmmm. Well, it certainly wasn't my ambition to become a judge. But after we moved down here with the boys, Vincent got into politics, and he was gone a lot of the time, often to Paris, for weeks. When the boys went to college, I became bored, just sitting at home by myself most evenings. The opportunity came up, and I was in the right place at the right time. I thought it would be an interesting challenge. And I do like the title—*juge d'instruction*." she added flippantly. "Of course, Vincent helped with a nudge too."

Max scrutinized her face. "Do you enjoy it?"

"I do. It gets me out of the house and keeps my mind active."

"*Bon*. A British *juge d'instruction*. That must put a few Frog noses out of joint."

"Monsieur Dempsey," said Claire. "I am married to a Frog!" She laughed again, a warm throaty chuckle. "I haven't heard that word in a long time."

"I never was very PC. Emma used to scold me a lot."

At that moment the first course arrived—Coquilles Saint-Jacques for Claire and duck carpaccio with apricot curry emulsion for Max. Max peered over at Claire's dish: plump white scallops, caramelized on top and served in the clamshell bathed in a creamy sauce of shallots, mushrooms and white wine. The aroma was alluring, but he didn't eat shellfish. Claire saw his inspection.

"I know, I shouldn't eat them, So rich and decadent, but…" she held up her hands in surrender.

He smiled. "So very different from home then, the inquisitorial system?"

Claire nodded. "Yes, I like it actually. It doesn't matter as much who has the best lawyer. Only the truth is important."

Max frowned, contemplating his own previous court career. "I can't imagine working in this system. So, you investigate crimes along with the police?"

Claire nodded.

"And obviously you are investigating the death of Madame Borrell."

Mouth full and sauce lingering provocatively on her lip, she nodded again.

"It's not really surprising that Jacques didn't want you to have dinner with me."

He forked a sliver of rare duck into his mouth and savored the sweet spiciness of the emulsion. She licked her lips.

"I can't really talk about it, but I think you can safely say you are in the clear. One Hans Beeker places you on your balcony immediately after the scream was heard. So as far as I am concerned, you are not a suspect no matter how much Capitaine Jacques would like you to be."

"That's true; I did talk to Hans in all his glory then."

She arched one eyebrow.

There was another awkward pause. He hadn't seen this woman in almost thirty years, and they were never close friends back then. But he could feel a genuine empathy emanating from her and, weirdly, felt they were friends now.

"Have you met him?" asked Max.

She shook her head. "Just read his statement."

"Wait until you meet him, a large, overweight bear of a Dutchman, and then try and imagine him naked except for a very small and tight pair of Speedos."

Claire's laughter rang around the room, and several heads turned in their direction.

"Then, if it's not too much to ask, imagine him reaching in to scratch his testicles."

"Stop, stop," she spluttered. She wiped her eyes. "You are hilariously influencing *un juge d'instruction.*"

"Sorry. Just trying to add a little color to your investigation."

They finished their appetizers, and a now dourly professional Beatrice whisked the plates away to be replaced with the entrée. Her coolness towards them, and in particular Claire, was clearly a source of great amusement to the judge, but Max was disappointed. It was so unlike the Beatrice he knew.

"Do you think she is just a tad jealous?" Claire asked, smirking.

"Don't go there," Max replied, grinning despite himself.

Over their saddle of lamb, they filled each other in on their lives since university. It was more sharing than Max had done in a very long time, and it felt good to relax and talk. When they rose to leave, Claire held out both hands to him, and he reached out to clasp them.

"This has been *formidable*, as the French say," she said.

"Yes," he replied. "It makes me think I missed something back at Uni."

She tilted her head to look at him. "I think perhaps me too."

Side by side they strolled out of the high-arched entrance and along the Rue de la Poste past the post office and pharmacy to the parking lot. The night was clear, and the air aromatic with the fragrance of wild herbs. The rolling burble of conversation and the splash of laughter from café terraces rippled through the otherwise quiet streets.

Max was gratified when Claire stopped by a Citroen C4 Cactus in metallic teal. Somehow, she intuited what he was thinking.

"Vincent has the BMW. Luxury cars are not my thing."

"Brava, you. That's my ride over there." He nodded at the 2CV6, shining lime green under the streetlights.

"I love it. Let's do this again."

"*Absolument!* You can even bring your husband."

There went that uneasy smile again. "We'll see. *Bonne nuit*, Max." She stepped forward and kissed him on the cheek. Her soft skin smelled of apricots.

"À bientôt, m*a amie.*"

As he walked home Max couldn't help but smile. The evening had been lovely. It had been so good to talk to and enjoy the company of a woman again. Claire felt safe because she was married to Vincent. He'd felt free to talk about Emma, about Luke, about the past six months. She had listened intently. He was glad she had come back into his life. Even if it was under the strangest of circumstances.

* * *

Claire didn't even wait until she reached home. She speed-dialed the moment she got into her car. After a few rings Samantha picked up.

"Hello, you. To what do I owe this honor? It must be quite late your time."

"You will never guess who I just had dinner with."

There was a pause. "I don't know. The President of France?"

"Better."

"That guy who stars in *Balthazar*."

"You mean Tomer Sisley. Better."

"Come on, who could be better than Tomer whatshisname?"

"An old flame of yours."

"Now you're just sounding old. Who says flame anymore?"

"Okay, *ton ancient amant.*"

"Sounds much better in French. I have no idea. You'll have to narrow the field a bit more. Or you could just cut the suspense and tell me what the hell you are talking about."

A prolonged silence ensued while Claire thought about what to say.

"Claire?"

"I'm still here." She paused and then said, "I think you still have a thing for him."

There was a small gasp. "I do not."

"Ah, so you know who I am talking about."

Samantha sounded abashed. "Well, yes, I suppose. What is Max doing there?" Her tone turned accusatory. "And what are you doing having dinner with him?"

Claire could not keep the smirk off her face. Max had said he and Sam still got together in London. The rest had been a guess. Who wouldn't have a thing for Max Dempsey? She had a thing for him after only one dinner. And the waitress was positively possessive. Her thoughts sobered. "He moved here recently with his son after his wife was killed in a traffic accident. He said they needed to get away from the house, the relatives, the constant reminders."

The silence stretched between them.

"That's awful," Samantha finally said. "He was madly in love with her." She sounded dismayed, and Claire wasn't sure whether her friend was sad that Max had lost the love of his life, or that she had never had that opportunity—possibly both. She could tell that Sam was thinking about her own failed marriage and decided to lighten the mood.

"You'd better get across here soon. I know of at least one very attractive waitress who has designs on him. There are probably dozens more."

Samantha laughed. "Probably," she agreed. "How is he?"

"Even handsomer than in college but still with a boyish charm. And smart and interesting. Oh, and funny. He still plays competitive football and he likes to cook. A real catch. But then, you know that."

"I meant, how is he coping, you fool?"

Claire hesitated. "I know. The truth is, I don't know. I've only really seen him the once. He seemed okay, but you can never tell. When he talks about her, he has a thousand-yard stare as if he's not in the moment. I'd say he has been putting on a brave face for his son, Luke."

"Hmm!"

"Come and see for yourself. I haven't seen you in ages. I know Vincent will be pleased to see you."

"If he's there."

Claire emitted a sad sigh. "Yes, if he's home."

"I don't know that Max needs to see me at this time."

"I think it is exactly what he does need. Another friendly face that reminds him of better times. One that presumably holds only good memories if you guys used to catch up in London."

"Hmm. Let's say memories of unfulfilled promise. Bitter-sweet for me."

"Do come over. I could use a friendly face too."

"I'll think about it."

"Think hard, my love. Think hard."

19

The following morning Max and Luke were up early. For once Max had managed a good night's sleep. While Luke went for a quick swim, trying to beat Madame Hojberg, Max caught up on his emails. There was already one from Claire:

Had a great time last night. Can't believe we weren't more friendly at Uni. Let's do it again soon.

He pecked out a reply: *Then you don't remember how popular you were, running with the in-crowd and how geeky and insecure I was.*

A reply came almost immediately: *Geeky? You? According to Rachel you played football for the university, had a wicked tennis serve and were a table football legend.*

Max winced and responded: *Rachel exaggerated. Well, at least about the tennis and table football.*

The reply pinged immediately: *So how does that make you geeky?*

Max thought for a moment: *Perhaps geeky isn't the right word. I wasn't cool - particularly where women were concerned. Someone like you was out of my league.*

He waited with interest for her reply.

Hah! I was just as out of my depth as you, but better at pretending. And I'd hardly call hooking up with Rachel and Sam a bad track record with women, although the cheating...

Max looked at his keyboard for a long moment before replying. *You're right. I said I wasn't cool. They both deserved better.*

Well, now look at us. How does Sunday sound? The following day is our national holiday so Vincent will be in Paris again celebrating with the important people.

Max sat back, contemplating. Was she being flirty? Or friendly? He wasn't sure how he would react if she really was flirting. Every time he thought about the possibility of another woman in his life, of being physical with anyone else other than Emma, he froze. The magnitude of what he had lost swept through him like an Arctic breeze. He took a deep breath that tugged somewhere down by his navel, and then let it out slowly.

Perhaps. I have Luke. Let's see how it goes.

The reply was again immediate: *Bring Luke and, of course, that cute puppy. I'll cook and he can swim and play with the dogs.*

If Luke was invited too then she couldn't really be trying to seduce him though, could she? That might depend on how French she had become, he thought wryly. Nevertheless, he felt relieved and then, despite himself, a little disappointed. He didn't want a relationship, but it was always nice to be asked. Quickly, he ended the conversation before making a decision on her invitation. *Got to go. Luke is back and we are headed to camp. Thanks for the invite. Will let you know when I see you later.*

Having dropped Luke at camp, Max met Helene Blanc, Claire and Dupre in the lobby of his apartment building at ten a.m. Claire gave him a sassy look, making him once more question her intentions. He exchanged the *bisous* with her, feeling that after last night they really were old friends now. He wasn't sorry to see the captain absent. He surely would have had a problem with him kissing the *juge d'instruction*. Dupre seemed not to care at all, and Maître Blanc simply cocked her raven head on one side with a contemplative expression of *Just how friendly were you back in college?*

"I'm missing my football for this," groused Max.

"What do you mean?" asked Helene.

"On Saturday morning at camp they play a World Cup competition and they let parents play if they can. I miss playing in my soccer league at home but here I get to play with Eric Cantona!"

He saw the policeman do a quick double-take.

"Do you play, Monsieur Lieutenant?" asked Max.

"When I was young," the policeman answered. "Then I hurt…" He cast around for the right word. *"Mon genou,"* he finally said.

"Your knee. *Moi aussi.*" Max rubbed his right knee where the partially torn meniscus gave him intermittent trouble. "But it can be fixed, no?"

Dupre threw his hands out. "It was fixed, but the injury was too bad." He patted his rotund belly, looking sheepish. "Now I only watch."

"Marseilles?" Max asked.

Dupre looked crestfallen. "I should, *mais non.* PSG!"

Max nodded his appreciation. *"Vous aimez Paris Saint Germaine!"*

Dupre finally smiled at him. "And you are a Manchester United fan."

"How did you know?"

The policeman smiled again, and his ordinarily impassive face took on a whole new aspect. "I am a detective. I have a friend who coaches at Bousquier. I was curious. They tell me your son is good... for an American."

They laughed. Claire cleared her throat.

"Sorry to interrupt this important male bonding, but can we proceed?"

Dupre flicked a sideways grimace at Max. *"Bien sûr, Madame le juge."* He swept one arm towards the elevator.

As they walked along the corridor to the apartment, trailing behind the lieutenant and the judge, Helene bent towards Max and whispered in his ear.

"Incroyable! You have turned Monsieur Dupre into a possible ally. Bravo."

Max grinned. "It was genuine. Talking about football is always easy."

When he walked in the door, Max's first impression of Madame Borrell's apartment was how out of place it was in Provence. This was a region of sun and light, captured in pale blues and tones of gold, peach and apricot. The apartment was a rococo fantasy that Louis XIV would have been proud of. He was so distracted by the weirdness of the décor that he barely glanced at the large wine-red stain on what looked to be an antique kilim rug.

He always thought you could tell a lot about someone from their books, so that was where his attention settled first. This woman was clearly highly educated. There were classic French novels by Hugo, Balzac, Molière, Proust, Dumas, and Camus, among leather-bound volumes of Tolstoy, Goethe, Mann, Melville, Wouk, and other European titans of literature. Less expected were the shelves crowded with complete sets of Dickens, Austen, Brontë, and Hardy in English. Other shelves held works by Shakespeare, Milton, and Chaucer. It was an unnerving portrait of his own grammar school literature education and not unlike the laden bookshelves he had at home.

But the section that piqued his curiosity held works by many Eastern European authors such as Andric, Crnjanski, and Sekulic. These books were in a Slavic language that Max couldn't read a word of, but he recognized the text font from the time, many years ago, when he had dated a Hungarian grad student in New York. What was Madame Maxine Borrell doing with books in a very uncommon language?

He turned away from the bookcase and scanned the room.

"Notice anything strange?" he asked Helene.

She expelled a spurt of air between pursed lips. "Are you kidding? Look at this place. Lots of money and no taste."

Max wrinkled his nose. "I'm not so sure about no taste. I think just different taste." Absent-mindedly he scratched his forehead. "There are no photographs."

"Yes, the police went through the apartment carefully but found nothing that identified a family. As far as they can tell, she had no family that she was in touch with."

Max wandered over to an ornate sideboard and opened one of the doors. Inside was a CD player.

"*Zut,*" exclaimed Helene, looking over his shoulder. "I haven't seen one of those in a while."

"Ni moi," Max agreed.

He began opening drawers until he found the collection of CDs. As he expected, having seen her bookshelves, they were mainly classical works with a heavy emphasis on Sibelius, but neatly stacked together were a few CDs of Slavic folk music. This only bolstered the idea that was now percolating through his mind.

He glanced around the room. No one was paying any attention to him. Helene had disappeared into the master bedroom. The others were talking by the doors leading out onto the balcony. One last thought. Max headed into the kitchen and began rifling through the cupboards. In moments he had uncovered a stash of Médélice Coconut Chocolate tea biscuits and Pionir Honey Heart Gingerbread Cakes. Max had moved to the United States more than twenty years ago, but he still craved British and Australian foodstuffs, particularly the sweet things. He largely shunned American desserts but always kept a package of McVities Chocolate Digestives to have with his afternoon tea and Cadbury's chocolate in the refrigerator. It seems that Madame Borrell also had a fondness for remembered childhood delights.

He sat on the couch and took out his phone. He was scrolling through Google when Helene Blanc reappeared at his shoulder.

"Seen enough?" she asked.

"Yes," he replied. "Are you ready to go?"

She nodded. "Find anything to help?"

He had already decided not to share his thoughts with anyone but Dupre. He didn't want to come across as a smart-arse, and they could use the policeman's cooperation.

"Not sure. I want to think about what I've seen. I'll just have a last word with the lieutenant to cement our rapport."

He gave her a lop-sided grin and she gave him that *men are hopeless* look.

"I'll leave you to your football talk," she said.

"Monsieur Dupre," he called across the room. "Perhaps we can talk?"

The policeman crossed the room, and they leaned toward each other across the marble-top kitchen peninsula. The lieutenant no longer seemed as distant. This close, Max noticed the amber dapples in the brown eyes that seemed to burn with a calculating competence.

"Quoi de neuf?" Dupre asked.

Max lowered his voice. "I'll tell you what's up. I don't think the victim is French. And I'll bet her name is not Maxine Borrell."

The policeman's forehead disappeared into his shaggy hair-line. Max outlined his thoughts: The apartment looked like something from another culture with Serbian books and music, and Serbian-labeled groceries were in the kitchen.

"Just between us, I thought you might want to investigate."

The policeman appraised him somberly and Max watched something flicker across the man's face. Dupre knew what he was being offered—an unseen helping hand, but would he be too proud to take it?

For a long moment, Dupre scraped at his straggly beard and then said, "That's an interesting theory. I'll look into it."

He nodded at Max. There was no *thank you* forthcoming, but they had established an understanding.

"That didn't look like football talk to me," Helene Blanc said as they left the others on the street afterward.

"Just doing my job and trying to keep the police on our side and our client out of jail."

"Do you want to share?"

He told her his suspicions.

"You see," she said. "I told you I could learn something from you."

They were standing by the pharmacy across the street from the town parking lot. Helene Blanc gazed vacantly at the milling tourists and at the view across the valley on two sides. Unusually, the sky was a lowering mass of swirling gray clouds.

As Max glanced at the sky, a roll of thunder reverberated across the valley. He felt his phone vibrating in his pocket.

"D'accord," he said, listening to the voice on the other end. "À demain. À demain." He turned back to the lawyer. "Zip-lining postponed until tomorrow."

"Ah, *oui,*" said Helene. "Not ideal to be swinging from the trees in that, no?"

"No," said Max. "Nor sitting by the magistrate's pool with a glass of wine."

Helene laughed. "I'd better go."

Max watched as she got into a sleek black BMW. It suited her. Thunder sounded again and the first few drops of rain splattered him. He ran for the car, quickly rolled the canvas roof into position and folded the windows back into place. It was going to be another dash to Cavaillon as camp was sure to let out early. Well, at least he hadn't missed that much football.

At camp, he watched as Luke ran toward the car and clambered in, soaking wet. He shook his mop of hair like a dog, sending a spray over Max.

"Can you believe this rain?" he said, sounding exasperated.

"Yeah, biblical," said Max, before breaking the news that their afternoon activity was postponed.

Within minutes he and Luke were sitting in what was little more than a tent on wheels while the storm raged around them, buffeting the car from side to side alarmingly. The wind howled like a thousand demons. The canvas roof of the 2CV6 was not known for noise suppression and it felt as if they were almost out in the open. It didn't often storm here in the summer, but when it did, the weather let loose all the humid energy it had been saving up, often dropping more than six inches of rain in a few hours, causing dangerous flash floods. Despite being midday, the sky was almost black, lit into a magenta tableau every few minutes by a spectacular blitz of jagged forks of crimson lightning. The windshield wipers whipping back and forth in a frenzy could barely clear the deluge, and Max hunched forward to peer ahead. The traction on the car was excellent but the suspension caused it to pitch and roll worryingly.

"This is almost as good as zip-lining," said Luke. "Maybe better."

"Huh! Perhaps for you," Max said through clenched teeth.

Luke grinned. "Blow winds and crack your cheeks. Rage and blow 'til you have drenched us."

"Wow. Paraphrasing Shakespeare. Your mother would be proud."

He and Emma had both been Shakespeare fans and much to Luke's dismay he had been forced to attend a Shakespeare camp the year before with his best friend and a gaggle of girls.

At that moment a large silver Mercedes shot by them into the blaring horns of oncoming traffic on the narrow road, the wake it threw up swamping Max's windshield and rendering him temporarily blind.

Max cursed under his breath. Of all the nights to have agreed to go out to dinner with Luke. "We may be joining her soon with these idiots," he muttered to himself.

Luke reached over and plucked Max's phone from the cupholder.

"I don't think I could concentrate on the book at the moment," Max said.

"Nah. I have something better in mind. Sticking with the Shakespeare theme..." He turned up the volume. "I give you 'The Tempest' by Tchaikovsky."

From the speakers blasted a wild cacophony of swirling strings, deep horns and rumbling drums that seemed to mirror the storm outside. Luke began throwing his arms around in a frenzy as if he was conducting an orchestra.

"You're a smart-arse, you know that? Is this what they teach you in band?"

Luke paused on a downstroke. "You know I take after you."

"No. The smart you get from your mother. The arse you picked up all by yourself."

Fortunately, they made it back in one piece, and by the time evening came around, the rain had lessened and the wind had calmed. Marrakech was situated on a quiet walkway in the town of Apt. It had a brick red façade lined with metal bistro tables with matching slat-backed chairs under a striped awning. The tables were covered with bright red tablecloths and separated from the street by a row of large concrete planters containing pink-blooming bougainvillea shrubs. Max thought it looked invitingly cozy despite being somewhat storm-bedraggled on the outside. The inside was even more charming and, more importantly, dry. A wide swathe of cream linen formed an un-dulating canopy overhead, and a banquette of crimson cushions lined the old stone walls. The yellow Moroccan tile-top tables were wrought iron to match the chairs. Brass filigree pendant lamps completed the ambience. The smell was like a warm bath of cinnamon and cloves. Max's mouth began to water as soon as he stepped through the door.

The place was crowded, but Zoya saw them and danced over in lithe, graceful strides. She beamed and held her arms out.

"Max. May I call you Max?"

"Please do, Zoya."

"We are so glad you have come."

It was then that Max realized Luke had already ducked around him and was greeting Yousef at the back of the restau-rant. Zoya showed him to a table by the window and after a few minutes Luke deigned to join him.

"Yousef has to work," he complained.

"Maybe we should find you a job to keep you busy after camp and on the weekends. I can ask around."

"Noooo!"

"Then don't forget how lucky you are."

The words were out before he realized, and he wanted them back immediately. He waited, but Luke just looked down at the menu in his hands. Yousef had both parents.

Max sighed and turned his attention to the menu. The entrées sounded so great that he struggled with what to choose. In the end he opted for the Chicken Bastilla, a savory pie cooked with saffron, ginger, pepper and cinnamon, then layered with crispy warqa pastry and topped with a herb omelet and fried almonds scented with orange flower water. He hadn't seen one in years, and it sounded delicious. But glancing down the rest of the menu he was a little concerned about what Luke would find to eat.

"Do you think they do this with pasta?" Luke asked, pointing to the Kefta Meatball Tangine.

"No. You get a loaf of bread to soak up the sauce."

Luke's eyes lit up at the mention of bread, his favorite food.

"But I'm sure they could do it without the poached eggs on top."

"That's okay. I'll take the eggs."

Max stared at him. "Who are you and what have you done with my son?" Were Luke's tastes changing or did he not want to be seen wimping out by his friend? Whatever it was, he was thankful for it.

As Max awaited their food, his anxiety rose that it wouldn't be very good. It would place him in a difficult position with Yousef's family and he didn't want Luke to feel uncomfortable. But he needn't have worried. The food was divine—an utterly amazing fusion of flavors and textures. He paired the food with a luscious Bandol from Château Pibarnon. Bandol, a commune on the coast east of Marseilles, was a wine domain of its own. Max wasn't a wine snob and could never taste the raspberry, or tobacco—who wanted to taste tobacco in wine anyway?—or any of the other affectations good wine was saddled with. But he knew a rich, velvety wine when he drank it. He smiled when he thought of Beatrice who said there were only two types of wine drinkers in the world—those who love the wines of Bandol, and those who don't know the wines of Bandol. He had already made some good friends since he came to Provence.

Luke was still scraping the last of the tomato sauce from his dish with a hunk of crusty Moroccan bread when Zoya came over with a man of about her age dressed in a chef's jacket. He had an oval face, covered by a sparse, close-cropped beard. His oversized mouth smiled widely in greeting. He was as tall and slender as she was short and stout. They made an almost comical pair.

"This is my husband, Mourad," said Zoya.

Max stuck out a hand, and Mourad wiped his on his jacket front before reaching out.

"That meal was truly exquisite," Max said, kissing a blossom from his lips. "The last time I had Bastilla was in Manhattan about twenty years ago, and it was nowhere near as good as this."

"*Fantastique,*" Luke mumbled through a mouthful of bread.

Mourad looked confused and glanced at his wife. "*Desolée.* My English is not so good as Zoya," he said apologetically.

Zoya translated Max's comments, and the chef looked sheepish. "*Merci.* You are kind to say it."

"De rien," Max replied.

"Oh," Zoya said in that by-the-way voice. "I understand we have a friend in common."

"Really?" Max didn't have that many friends here to choose from.

Zoya's face was suffused with delight. "Yes, Hassan. He is the concierge in your building, no? He is my cousin."

Max could feel his face fall. His mind went blank. *Merde!*

"Max, what is the problem? Is Hassan not a friend?" Zoya looked confused.

"Dad…" Luke began to say, but Max held up his hand, and his son fell silent.

"Oh, Zoya. I'm sorry." Max looked at her with great sympathy. "I guess you haven't heard."

"Heard what?" Now she sounded frightened, and Mourad followed their conversation back and forth like he was watching a tennis match.

Max rubbed the back of his neck. "I don't know how to tell you this…"

"What? Tell me."

"Hassan's been arrested for murder."

Zoya threw a hand to her mouth and crumpled into a chair. Max watched as she tried to process it.

"No, that can't be," she finally said. Tears were beginning to smear her kohl. Mourad was kneeling next to her, holding her hand. They conversed in rapid Arabic, and Mourad began to look very angry.

"Look, I don't think Hassan is guilty," Max said using his most comforting voice. He wanted to add *I'm sure the police will realize that soon and release him*, but he knew he couldn't. Guilty or innocent, Hassan was in real trouble.

Zoya suddenly lurched up as if she would run to the door. "Does he have a lawyer? He doesn't have much money. He has been caring for his father. The medical bills." She waved a desperate hand.

Max put his hand on her arm. "He does. I couldn't do much, but I found him the best lawyer. Don't worry about her fees."

She visibly pulled herself together, drawing her short stature up in a prideful stance. "Thank you, Max. Thank you for your concern and friendship. But we will pay whatever it costs."

Another guest shouted to her and she blew out a long breath. "Excuse me, but I must get back to work."

Max turned to Mourad and indicated a chair. *"Asseyez vous, s'il vous plait."*

With a backward glance to assess the waning dining room situation, the chef perched on the edge of the chair. Max did his best to assuage Mourad's anger fueled by years of being treated as a second-class citizen by the police and almost everyone else. But the best he could say was that the investigating judge was a foreigner too and known to be very fair. When Mourad was called away they got up to leave.

"You have to help him now, Dad."

Just great. No pressure, then.

"We'll be back," Max told Zoya as they left, the warmth of good food and friendship now entirely evaporated.

Luke was yawning as he slapped hands with Yousef.

"A bientôt," Zoya said waving them out. "And thank you, Max."

What a terrible ending to a wonderful evening, thought Max, ducking out into what was now light rain. Perhaps coming to Provence hadn't been the right decision after all.

21

That night, after the full fury of the storm had subsided, Gendarme Sergeant Armand Da Silva slipped into the police headquarters in Aix. He paused inside the main door and glanced surreptitiously around while he beat the water from his dark uniform. He kept his head down and away from the surveillance camera, his kepi pulled low. No one was on the front desk, and the place had all the activity of a morgue at night.

It was as he had expected. In a vicious storm like this, any officers on duty would be out on the roads. They were perpetually understaffed. He had been here many times before and knew where he was going.

One floor down, he keyed in the access code for the evidence room and peered around the cracked door. The custodian was long gone. Quickly he entered and began to search the bins. They were arranged by date order, with the newest additions at the front. It took him only a few minutes to realize the laptop wasn't there. He cursed and cracked his knuckles while he thought. Failure was not an option.

Michel had been non-stop calling from a blocked number, his last ending abruptly with the words *Battistu is not long on patience.* If it was not here, then where? He had recognized Arielle from the description Michel gave him. He didn't know her, but he had heard about her. Her looks were eye-catching, especially in the male-dominated police force, and her computer skills were legendary. Of course, she would still be working on it. He had heard she kept strange hours so that meant she could be working on it this very moment upstairs.

How far was he prepared to go? He thought of Michel and the evidence he held against him. He thought of the threat that Battistu posed to his family and career. He needed help and he knew it, but what could he do? Without the coke he couldn't function, couldn't work, couldn't support his family. He could use a hit right now. His jaw clenched and he fingered the gun at his hip. He had no choice. He would go as far as he had to. He took his cap off and passed a shaky hand through his thick hair. He'd have to go upstairs.

As it happened, fortune was with him and with Arielle. As he came up from the basement, he saw Arielle's back heading down the corridor that led to the garage. He hurried up to the second floor. He found Arielle's cubicle—the only one with a desk lamp on—and there it was. The laptop was still warm, so she had been working on it. There was no time to lose.

He picked it up and was headed out when he heard voices. Stupidly, he hadn't thought to bring a bag and could hardly just stroll out of the building with a laptop tucked under one arm. He stood irresolutely as his nerve failed him. If he was discovered here at this time of night, questions would be asked. The voices were coming closer, and he fought down the rising panic. Desperately, he ducked into the adjacent break room where his eyes fell on the microwave. He frowned. Perhaps there was a better way.

He cowered as the voices approached, and he sagged with relief as they passed by and diminished. He closed the break room door and placed the laptop in the microwave. Three minutes should do it. He didn't want to melt the outside casing.

He hadn't appreciated how noisy it would be or reckoned on the smoke. It seemed an eternity of loud fizzing and crackling that accompanied the pyrotechnic display visible behind the microwave door. His heart pounded as he held his ear to the door expecting someone to investigate. By the time it was over he was choking on the stench of cooking plastic and silicone. Hands trembling, he finally slid the laptop back where he had found it.

22

Sunday dawned bright and clear. The heavy rain had dissipated some of the oppressive heat and enhanced the terroir in the same way any herb springs into fragrant life when run under a faucet.

Max sat on the terrace savoring his coffee and croissants and mulling over the events of the previous evening. Shit! Shit! What were the chances? Still, it was Sunday, and there wasn't much he could do for Hassan today. Luke was still in bed, but Dickens came out to join him. He was staring Max down with his head cocked on one side, hoping for a tidbit.

"Well, what do you think, *Chien*? Should we go visit Claire? Is it safe?"

Dickens yipped.

He swirled the last of his coffee and drank it off. "Okay, but first zip-lining. And you can't come. Let's see if Angela will look after you."

Angela took the puppy into her arms in a shower of whiskery kisses. She laughed. No one could resist a puppy, especially Dickens, and she waved them off with the dog clutched under her arm like a baby.

Half an hour later they were billowing along the D100 towards Lagnes. The roof was open and the windows were down.

Following the storm, the air rushing in felt fresher and cooler. To Luke's dissatisfaction, "O Mio Babbino Caro" by the incomparable Maria Callas soared from the speakers. Despite the somewhat tragic lyrics, Max always found the aria uplifting. It was good for Luke to be put out from time to time and also to have a little classical opera education. Pavarotti and "Nessun Dorma" next, followed by "Libiamo, Ne'Lieti Calici." To soften the blow, he allowed Luke to play games on his phone, which was usually prohibited in the car.

Passarelles des Cimes made every other zip-lining course they had been on seem like a toddler's playground. The lines, rope ladders and climbing nets were strung between soaring pines at a height sufficient to promise death in the event of a fall. The speeds they achieved threatened to smash them into tree trunks. Luke loved it. For Max it was a lot like watching Luke play American football—a mixture of elation and foreboding. They survived, and two hours later, tired and hungry, left, heading for the address outside Ménerbes that Claire had given him.

As they drove up to the high wrought iron gates, Luke whistled. The crushed white limestone driveway lined with narrow Italian cypresses was long, bending out of sight toward a house, the roof of which peeped between towering pines and poplars. The house itself was a magnificent 18th-century farmhouse of honey-colored stone with terracotta roof tiles and gray shutters. It reeked of expensive antiquity.

"How rich is this woman?" Luke demanded.

Max gave his son a disconcerted glance. Were those rich kids at camp getting to him? "No idea. Does it matter?"

Luke chortled. "As you say, Dad, if you can't be rich, it's good to have rich friends."

As parents, they had always played down their wealth, so Max was always relieved when Luke downplayed it too. Being rich was relative, but even being a little rich was something Max would never wrap his head around.

They parked on the large circular driveway which surrounded a bubbling fountain bordered with lavender. On one side stood an old stone archway hung with a luxuriant violet wisteria vine. Through it, Max glimpsed a gravel walkway and the periphery of a well-tended garden.

The scarred front doors looked like they had withstood centuries of attack with axe and battering ram. Max pulled the long iron pull chain, and they heard the jangle of a bell deep within the house. Moments later Claire opened the door dressed in pink capris and a white sleeveless blouse. Her feet were bare. Her smile was radiant. A black lab barreled past her, tail wagging furiously, and all but knocked Max over. Luke instantly dropped to his knees to pet the big dog as it attempted to lick his face.

"Max, I'm so glad you could come. Do I have a surprise for you!"

Max raised his eyebrows. He pulled Luke up from where he squatted behind him. "This is my son Luke. Luke, this is an old law school friend, Madame Lejeune."

Luke appraised her frankly as teenagers do and must have decided he liked what he saw. He stuck out a hand and said, "Hi, I'm Luke. Sorry about the sweat. Zip-lining, you know."

Claire laughed again. "Don't worry, I have had teenage boys of my own. What's a little urea among friends?"

Luke grinned. "I must remember that. It's nice to meet you."

"Oh, and this is Rasputin, by the way." She nudged the big dog aside with her leg. "Come in, come in." She stepped aside to usher them through the door. "You can cool off in the pool before lunch. I take it you haven't eaten."

Luke shook his head vigorously. "I'm starving!"

Max rolled his eyes, but Claire laughed. "Of course you are. When are teenage boys not?"

She ushered them into a spacious foyer dominated by a curved stone stairway with a black, barley sugar twist iron balustrade. The interior of the home was a combination of the same exposed honey-hued stone and smooth stucco. The floor was pale gray limestone flagging.

Eyeing them both, she asked, "You did bring a change of clothes, right?"

Max swung a canvas hold-all off his shoulder. "Of course."

Claire led them up the stairs and into a large bedroom with round hand-hewn ceiling beams the dimensions of telegraph poles, leaving them to change into bathing suits.

"When you're ready," she said, giving Max a mischievous grin which made him wonder what surprise she had in store for him, "come down. You'll find us on the back patio."

Us. She said *us.* She had said her husband was in Paris. Her children perhaps? But why would that be a surprise for him? Luke had already changed while Max was still puzzling this over.

"Come on, Dad. I'm starving."

"Yes, so you said. Hold your horses."

Max changed into his board shorts and T-shirt, feeling more than a little self-conscious. After all, he didn't know this woman very well and this wasn't like being at a public beach. *Us?* He could be walking into a party for all he knew. She had been dressed with casual elegance, and he… well, he cast his eyes up and down his clothes, was decidedly not. Luke obviously had no such concerns.

He bounded ahead down the stairs and paused, mouth agape, when they entered a living room that soared twenty feet to a vaulted ceiling framed with massive oak beams. One end housed a giant stone fireplace, and the back wall was entirely glass looking out to a vista of undulating green lawn and flowering gardens, which in this heat, Max thought, was no mean feat. Clearly, this old home had been expertly restored and modernized.

"Wow!" Luke whispered, staring out the wall-to-ceiling window.

Max was feeling all shades of envy. This was the type of home he had always aspired to. "Yes, wow!"

They made their way through a state-of-the-art kitchen, with sleek stainless-steel appliances and black granite counters, and into an outside dining room with more timeworn beams, stone walls and a blue mosaic floor. Claire and another woman whose back was toward them sat at an old farmhouse table. Max stopped in the doorway feeling a tingling heat rising up his neck and into his scalp. He would know that figure anywhere, even from behind.

Feeling practically naked in his T-shirt and shorts, he summoned up the fortitude to walk forward. Luke sensed something going on and stared from him to Claire. As Max approached, the other woman stood up and turned around. She was still slender, although the years had added a few curves. Her dark, shoulder-length hair, frizzy back in college, was now pin straight with amber highlights, framing a pale oval face with prominent rosy cheeks and high arched, carefully manicured, eyebrows. Her customary generous smile seemed a little uncertain.

"Sam," Max murmured, clearing his throat in confusion. "I had no idea you were here."

"Hiya," Sam replied, apparently unsure how to respond.

"She arrived yesterday afternoon for a short visit," Claire said brightly.

Max looked up to the ceiling trying to gather his thoughts. He was pretty sure this was Claire's doing, and he wasn't sure how he felt about it. He was always happy to see Sam in London, but the present circumstances didn't feel ideal. He glanced sideways at Luke, who was scrutinizing her suspiciously. Then, stepping forward tentatively, he enfolded her slim body in a deep hug and felt her soft lips against his cheek impart a long measure of condolence in the way only old friends might. He lingered in the moment, blinking away instant tears. Words were unnecessary. Collecting himself, he reached for her hands and pulled back slightly, gazing deeply into her hazel eyes. "It is really good to see you. You look well?"

His observation was more of a question than a statement. He had, of course, heard about her divorce. Her reassuring smile put him at ease.

"So do you."

He smiled deprecatingly. "Yes, well, looking at you two, I feel a little underdressed."

She pulled him back into a quick hug, her whisper feathering across his face, "I've seen you with less," before stepping back.

He swallowed hard and turned to Luke. "And this is my son, Luke. Luke, this is another old university friend, Samantha..."

He paused, unsure whether she was still using her married name.

"Sam will do. That's what my stepchildren called me."

Luke hesitated momentarily and then stiffly thrust out his hand. "Pleased to meet you," he said, with none of the warmth he had bestowed on Claire. There was a moment of tension, and then Samantha put her other hand gently over his and said in her plummy British accent, with obvious feeling, "I'm really sorry about your Mum. I never met her, but your dad talked a lot about her when we met in London. She must have been a special person."

Luke gazed at her, and Max saw him struggle against the beginning of tears. "Thanks," he finally croaked out.

Max caught Claire's sympathetic regard and squeezed his son's shoulder. "I think we could both do with a swim," he said. "We'll be right back."

He steered Luke toward the rectangular pool which lay beyond a wide swath of lawn, sparkling like a multi-faceted turquoise gem in the bright sunlight. As he dawdled in the refreshing water, Max contemplated his surroundings. The house was nestled in a depression among the heavily forested surrounding hills. Beyond the immediate semi-walled garden, he could see a regimented grove of olive trees, flanked by more neat rows of lavender, and a large pond. The scent in the air was intoxicating, and it was so quiet that he could hear the bees buzzing among the flowers and the clink of glasses from the house. The whole setting composed a scene of peace and beauty. He fully understood why Claire lived here. He would be ecstatic to do the same.

When he'd taken in his tranquil surroundings, his thoughts turned back to Samantha. He had last seen her in London two years before. She had been in the throes of a difficult divorce at the time. The second one. Was she hard to live with, he wondered? Behind closed doors? Behind the glossy, sultry presence he had known? Or had her husbands been the problem? Controlling. Argumentative. Or perhaps they'd grown bored, their interests diverged, the decision to live apart the only answer to their unhappiness?

He had been very lucky with Emma—better than he deserved. In hindsight, Sam had been his first real love. If he had recognized it then, his life might have been very different. He glanced at Luke who was doing backward flips off the springboard. He could certainly have no regrets on that score. He had known the best possible marriage. He turned his head sideways, biting his lip at the sudden ache in his chest. He struggled to gather himself, willfully picking up his train of thought.

Max thought of the times he had spent with Sam, their fling only lasting a few months, but spent constantly together, mostly huddled in student digs before graduation had separated them. No, he was fairly confident that, for the right person, she was easy to get along with. In fact, despite being a fierce litigator, she had always seemed somewhat vulnerable to him. Today, she was wearing a reassuring smile, but he wondered how she was really coping? He, too, could turn on a façade in the same way when needed. He found himself doing that a lot around Luke these days. Sam had no children of her own, and if her stepchildren cut her out in the wake of the divorce... well, that would be awful and unfair. So, what was she doing here? If the trip had been planned for a while, why hadn't Claire said anything?

Suddenly he was jerked from his reverie by the arms of a teenager around his neck from behind.

"Are you ready? I'm hungry."

Clearly, Luke's equilibrium had been regained after horsing around in the pool. They returned to the house to find a feast laid out on the antique sideboard. Luke dived right in while Max took a chilled glass of Chablis from Claire.

"Now you see, Dad, this is real food," Luke said through a packed mouth. His plate was laden with salmon and bread, with a smattering of grilled courgettes and a slice of melon.

"He's not a huge fan of French cooking," Max said by way of explanation.

Claire chuckled. "Next time, I'll make you a burger," she said, and Luke gave her a thumbs up, his mouth too full to speak.

Max prepared himself a plate of Serrano ham and melon with some undefined white cheese.

"So, you and Claire are against each other, I hear," Samantha said.

Max scratched his head. "Are we? I suppose so."

"Oh, I thought we were working together," Claire said, pretending hurt. "This is not supposed to be an adversarial system."

Max paused, about to fork a cube of melon into his mouth, and stabbed the fork in her direction. "Your job is to get to the truth. My job is to get my client off. Not the same."

"So, I should stop helping you then." Her voice was light, but there was an undercurrent of pique.

"Uh, oh," said Samantha. "I didn't mean to start something."

Max waved his hand, batting away her concern. "In this instance, I think the two are one and the same thing."

Claire visibly relented. "As it happens, I tend to agree with you. Your client doesn't look to have the stomach for gutting a person."

Samantha choked on her wine and coughed.

"Sorry," said Claire, glancing first at her and then Luke.

Max snorted. "Don't worry about Luke. He relishes this kind of gore. It makes him very popular at camp."

Luke nodded vigorously, his mouth still full.

"Anyhow," Claire went on. "I can tell you that based on what the police have discovered, the field has opened up considerably. It seems the victim was in business with some very unsavory characters."

"Who?" asked Luke, swiping his mouth with the back of his hand.

Claire looked at Max, who shrugged.

"Okay, but you cannot talk about this in camp," Claire said pointedly at Luke.

His face fell. "Okay," he said reluctantly.

"She had dealings with the Brise de Sang and the Russian mob."

"Brise de Sang?" Max asked.

"A Corsican gang into organized crime. Gun running, human trafficking, drugs. You name it."

"Fantastic," said Luke, his face alight with interest. "Breeze of blood. Or breath of blood. Take your pick. Either way, that's some name."

Ignoring his son's apparent morbid relish, Max asked, "So, will you let my client go?"

"Already done," replied Claire.

Max's relief was palpable. He no longer had to be involved and he no longer had the pressure of letting down Yousef's family and Luke.

"Great," said Max. "Now maybe I can get back to retirement."

"Great for you, perhaps," their hostess said with a resigned sigh. "Not so great for me. We are going to have a very challenging time pinning the murder on the Corsican gang or Russian mafia. I much preferred an individual suspect." She scrunched her face. "So, your guy is still very much a person of interest."

Oh no. He wanted Hassan well and truly off the hook. Max waved his hand. "If it's an individual you want then perhaps you should look at Jeremy Nash."

Claire's brow creased in puzzlement. "Oh?"

"Well, I hear he had quite the row with the deceased in the town square."

"That's interesting. He told us he didn't know the woman. And where did you hear this?"

For no conscious reason, Max looked at Sam and colored. "Beatrice," he admitted. "She saw them from her shop."

Claire met Sam's eyes, amusement apparent on her face and in her voice, and said, "The waitress I told you about."

Max cast his eyes skyward. "We were just talking while I was choosing a melon for lunch. Anyway, the whole town is talking about the murder."

"I bet," replied Claire. "The mayor is very concerned about the effect on tourism. Now let's talk about something different."

Seeing that they were not going to discuss the murder anymore, Luke said, "I'll leave you to your reminiscing," and went back out to the pool, trailed by Rasputin.

Max spent a relaxing, wine-infused afternoon talking classmate gossip, books, travel and food. They stayed for dinner that had Max grilling steaks.

It wasn't until eight that Max tore Luke away from the giant television screen in the lounge to head home before full darkness set in. The unlit, narrow, winding country lanes, coupled with crazy French drivers, were a challenge better avoided.

On their way out, Max nudged his son, and Luke turned back. "Thanks for having us," he said to Claire, reaching out to shake her hand.

"You're welcome," she said.

Then, to Max's relief, he offered the same hand to Samantha. "It was nice to meet you."

She clasped it again. "You remind me of your father," she said with a soft smile, and something behind her eyes told Max she was looking back fondly. He wondered what part of his youthful, insecure college identity she had seen in his son.

But whatever it was, in that moment, she won Luke over. To Max's surprise, his son stepped closer and briefly embraced her. They were about the same height. His voice cracked slightly as he said, "Thanks for being Dad's friend."

Samantha looked momentarily nonplussed before giving Max a contemplative glance. Picking her words carefully, she replied, "It has been my pleasure, for the most part."

"And what part wasn't a pleasure?" Max said huffily. Then he glanced at Luke. "Never mind."

Claire gave Max a mischievous wink. "See you tomorrow for *La Fête?*"

Max nodded.

"Next time, I'll make burgers," she called after Luke.

"I'll be back soon!" he tossed back over his shoulder.

As Luke climbed into the car, Max ruffled his hair.

"What was all that *thanks for being Dad's friend* about?"

Luke squinted at him. "We both need friends. I have a bunch at camp. I'm worried about you."

"Hmm." Max was more than a little troubled by the comment. He thought he had been doing a better job of hiding his ache.. "When did you get so old?"

They both knew the answer to that one, and a brief silence hung between them.

"You don't have to worry about me. I have you," said Max, snapping his contented façade into place.

"They're very pretty," Luke added, in a thoughtful sort of way.

"Who?" Max asked, although he knew.

"Your two university friends."

Max looked at Luke keenly. This was the first time he had ever heard Luke pass favorable judgment on the looks of someone of the opposite sex. Mostly, he thought of girls as annoying, particularly if he had to play soccer with them.

"You have nothing to worry about there either, you know," he said, recognizing that this statement was somewhat abstruse.

Luke smiled enigmatically. "I'm not worried." Then, to Max's overwhelming contentment, he leaned over, put his head on his dad's shoulder and turned the playlist of arias back on. Max found that he was teary again.

"La Donna è Mobile," Luke read on the screen. "Can you tell what they are saying?"

Max laughed his tears away. "Let's just say it is not very flattering about women. Trust them, and they will break your heart."

"Hah!" his son exclaimed.

23

It was the morning of La Fête Nationale, or Bastille Day. Dupre had dragged himself into the office, clutching a large bag of pastries and feeling tired and a little worse for drink. He made a stab at going over his notes, searching for a thread to pull and unravel this mystery. But his thoughts kept turning to Madeleine and her ready smile and the touch of her face against his. He would make another booking soon at Le Saint Amour. He had to see her. It had been a long time since he had allowed himself any romantic thoughts about a woman and not for want of prodding by his mother who craved grandchildren.

Eventually he sat back, took out a pain au chocolat and pondered the theory the *Anglais* had espoused. Could it be true? Making up his mind, he picked up the phone and asked Arielle—yes, of course, she was sitting at her workstation, even on a national holiday—to send Borrell's fingerprints to Interpol.

An hour later she appeared beside his cubicle. Her face was set in hard lines, her lips screwed tight. "You were right. She's not French. She's Serbian. Her real name is Biljana Markovic, and she is wanted for war crimes during the Balkan conflict."

Dupre whistled. "That would explain a lot."

"Frankly, from what I read, we should be looking for her killer to give them a medal."

Dupre looked at his colleague. He had never seen her angry before. Two red spots burned high on her cheeks. He spoke sympathetically. "Perhaps, but that is not our job."

Her voice blasted on. "She was convicted in her absence of genocide, extermination, rape, mutilation and other atrocities. One teenage Croatian nurse was made to strip and dig her own grave before Markovic's unit gang raped her and did foul things to her body before someone mercifully shot her."

Dupre swallowed hard, tasting bile.

"I'm glad she's dead," Arielle fumed.

"You're glad who's dead?" came a gravelly voice behind her.

Dupre looked past Arielle and saw Jacques approaching down the aisle looking buttoned down in a dark suit as though it was a regular workday. He shot Arielle a warning look. Chill out, it said, but she was shaking with rage. She turned to Jacques, scowling.

"Borrell!" she hissed. "Only her name's not Borrell; it's Markovic, and she is a wanted war criminal who has committed unspeakable atrocities."

If she had punched her superior in the face, he could not have looked more startled. His brow furrowed and he passed a hand across his bald pate. He clearly struggled to take in the significance of what she had said. With a deep breath, he squared his shoulders. "Tell me. How?"

"I received a tip that the victim might not be French," Dupre said quietly. "I asked Arielle to run her fingerprints through Interpol and this is what turned up."

Jacques seemed scandalized. "A tip! From whom?"

Dupre's posture slumped. "The *Anglais*," he admitted softly.

Jacques' eyes grew wide. He choked, stopped, and then started again in a dangerously venomous voice. "And how did he know?"

"He's smart," Dupre said in a matter-of-fact voice. "He noticed things we did not."

"Such as?"

"Serbian books and music, Serbian cookies, heavy furniture. He said that he recognized the signs of an expat living abroad."

The captain looked down, ran a palm across his head again and massaged his thick neck, an expression of anguish screwed on his rugged face.

"Oh my God," said Jacques. "The painting."

"What painting?" asked Dupre.

They watched Jacques' mind turn over.

"She has a Yazmin painting at the BRDO offices. The disturbing likeness of her and some guy. I've just realized who he is now. The Butcher of Bosnia. Radovan Karadzic."

He shook his head ruefully.

"That is why no one was sure what language she spoke," continued Dupre. It sounded vaguely Russian but was probably Serb."

Jacques looked up. "You realize what this means?"

"*Bien sŭr*. I imagine a lot of people would have a reason to kill her, but who knew she was here?"

"Back to square one," Jacques murmured. "We have already been ordered to release the Arab." His lip curled as if being Arab in itself was sufficient reason for detention.

"What I don't get is how she passed for French all these years?" said Dupre.

"Oh, I can answer that," Arielle broke in, disgust evident on her face. "Her mother, Stephanie Borrell, was from Strasbourg. Borrell herself was a professor of modern languages at the University of Zagreb who spent three years at the Sorbonne, so her accent was flawless."

Dupre nodded. "And easy enough to get papers in her mother's maiden name."

"Where are her parents now?" Jacques asked.

"Dead," replied Arielle.

"Siblings?"

"Only child. No other known family." She sniffed. "With her DNA that seems just as well."

"Hmm. Well, we still have to find her killer," the captain said curtly. "Given the type of people she was dealing with, they could be even more repulsive than her. At least I have some progress to report to the judge, even if it is in the wrong direction in terms of finding our killer. What about the prints at the restaurant? From her dinner date?"

"Ah yes," Dupre said. "That took some time, but we finally matched them up through Interpol again, and the result makes sense in the light of the victim's true identity. Her companion was one Zoran Zemunac with ties to Serbian crime gang Senjicari. Gun running, drugs, trafficking, prostitution, extortion."

"Perhaps Markovic was a go-between with Senjicari and Brise de Sang and pissed one, or both of them, off?" Arielle suggested.

"Perhaps," said Dupre, throwing himself back into his chair, worrying his bottom lip with his teeth. "But this doesn't particularly seem like a gangland killing. She wasn't tortured as though she offended someone important, and it wasn't a clean bullet to the head. It seems personal, visceral even. Like someone with a score to settle."

"Well, all this is fantastic police work," the captain growled, "but it doesn't get us anywhere."

"Speaking of which," Arielle took a deep breath, her face drooping with dismay. "I almost forgot, what with the Markovic thing and all..." Her face screwed into an apprehensive expression. "The laptop is kaput."

Jacques' stare was uncomprehending. "What?"

Her shoulders hitched meekly. "Markovic's laptop has been destroyed."

His eyes went wide. "How in God's name did that happen?"

"Er, I left it on my desk yesterday, and it wouldn't power on this morning." Arielle winced.

Dupre was also wincing, hunched against the tirade he felt sure was coming. Jacques gaped at the young tech, seemingly lost for words. Finally, he spoke.

"You left our most valuable piece of evidence on your desk?" His voice was taut. "You are aware that we have an evidence locker and what it is used for?"

"I know, I know," she said, wringing her hands. "But what could happen in a police station? I was working on it until late last night..." Her voice trailed off into an anguished whisper. "I was tired and worried about getting home in the storm. I just didn't think."

Dupre watched a range of emotions play across his boss's face. Then, surprisingly, there was a softening and Dupre guessed he was thinking of his daughter.

"Are you sure it's dead?" Jacques asked.

"Oh, I am quite sure," Arielle responded. "I took the hard drive out and tested it. It is completely shot."

Jacques released a deep sigh, blowing out his cheeks and shaking his head as though he had expected something like this. "It seems we are going backward. How could this have happened?"

Arielle's demeanor lost its apologist attitude in an instant. She squinted angrily. "At a guess, from the internal damage and a lingering smell of burned plastic, I would say someone put it in the microwave in the break room."

Again, Jacques' hand ran across his bald pate and down his thick neck, rubbing hard while he stared at the ceiling. When he finally spoke, his voice was quiet with suppressed anger. "I want to know how this happened. Who was in here?"

"Arielle, what time did you leave?" Dupre asked.

"I waited until the worst of the storm had passed and left around ten. The place was a ghost town."

"It would have been," Dupre observed. "Every available man would have been out in that storm."

"Hummph!" Jacques grunted. "No doubt that was what they were counting on. There should have still been a skeleton crew. I want to know exactly how a total stranger managed to get past security, come up here and nuke an important piece of evidence."

As he said the last piece, he peered accusingly down his nose at Arielle, and she looked like a naughty child caught in the act.

"If it was a total stranger," Dupre posed, tapping a forefinger against his lips.

"You don't mean one of our…" Arielle's voice faltered as she put a hand to her mouth.

Dupre and Jacques exchanged sardonic grimaces.

"Check the cameras! Find out," Jacques commanded. "In the meantime, I guess we are not going to discover what our victim was up to." He gave Arielle another penetrating look.

"Victim!" exclaimed Arielle. "She's—"

"Our victim," interjected Jacques firmly. "She is still a murder victim, and we need to find her killer among the growing list of suspects. Or do we let murderers go free if they are selective about who they kill?"

"No," admitted Arielle. "No, we don't."

"*Bon,*" said the captain. "So, what now?"

"Ah, well, *mon Capitaine.* All is not lost," Arielle said, her face brightening slightly. "Whoever destroyed the laptop didn't understand how the cloud works."

Jacques waited silently, encouraging her to go on.

"They didn't understand that her data was not stored on that hard drive, so they destroyed only one access point for her data. We still have the access information stored on her smartphone, so I may still be able get into her remote server." She smiled hopefully at her boss, then added, "Eventually."

Jacques looked up in a *heaven-help-me* way. "Why didn't you say this in the first place?"

"Well, you didn't give me a chance."

Jacques scratched his furrowed brow. "Okay, go work your magic. And for God's sake, protect that phone with your life."

After Arielle had left, the captain pulled over another chair and slumped into it, briefly closing his eyes. Then they popped open and he cleared his throat.

"Is there any chance that one of the residents is Croatian?"

Dupre shook his head. "Some Dutch, a Swede, a few Germans, and of course the American lawyer and the Englishman, Nash, but no Croats. No one even from the Balkans."

Jacques closed his eyes again and spoke wearily. "Of course not. This is likely to be just another wild goose chase."

At that moment Dupre's phone rang and he picked it up. As he listened, he held up his index finger and jotted down a few notes.

"Well," he said, putting the phone down. "The circle of suspects grows still further. The Englishman, Nash, who said he didn't know Borrell, I mean Markovic, was seen having a heated argument with her the day before she was killed."

Jacques was staring at him, apparently struck dumb.

"That was Judge Lejeune," Dupre offered.

Jacques found his most scathing voice. "And she knew how?"

"She didn't say."

"The *Americain*." Jacques sneered. "I can just feel it."

"Does it matter how she knows?" his lieutenant asked. "Perhaps she found out directly from the source."

"Which is?"

"The young woman who keeps the co-op produce store in Roussillon." He looked at his notes. "Beatrice, no last name."

Jacques was massaging his temples. "Is there anyone in France, no Europe even, that did not have a reason to kill this woman?" He batted his forehead with a clenched fist. "I knew I should have passed this one to the Gendarmes."

Dupre waited silently while his boss composed himself.

"Ah, well," Jacques finally said. "What's one more to the party? Talk to this shopkeeper and bring Monsieur Nash in for a little tête-à-tête."

He was thinking that in all this chaos, perhaps there was a glimmer of hope. If there was anyone he would like to be the murderer more than the American lawyer, it was the obnoxious Englishman.

24

"So, explain Bastille Day to me," Max demanded.

He had set this project for Luke the week before as a learning experience in the lead-up to the national celebration. He raised his bowl of coffee to his lips and took a satisfying draught as he waited for a reply. They were sitting on the patio, bathed in sunlight with the hum of bees plundering the lavender that perfumed the air. The sky was blue, and the morning air was still slightly cool. It was going to be another scorcher.

Luke's shoulders slumped. "Really? Over breakfast?" As if to stress his objection, he crammed a wad of croissant smeared with apricot preserve into his mouth and folded his arms.

"Yes. Today's the day. I want to know that you understand the significance of what we are about to see."

Luke swallowed and then belched. "Oh, alright! For a start, it isn't called Bastille Day, except by us. The French call it Quatorze Juillet or July fourteenth. It's wrong to think it celebrates the storming of the Bastille in 1789. It's more complicated than that."

He paused to take a swig of orange juice and insert another chew of croissant into his mouth, tucking it into the pouch of his cheek like a hamster so he could continue in muffled tones.

"In fact, the day commemorates two things. One was a gathering in 1790 when loads of people from all over France got together in Paris for a military parade led by some guy called Lafayette. Some other guy called Talleyrand held a mass, and everyone took some sort of oath. The whole thing was supposed to be a national unity thing, sometimes called the Fête de la Federation. King Louis XVI and his wife, Marie-Antoinette, gave rousing speeches to the people." He laughed sardonically. "Those same people who chopped off their heads just a few years later." He furrowed his shaggy mop. "Some unity."

He took another swallow of orange juice, followed by another plug of bread.

"Is that it?"

"Nah. Apparently there was a lot of disagreement over when to celebrate France's independence. Napoleon wanted it to be July fifteenth, his fake birthday." He snickered. "And some fools wanted it to be some other day to celebrate something called the Tennis Court Oath." He laughed again and specks of croissant flew across the table. He wiped the back of his hand across his mouth. *"Pardon."*

It didn't escape Max that the French word for *sorry* had come to Luke's lips without thinking. "And?"

"Well, this politician, Raspail, suggested that it be July fourteenth because that date satisfied the Fête de la Federation guys and also the lefties who wanted to celebrate the storming of the Bastille." He put his hands behind his head and leaned back. "That's pretty much it."

Max nodded appreciatively. "Well, I never knew all that. Excellent job. Now that Hassan has been released, what shall we do with the day?"

"Can we go canoeing? You said we could weeks ago."

"Well, you've been busy with camp. And you know that Claire has invited us to go to the parade in Aix with her."

Luke wrinkled his nose. "That's not until tonight. We have plenty of time before then."

"All right, I'll call and see if Canoe Collinas is operating today."

"Can we take Hans and Angela? Remember they wanted to go with us?"

Max hesitated. What on earth would Angela wear on a canoeing trip? He peered at Luke in confusion. Was he interested, or even aware? Luke was staring back at him with a matter-of-fact *I'm waiting* look.

"Er, I guess so."

"Great, I'll go and let them know."

"Wait till I make sure..." said Max, but Luke was already on his way out the door, closely followed by the prancing puppy.

The kayak tour company was open, and their Dutch neighbors were excited to go, although Hans refused to travel in the green tin can, which he liked to call the 2CV6. Instead, they went in Hans' large Mercedes. Luke, who had a teenager's lack of appreciation of vintage charms, wallowed in the luxury of the calfskin back seat.

"Now this is the way to travel, Dad."

Max grinned. "Yes, the Germans do make a nice car if you like that sort of thing."

It took them an hour to get to Remoulins where they checked in at the yellow shack of the kayak company. After a short trip by minibus, they reached the departure point and were equipped with two plastic canoes in amorphous shades of orange, pink and yellow. Max was relieved to see that Angela was wearing a swimsuit that obscured all but the top of her cleavage. He knew he shouldn't worry about what she was wearing, but he couldn't help himself. It was a mixture of fretting about what Luke might think, as well as making sure that his eyes didn't drift where they should not. Not that Hans would mind, he knew. He was very proud of his wife and her ample assets.

Each canoe had a watertight barrel attached to the stern, where Max put his wallet and their phones. Hans preferred to use his to store a multi-pack of Heineken on ice. The Gorges du Gardon, with its wide shallow river, lay ahead, flowing slowly down towards the Pont du Gard. It was a lazy ride, and they only needed to paddle to steer. The water was clear enough to see fish swimming among the green fronds waving on the bottom. The riverbanks were heavily forested, interspersed with high rocky outcrops. They were not the only people on the river, and the gorge reverberated with shouts and laughter. Occasionally, having baked in the fierce sun and worked up a sweat, they would jump out of the canoe for a swim.

When they rounded a bend in the river and saw a stony beach with a dozen canoes pulled up and a crowd of young people leaping off a towering escarpment into a deep pool, Luke begged them to stop so he could join in. Hans needed no second invitation, but Max and Angela declined to join them in the climb to the top of the cliff.

"He's just a big boy," Angela said, laughing as Hans, with his considerable bulk, leapt whooping from the cliff to land in a tremendous fountain of water.

"And sometimes, I feel he is still just a small boy," Max said, his heart in his mouth as the diminutive figure of his son followed Hans.

Hans climbed only once more to the top before he plopped down, winded, into the canoe next to Angela, who gave him a laughing kiss. They were clearly very much in love, and with Angela's maternal instinct, Max couldn't help but wonder why they did not have kids of their own. Had they chosen not to, or had it simply not happened for them?

"Haven't you had enough?" Max called to Luke after his fifth jump.

"One more. I think I can flip."

"I don't think that is a good idea," Max said, then felt Hans' hand on his arm. The Dutchman nodded at him, his expression saying that sooner or later you had to let go. Max took in a deep breath and with a sinking feeling said, "Go on then."

By now Luke had insinuated himself as one of the group of twenty-somethings and was chattering away with them while he waited his turn.

He really was an amazing child, Max thought, tears welling in his eyes. He deserved to have his mother, although she would not be too happy with all these shenanigans. She hadn't been very fond of his antics on the trampoline at home.

Then Luke was at the edge and executed a faultless somersault before striking the water feet first. A chorus of cheers and whistles broke out from the other jumpers on the clifftop, and Luke waved up to them as he climbed back into the canoe.

Hans high-fived him, and Angela ruffled his wet hair.

"That was quite an exciting finale," she said.

Exciting was not the word that Max would have used. Releasing a breath he hadn't known he was holding, he thought with a wry smile how hard it was to be a parent sometimes.

Half an hour later they paddled round the last bend and saw before them the spectacular Pont du Gard. It towered into the blue sky, although it was still some distance away. Like many other canoeists, they paused, simply floating, to gaze in awe at the three tiers of limestone arches. Each tier housed a row of smaller arches than the one below, and the whole structure spanned nearly three hundred meters across the gorge. Even Luke seemed slightly impressed. Originally a marvel of Roman engineering built in the first century, it was designed as an aqueduct to carry water from Uzès to Nîmes over thirty miles away.

"*Mijn God*," Hans said. "Can you believe this was built without backhoes or cranes? It was built so precisely to a grade of one centimeter in almost six hundred feet."

"Well, there's a little-known useless fact," said Luke, grinning.

Max pretended to swat him.

Luke clucked. "How, why, do you even know that?"

"Don't forget I'm an engineer, smart-arse," Hans growled.

Angela scrambled to her feet, rocking precariously in their canoe. "I want a picture," she said, holding up her phone. "Here, Hans, sit up there at the front."

Hans began to edge his girth backwards towards the prow, the canoe rocking dangerously beneath Angela's straddled legs. It was inevitable. As Hans crouched in the well at the front of the canoe, his considerable weight over-balanced the boat, and with a shriek, Angela toppled over the side. She came up spluttering. "*Jebi Ga!*" she gasped. Then she glanced guiltily at Max. "Sorry, my phone." She held up the dripping instrument and flung it into the canoe.

Hans was hooting with laughter, but Angela did not look amused.

"Will you help me back into the boat?" she snapped.

Max and Luke held Hans' canoe steady while he hauled Angela over the side. "Come on, my darling," he crooned. "Let's go and get a drink."

She stared at him, narrowing her eyes, lips compressed, and then abruptly tipped the canoe over. They both went into the water, but this time when Angela came up, she was grinning. Transfixed, Max watched them in a daze.

When they finally paddled under the aqueduct, staring in awe at the arches soaring almost fifty meters above their head, Luke spotted an ice-cream stand on the shore and they pulled up the canoes onto the adjacent beach. He and Angela went off arm-in-arm in search of something sweet while Max and Hans popped beers. Afterwards they all strolled along the modern concrete road that ran parallel to the old stone aqueduct, Hans adoring every meter of the ancient stone structure. And through it all, despite the setting, the surroundings and the wonderful company, Max was more troubled than he had been in a long time, facts coming together like a completed jigsaw to reveal a very unhappy picture.

25

While the entire nation of France was enjoying the day's Quatorze Juillet celebrations, Jeremy Nash was sitting in an interview room at the Aix police station. Dupre sat across the table feeling very disgruntled. He was staring at the Englishman with a good deal of animosity. There was something about this man he didn't like, but admittedly, it was probably the fact that he was not in his favorite bar celebrating with his friends.

One finger slowly tapped the manila folder on the table before him. Nash had initially assumed a bland, unconcerned expression, but as the clock ticked away in the silence, he traded it back and forth with a look of confusion. Dupre had done his homework and knew exactly who this man was. Doubtless he had heard that Hassan had been arrested for the murder of Borrell and then later released. Now he, Jeremy Nash, a well-known figure in London, was sitting here in this French jail being studied in silence by a deliberately unpleasant policeman.

Finally, Nash appeared to summon the courage to snap, "Well, officer? What are we waiting for?"

Dupre's English was decent, courtesy of his expensive private school education, an exchange year studying international politics in Washington DC, and his many interactions with British tourists, but he said nothing. His dark eyes bore into Jeremy.

Finally, he opened the folder and began a leisurely review of the contents. More minutes passed while he read. From the corner of his eye, he watched Nash nervously stroking his goatee.

"Look, if you have nothing to say, then I'm leaving," Nash scowled. "I have some powerful friends in Avignon who will hear about this."

Dupre looked up languidly and stared some more at the Englishman. His mouth worked to give the impression of thoughtful consideration. "No, Monsieur Nash, I don't believe you will be leaving soon." He frowned. "You may not leave here at all." Dupre was well aware of the reputation the French police had.

Nash swallowed hard. His voice shook slightly as he said, "Look, what is this about?"

"You don't know?"

"No, of course, I don't know. How would I?"

"Come now, monsieur. Perhaps you will tell me what you were looking for in the murdered woman's apartment?"

Nash blanched, pinned against the back of his chair by Dupre's knowledge like a moth against a board. Dupre could see his mind scrabbling for a response before it came up with blustering bravado.

"What the hell are you talking about? I was never in that apartment. I didn't even know the woman."

Dupre clasped his hands together at the edge of the table and stretched his neck forward like a chicken watching a worm. "I know what you told Capitaine Jacques, just as I know it wasn't true."

Nash's eyes roved everywhere, as though avoiding the policeman's face could make him disappear.

"You were seen having a heated argument with the victim outside the pharmacy the day before she was killed. Also, we found a drop of fresh blood in the victim's apartment. The cup from the coffee we gave you has been sent to forensics and we will soon have your DNA. I think we can find a match, *n'est-ce pas*? That doesn't look good for you. Perhaps you would like to revise your story?"

He could tell that Jeremy was scared. But what was he hiding?

A cursory check with the British police told him that Nash had been in police custody before over an incident with a young woman and for several DUIs. But he had never been charged—possibly due to some influence brought to bear. Now he was a suspect in a homicide in a foreign country, and he had no such influence here. Or did he? Who were these powerful friends?

"You can't get my DNA that way," Nash croaked. "I want a lawyer. I'm not saying anything else until I get one."

Just those few words—the acknowledgement that he needed a lawyer, seemed to sap Nash's bravado. The one visible hand, picking at his goatee, was trembling. Good. Dupre rolled a shoulder, a gesture of nonchalance.

"*Bien sûr.* Who should I call?"

There was a long pause while Nash was clearly considering his options. Did he know any French criminal lawyers? If he did have friends in high places, why hadn't he already called them? They surely would have access to a top-notch criminal attorney. The American lawyer had tracked down a very good one in a matter of hours.

"I want Max Dempsey," Nash finally blurted out.

Dupre's face betrayed his surprise. "But Monsieur Dempsey is not a French lawyer."

"I don't care," Jeremy snapped, regaining some composure. "That's who I want, and I'm not saying another word until I get him." His mouth curled in a sneer. "I wouldn't trust a French lawyer. You're probably all in it together. I'm not about to be railroaded by some Frog conspiracy."

Dupre suppressed a smile and shrugged. "I will see what can be done."

He left the interview room and found an outraged Jacques already in the corridor waiting for him. He had been watching the interview.

"Pas de chance," the captain snarled before Dupre could even get a word out.

"But if it will make him talk?"

"Hein. I have had enough interference from the American lawyer."

Dupre frowned, his disappointment in his boss evident. He thought Monsieur Dempsey had been nothing but helpful. Jacques was surely pissed off about something, and he knew that was clouding his superior's judgment.

He scratched at his beard and then said in an offhand way, "We should probably call the judge and let her know what is going on."

He knew Jacques could not afford to make a unilateral decision.

Jacques contemplated the matter for a long moment and eventually came to the same conclusion. After all, why would he care if the suspect had a lawyer who didn't know the system? Let that be her decision. Jacques uttered another muttered curse.

"Fine! Call Monsieur Dempsey's good friend, *le juge*, and see what she says."

As it happened, the judge was already on her way to the station to interview the Englishman. Dupre brought her up to speed when she arrived.

"So, we don't have the DNA yet?" she asked.

"Soon. But from Nash's reaction, I would bet a month's salary that it's his."

He showed the judge to the interview room and sat in a corner while she took a seat across from Nash. Nash eyed her suspiciously and then she spoke in English.

"Good morning, Mr. Nash. It seems you have got yourself into some trouble."

His eyes widened and then he frowned. "I asked for a lawyer. Are you from the British Embassy?"

"No, Mr. Nash. I am the local examining magistrate."

His frown deepened. "But you're British."

"Scottish, yes."

A sequence of confused expressions whirled across Nash's face. Dupre could imagine what he was thinking. Was this some kind of EU thing? Well, if it was, so much the better for him.

Some of Nash's bravado returned in the face of this attractive British woman. He clearly believed she would be on his side.

"Look here. I don't know what's going on, but these damn Frenchies have it all wrong, and I demand to be released."

The judge addressed him with an icy smile, her expression as hard as flint. She leaned forward.

"Mr. Nash, my name is Judge Lejeune. I may sound British, but I assure you that for these purposes, I am completely French. It is my sworn duty to get to the truth of the matter and decide whether to charge you with Madame Markovic's murder."

Sitting in the corner, Dupre grinned and hoped Jacques was watching the interview from outside.

Nash jerked his head up from where he had been staring at his hands. "Eh? Who the hell is Madame Markovic?" he spat. "I've never heard of her. I thought this was about the Borrell woman."

So that wasn't his connection to her, thought Dupre. Clever of the judge.

"That was the real name of the victim—Biljana Markovic," she emphasized, looking closely for a reaction. "She is a wanted war criminal."

It was clear from the way Nash's eyes flew open and his jaw dropped that this news was a shock to him, and an unpleasant shock at that. So, what was the connection?

"Would you like to tell me how your blood came to be found on the victim's balcony?" the judge continued.

The hurried way Nash gabbled out his explanation told Dupre that he had been working on his story while he was waiting.

"Well, the only thing I can think of is that I cut myself yesterday while I was out on my balcony. It was quite painful, so I waved my hand about. A drop of blood must have flicked over onto her balcony." He stared at the judge confidently. She gave him a withering look.

Dupre blew out an impatient breath. Was this the best Nash could come up with while he sat there for the last half hour? The man was just digging a deeper hole. Could he actually be the murderer? Looking at the guy, that would surprise Dupre, but he had been surprised before.

The judge nodded politely at Nash as if this was a very plausible story. "So, I can send Lieutenant Dupre here to your balcony and he will find traces of this accident?"

Nash started.

"Well, no. I cleaned up the blood on my own balcony."

"How very conscientious of you," the judge said with more than a hint of sarcasm. "Just the sort of vacation tenant I would want."

"Is it a crime to be a little fastidious?" Nash said defensively.

The judge appraised his dress with the pocket handkerchief and ascot. Her expression suggested she thought it ought to be.

"Of course not," she said soothingly. "Do you mind if I see?"

"See what?"

"The vicious cut that bled so profusely that it shot blood ten feet onto the adjacent balcony?"

"Well," Jeremy faltered. "It wasn't that bad. It just took me by surprise."

"I'd still like to see."

Reluctantly Jeremy showed her a small scratch on his wrist. "It was worse than it looks."

"It must have been considerably worse," she said drily.

"Look here, I asked for a lawyer."

"Of course." She adopted a sympathetic tone. "I believe you wanted to see Max Dempsey. Do you know him?"

"Not that well. But I have heard he is a good lawyer. And he got the concierge off, didn't he?"

"Mr. Dempsey was working with a French lawyer and did not get Mr. Aamara off, as you put it. He is still a suspect in an ongoing investigation."

"Well, I'm done talking until I see Max."

"Fine, I will let you see Max, who, by the way, is an old college friend of mine. Of course, he may not want to represent you." She sounded like she thought this was highly likely. "But I happen to know that he is out for the day with his son, so you will have to remain in custody until tomorrow, and if he should decide not to help you..."

"Really? This is ridiculous. All over a drop of blood? It's Bastille Day and I have plans."

"Your plans will have to wait. You are a murder suspect and, therefore, a flight risk."

Nash looked suddenly panicked. "Look, couldn't you just keep my passport or something?" He gave her a pleading look.

The judge took a deep breath as she pretended to consider this. She obviously didn't like this man, and Dupre was not surprised. He was everything that gave the British a bad name.

"'Fraid not!" she finally said, wrinkling her nose in a way that almost made Dupre laugh out loud. "That's just not the way we deal with murder suspects here in France."

After they had taken Nash to a cell, the judge met with Dupre and Jacques.

"*Brava*," Dupre said with open admiration. "He obviously thought that as a British person you would go easy on him."

"He was wrong."

Claire glanced sideways at Jacques. Dupre thought he had detected a slight thawing on the part of his boss, but apparently, Judge Lejeune felt the need to clear something up.

"This is my home," she said. "It has been for twenty-plus years. I'm not here because of the EU. I'm here because I married a Frenchman and have two French children. I love France, and I consider myself as French as anyone else here."

Dupre felt his admiration mount. Jacques seemed nonplussed by her speech. The captain cleared his throat before giving the judge a begrudging smile.

"We understand that, Madame. We are all proud to be French no matter our beginnings."

She eyed them both shrewdly as if to say *Hmm. Let's see how we get along in the future.*

Then, giving them both a wry smile, she said, "I will see if Monsieur Dempsey wants to help this idiot. I doubt it, but it might be the easiest way forward."

Noting the captain's frown, she added, "I'll suggest he bring Helene Blanc."

She grinned wickedly. "Until then, let's keep Nash locked up as uncomfortably as is legal."

Finally, Dupre heard Jacques laugh.

26

Upstairs on the second floor, Arielle tapped feverishly on her laptop keyboard. She waited and watched as the computer screen stalled, caught in its process. Could it be?

"Yes!" she cried out. "Yes!"

Gaston and Benny looked over the desk dividers.

"Are you in?" asked Gaston.

"I'm in!"

Arielle beamed as she scrolled her mouse down through the files she had just gained access to in Markovic's cloud. Whatever she found would help the investigation, she knew. But the fact that she had cracked it meant that she had redeemed herself somewhat in the fiasco over the melted computer.

She was really pissed with herself over that. She was not a careless person. And she knew she should have locked the laptop away in the evidence locker. It bothered her that someone, someone on the inside, had managed to damage such vital evidence. She was gratified that the fact that someone in the police was working against them had diffused some of Jacques' anger away from her.

Arielle's eyes darted through the file icons neatly laid out against the white background of the cloud. There were dozens, titled in Cyrillic. She opened a few at random. They seemed to contain documents, invoices and lists, much of it in the same language, but some in French. They were going to need a translator. But in one folder she found images.

She held her breath as she clicked on one. She saw the naked flesh as the image appeared on her screen. She knew it. She knew before she even opened it—of course it would be a sexual image. She clicked another. It was the same young woman, but a different man in the same bed in the same place. Another and the same thing—the same woman but a different man. Was the woman a prostitute or a trafficking victim? Porn, or was it blackmail? She guessed the latter because the woman's face was not the focus. Each shot showed the man's identity very clearly. Another folder contained videos. She closed it quickly. She wasn't prepared to view live action as she was already disturbed by the still images.

Finding a translator would take some time, and she couldn't wait. Impatiently she went back into the document folders to lift some of the text to Google Translate.

As she worked slowly through them, she realized that many were simply agreements, invoices and shipping manifests reflective of any business. But some were ransom notes and journal entries reflective of a darker purpose.

She needed to take this to the captain now. Here was the proof that Markovic was in bed with the Brise and the Serbian crime group Senjicari. Extortion, drug smuggling and human trafficking—it was all here. She felt unclean just reviewing this shit. Without a single qualm, she felt that whoever killed Markovic had done the world a favor.

Unplugging her laptop, she walked out into the corridor. There she met Dupre, looking rather smug with himself. "Good news," said Arielle. "I've cracked it."

"*Ah, ma cherie*," said Dupre. "I never doubted you for a second."

"Ha, well, after yesterday, I think the captain did."

Dupre waved a hand in a gesture of dismissal.

"Have you found anything of interest?"

Arielle blew out a long breath. "Oh, yes!" Her face screwed into an expression of disgust. "Come to the captain's office and see?"

Dupre nodded. As they walked, he asked Arielle if she had any grand plans to celebrate Quatorze Juillet.

"Well, now that I've hacked the server, perhaps I will allow myself to relax a little," she said. "I cannot stop until I finish what I set out to do."

"I know that feeling," said Dupre. "But if you are going to relax, perhaps you would like to accompany me? I've made a reservation at Le Saint Amour for one, but it would be much nicer if there were two."

Arielle frowned. "Is this a date?"

Dupre blushed. "Not exactly."

Areille's face was expressive of someone putting two and two together. "Ah, the kissing woman. There is someone at the restaurant that you want to see?"

Dupre looked sheepish. "Perhaps."

Arielle looked slightly relieved. "*D'accord*, Dupre," Areille said. "I will be your wingwoman."

At this, Dupre's shoulders physically relaxed, and he smiled. *"Parfait,"* he said.

Capitaine Jacques threw up his hands when Arielle told him she had managed to access the victim's computer records. He sat up in his chair and leaned forward eagerly.

"*Enfin*," he said. "Let's see what's in there."

As the three crowded round the laptop, Arielle explained her theory that Markovic was some sort of go-between with the Serbian gang and the Brise de Sang. The sexual exploitation images were of men being extorted for money.

"What if," she said, "Markovic was killed by one of the men in the pictures? Someone terrified of being identified?"

"Well," said Jacques. "Let's see who we've got."

Arielle carefully began clicking through the images. On one of the shots, Dupre stopped her. "Wait," he said. "Stop. Can you zoom in?"

Arielle clicked her mouse and zoomed into the background of a photo where a man was standing with his back to a wall.

"Isn't that…?" Dupre stared.

"That's Michel Briancon. From the café? It seems he was more acquainted with the victim than he said."

Arielle nodded. "Yes, that's him. For sure."

"Bring him in," said Jacques. "Right after we're finished here."

"Now, Arielle," he continued, "we need to check out a few of these videos to get a general sense of what they contain. Do you want to step outside for a few minutes."

Arielle was surprised. Was the captain trying to protect her? She steeled herself. She may be a techie, but she was also a cop.

She could not afford to be seen as squeamish. She pulled back her shoulders and took the breath a diver takes before submerging. Then she clicked her mouse again.

They sat and ran through several videos, each equally disgusting, before Dupre told Arielle to stop on one that was even more repugnant than the rest.

"That's Nash," said Dupre, his mouth twisted in disgust.

"Those girls are clearly underage," said Arielle, her voice choking with revulsion.

"I've seen enough," said Jacques, leaning forward to close the laptop. "When will I cease to be surprised at the depravity of humans?" He shivered as though casting off a bad dream.

"Louis, I'm afraid you will have to watch the rest of these to see if you recognize anyone else." He looked purposefully at Arielle. "But not you."

"Don't worry," said Arielle. Her pretty face was distorted with a mixture of rage and loathing. "I wouldn't watch any more of this filth if my life depended on it. I don't need the nightmares."

"No, you don't," Jacques agreed.

"Nash," said Dupre, whistling. "Even worse than we thought."

He looked like he wanted to spit the taste of it out of his mouth, but instead, he took out a crumpled handkerchief and wiped his brow.

"Nash is going to need a better lawyer than that English American," Jacques snarled.

"I hope they lock him up and throw away the key," said Arielle. "Worse, I hope they put him in the general population so the other prisoners can get at him. I've heard that the other convicts really love pedophiles."

She turned away. "I need to get to the bathroom. I think I'm going to vomit."

"How convenient that we already have him in custody," Dupre said.

Arielle whirled back around. "What?" She hadn't heard this. "For this?" she was confused.

"No," said Jacques. "He was seen fighting in public with Markovic the day before the murder. And we suspect the drop of blood in the apartment is his. We know what he was doing there now, don't we? Looking for these videos. Undoubtedly, she was extorting him." Silence descended on the office as they struggled to digest what they had seen. Finally the captain roused himself.

"Dupre, take whoever's available and go and pick up Michel Briancon. Nash is here until tomorrow, waiting for Monsieur Dempsey to see him."

"Good, that will give us more time to build the case," said Arielle.

Dupre puckered his face in doubt. "It's not likely. I doubt the lab will have the DNA blood tests back in view of the holiday."

"No matter," said Jacques. "He will keep."

"One can only hope that Nash will never be free again," said Arielle.

"Not for a very long time if I have anything to do with it," said Jacques.

27

It was late afternoon when Max and Luke drove up to Claire's mellow stone bastide. No one answered the bell pull that triggered a resonant jangle deep in the house, so they walked around the back where they could hear the rhythmic clop of tennis balls. Claire and Sam, dressed in tennis whites, were doing battle on the clay court. They paused to wave hello.

"Help yourself to a drink," Claire called.

Rasputin, relaxing in the shade of a lemon tree, shuffled over to say hello. Both Luke and Dickens were happy to fuss over the old dog, although it seemed clear that the attentions of an inquisitive and energetic puppy were not all that welcome. Max sat on the patio and watched the game in a desultory fashion, feeling melancholy. The two women seemed evenly matched with long rallies.

Sitting in the afternoon sun with just enough breeze to set the lavender heads bobbing, Max tried to salvage a good mood. He was thinking of a second glass of Chablis when the women sauntered off the court, perspiring and looking sexy as hell.

"Well, that was quite an exhibition," Max said, attempting a grin.

Claire squinted at him. "The tennis?"

He winked. "That too."

Samantha flicked him with her towel.

"Since when do you play tennis anyway?" he asked Samantha. "I seem to remember you weren't very sporty back in college."

She tendered a sardonic grimace. "Lot of bread baked since then."

"And yet you both look just the same." He was rolling the banter around himself like a protective shell.

Samantha turned to Claire. "Is he being sarcastic? I can't tell."

Claire pushed her sunglasses up to her forehead and peered at Max. "Hmm. I don't think so. He's just trying to be cute."

"Well, it's not working. I certainly do hope I have changed from that thin, gangly girl with frizzy hair."

"Hey," Max protested. "I loved that slender girl with bushy hair." His voice tapered off, and an awkward silence set in.

Claire broke the silence, handing Sam a glass of wine and clinking glasses with her and Max. "Here's to old friends." She looked at her watch. "Come on, Sam. We need to crack on or we'll miss the start of the parade. Max, there's some chicken marinating in the fridge. Can you put it on the grill while we shower?"

"Of course." Max was glad of the distraction, but it was a fleeting respite. He had fallen back into troubled contemplation when Claire's voice broke his train of thought, making him jump.

"Another glass of wine?"

His pained expression must have registered before he could wipe it away.

She paused while pouring herself a glass. "What's going on, Max?" she asked cautiously.

Had he somehow given himself away? He had been thinking about Borrell's killer. For a split second he thought about telling her. He longed to unburden himself. But after the mess with Nash, he had to be sure. And he had to come to terms with what he would do with the truth. His delay in answering must have spooked her.

"Is it too much to have Sam here?" she asked, now sounding anxious.

"No. No, it's not that. It's great to see her." He struggled to switch gears. He gave her a reassuring smile. "It really is."

"So, what is it?"

Max tried to lighten his voice. "Oh, it's… just something I'm trying to figure out. Nothing to worry about." That was such a lie, and he looked at her guiltily. But Claire had decided not to press the issue. She nodded sympathetically and placed a gentle hand on his arm. "You've been through so much. I can imagine that days of celebration bring up a lot of memories."

Claire clearly mistook his melancholy for his grief over Emma, an understandable mistake, and he was happy to let her think that for now.

He mustered a brave voice. "Well, we are all here together and we will try to have the best day we can."

She looked over to where Luke was lying on the lawn next to Rasputin who was still being worried by Dickens.

"So, this is your Dickens?" she called over to Luke. "Come, let me meet him properly."

Max had never been more comforted by an old friend.

Sam came down dressed in fashionable taupe shorts and a lacey white cotton blouse.

"That top is lovely," Claire said, sounding slightly envious.

Sam glanced down as if surprised to find she was wearing something. "Oh, this," she flung out nonchalantly. "It's something I picked up in a street market when Peter and I were in Argentina."

There was an awkward pause while Samantha tossed her head as though dispelling a bad memory.

Claire picked up the slack.

"Boy, I thought I was adventurous living in Provence, but compared to you two jet-setters..."

While she spoke, she seemed to be effortlessly throwing together a sumptuous meal. "Anyway, you will fit right in—in Aix."

Sam frowned. "Why is that?"

Claire laughed. "That's right, you've never been. Tell her, Max. I have to get the chicken off the grill."

"Well," said Max. He had to choose his words carefully. "Aix, the city of a thousand fountains, is the fashion capital of the south. Très chic. Lots of rich foreigners!"

Sam laughed.

"What's that about rich foreigners?" Claire asked coming in through the French doors from the patio carrying a platter of aromatic chicken.

"Aix," Max replied.

"Ah, *oui, certainement.*" Her nose wrinkled as if there was a bad smell under it. "Oh well, you'll see soon enough. Let's eat."

When they reached Aix, it was approaching dusk. Fortunately, Claire's status as a judge allowed them to park at the Palais de

Justice, only a few blocks off the main thoroughfare, the Cours Mirabeau. A welcome breeze had sprung up, making the short stroll quite pleasant.

"Perhaps we should have left Dickens at home to keep Rasputin company," laughed Claire as the puppy strained to tangle himself with yet another couple walking past.

Luke jerked the leash to haul him back. "He thinks everyone is just dying to pet him," he said through gritted teeth.

"From the looks he is getting, I think most people are," Claire said, earning a warm grin from Luke and a *Don't encourage him* look from Max.

Eventually Max had to pick up the inquisitive puppy. There were too many people on the street, and the noise only excited the small dog. They struggled through the crowd thronging the wide avenue lined with ochre buildings adorned with the ubiquitous blue shutters.

Samantha's eyes lit up as they passed boutique after boutique.

"How is it you have never brought me here before?" she said accusingly to Claire. "Can we come back here without the men?"

Claire hooted. "I said you would fit right in."

Sam pouted theatrically. "So I like nice clothes. Sue me."

As they walked along the street, Max felt a hand creep into his, and for a moment thought it was Luke, who, in his younger years, had always held his hand but now, sadly, didn't. But Luke was walking in front, and the fingers were longer and slender and the memory of those fingers was imprinted on his psyche. He smiled inwardly, knowing this wasn't a pass or a suggestion, but an expression of support, a reminder of long ago.

He squeezed Sam's hand, and she smiled up at him before letting go, linking her arm through his and pulling him close until she leaned into him as they strolled. Luke weaved through the crowded sidewalk ahead like a football blocker, and they followed, hitting the gaps he made.

Eventually they reached the Mirabeau rotunda, dominated by a large fountain flanked by a quartet of supine stone lions. Claire led them to an apartment conversion housing Sephora, the multinational retailer, on the ground floor. She fished a key out of her pocket and opened one side of the arched, double mahogany doors. They entered a cool, mosaic-floored lobby.

"Where are we going?" Max asked.

"A friend's apartment. They are on call at the hospital and don't mind if we use it to watch the parade."

She cast Max a sideways glance, and he saw that there was something to it, a mental blush that made him think there was more to the story. He decided not to ask.

They tramped up two flights of stairs to a spacious apartment, the sleekness of which stood in stark juxtaposition to the ancient walls and exposed beams. From the décor, it was undoubtedly a man's apartment.

Claire opened a set of French doors and stepped out onto a wrought iron balcony. From here they had an unsurpassed view of everything happening on the street. She quickly rounded up a set of glasses and a chilled bottle of white, and they sat on the outside chairs just as the first wave of marching soldiers appeared down the street. Like the dozens of parades he had seen before all over the world, this one had drums, trumpets, saluting and cheering and overspent its welcome in Max's mind. But then, with the darkness came the fireworks, and what a display that was—fountains of red, white and blue lit up the indigo sky. The horde below laughed and sang. But through it all, Max was nursing unwelcome thoughts. How on earth could he have the conversation that must be had? And what would be the repercussions when he did?

"Penny for them?" he heard Sam say, rousing him back to the here and now.

"Not worth a penny," he said with a deprecating smile.

Just at that moment, they heard the sound of a key in the lock, and the front door swung open as a tall man clattered in carrying a racing bike across his shoulder. With a flicker of surprise, Max recognized him instantly.

"Claude!" he said.

The cyclist looked around in equal surprise. He frowned in concentration as his eyes fixed on Max. Then he cocked his head to one side. "Max, *n'est-ce pas?* With the green *deux chevaux?*"

"That's me."

Claire surveyed them both with something approaching consternation. "You two know each other?"

"Not really," said Max. "Claude was kind enough to stop when he thought I was having car trouble."

He did not want Claire and Sam to know of that dark moment when he had lost it by the side of the road.

Claude seemed to understand. "*Oui.* But it seems he was okay." He looked at Max down his long aquiline nose and raised a questioning eyebrow.

Max nodded and smiled. "As you can see, I have the best of friends."

"*Bien sûr*. With friends like these two lovely ladies, who else do you need?"

Claire cast a look to the heavens as she stepped forward to give Claude the *bisous* and introduce him to Sam. "Watch this one, Sam. He's a smooth talker," she smiled. Her brows then contracted in a puzzled frown. "Anyway, I thought you were on call, that we wouldn't see you?"

Claude shrugged. "I just completed the last post-mortem, so I left early."

He looked at her in a way that left no doubt in Max's mind what was going on. He now knew that any flirting he thought Claire had thrown his way was just banter. She only had eyes for the tall cyclist, who, it turned out, was also a surgeon. What a catch. But what about Vincent? Sam flicked her eyebrows at him, apparently thinking the same thing.

He did not know Claire's husband, but it seemed he was never around. Claire had too much to offer to be alone and unloved, thought Max. And he liked Claude very much.

At that moment, Luke came in from watching the fireworks, and when Dickens saw a new visitor, he loped across the floor, skidding on the tiles to end up in a tumbled heap at Claude's feet.

"And who is this?" Claude asked, reaching down to ruffle the puppy.

"That's Dickens," Luke said, and to Max's immense pride, he put out a hand and added, "And I'm Luke." He jerked a thumb at Max. "He's my dad."

Claude took the proffered hand gravely. "Pleased to meet you, Luke." He took in Luke's football jersey and his nose wrinkled. "I see you're a Manchester United fan. That's too bad."

"Could be worse," Luke replied. "I could have to support a French team."

Claude clutched at his chest like he was having a heart attack. "*Mince alors. Quelle insulte!*"

"I'm sorry, Claude," said Max. "But you know what kids are like nowadays."

"For that, young man, I will call you next time Manchester get kicked out of the Champions League… that is, if they even make it in."

"Hah! You should get together with Hans and start a delusional club."

"Who is Hans?"

"He's our neighbor. He likes Ajax."

Claude nodded in amused understanding. "*Ah, je comprends.*"

Turning from Luke, he said to the room at large, "Is there any of my wine left, and perhaps some food?"

Claire bustled off to the kitchen. "Coming right out," she threw back over her shoulder.

It transpired that besides cycling, Claude participated in a pick-up football game on Saturdays, so they exchanged numbers, and Max promised to get in touch when his Saturdays opened up after camp was done. It would be lovely to play football again and make some new French friends.

When they left an hour later, Max had the distinct impression that Claire would have preferred to stay. It was late by the time they arrived back at Claire's to collect their car.

"So, when will we see you two again?" Max asked as they were getting ready to leave.

"I have to get back to London," Samantha said, sounding apologetic and sad.

"Really?" Luke frowned.

Samantha looked at him in surprise. "Well, I don't want to overstay my welcome, and I have a few matters I need to take care of."

Luke stared at his sneakers, scuffing the toes against the floor. "It's just..." his voice faltered as he tried to pick the right words. "It's just that Dad has been happy around you two, and he hasn't really been happy since, well, you know..."

Max closed his eyes at a sudden ache inside. Samantha cupped his son's cheek with one hand. "What an extraordinary young man you are."

Luke blushed.

"Don't worry. I'll be back from time to time to check on him." She smiled fondly at Max. "In the meantime, try and keep him out of trouble."

"Hah! C'est impossible."

Luke climbed into the car, and with a peck on Max's cheek, Claire disappeared into the house. Finally, Max and Sam were somewhat alone.

"It's been so lovely to see you," she said.

Max nodded, feeling his chest tighten as she edged up close in front of him.

He could smell her perfume, smell her hair, fragrant with a tropical scent.

"I know things have been tough," she said. "But I would like to see you again."

Max nodded, unsure of where this was going and terrified to think it was going anywhere. Suddenly her lips were on his, and the shock of the kiss and yet the familiarity of Sam, even after all these years, helped him to melt and respond. It was only a moment. Not exactly passionate, more tentative.

After a haunting, nostalgic moment he pulled back, terrified that Luke was watching. Glancing around he was relieved to find that Luke was engrossed in his phone and had not even seen.

He reached out and took both her hands. "I think I would like that too." His voice quavered. "It's just… you know…"

"Of course," said Sam. "Of course. There is no rush. I'm in no rush. But you know where I live, and if you are ever in London, you and Luke, you'd better look me up."

They embraced in a lingering hug, and Max felt a mixture of overwhelming emotions. He had not shared a romantic kiss with a woman other than Emma in almost twenty years. It had stirred deep forgotten feelings—feelings for Samantha that he had left behind long ago. He had not counted on this.

"Au revoir," quipped Samantha as Max climbed in and started the engine.

They waved to her until a bend in the driveway and darkness swallowed her.

"I like her," said Luke, holding a sleeping Dickens on his lap. "Do you think we'll see her again?"

Max smothered a grin. "You can count on it."

28

Dupre sped toward Cassis, having taken the first available colleague he had seen with him. Gaston was not thrilled at having been waylaid from his morning coffee and pastry and bundled into the small, cluttered Renault with the fast-moving lieutenant.

"Not my department," he muttered mutinously when Dupre demanded his company.

"Extortion and fraud!" replied Dupre. "Right down your alley."

Dupre had never wanted to get somewhere so fast. He turned on the blue roof lights and siren. Gaston looked at him in surprise. Detectives did not normally employ these measures, but Dupre had never felt so motivated.

"Where's the fire?" Gaston asked.

"We are close to wrapping this up," Dupre muttered, "and I am on a tight schedule." He put his foot down.

They rode in silence, Dupre's thoughts consumed not by the case for once, but by this evening's dinner at Le Saint Amour. Madeleine was all he could think about. He feared that bringing Michel in and questioning him would take hours and all his plans would come to nothing.

He pulled the car to halt with a jolt on the pedestrian walkway in front of Le Bateau Ivre and jumped out leaving the engine still running. Danielle was serving at one of the bistro tables, placing an expresso in front of a customer.

"Ah," she said when she saw Dupre approach. "You are back."

Dupre checked his rush. "Yes, we are back." He smiled at her. He liked Danielle. She had been helpful and seemingly truthful the last time he had been here.

Danielle followed the two into the café where Julien Briancon stood behind the counter. His face fell when he saw Dupre.

"Monsieur Briancon," said Dupre. "How are you this afternoon?"

Julien pasted an insincere smile on his face that fooled no one.

"*Comme si, comme ça,*" he replied, picking up his ever-ready dishcloth and rubbing at a wine glass. "To what do I owe the pleasure of a return visit?" he asked, scowling his displeasure on the glass.

"Your brother," said Dupre. "Is he around?"

A momentary expression of fear crossed Julien's face and he blinked to get rid of it. "No. Not this afternoon, *monsieur.*"

"Do you have any idea where I might find him?"

"*Non, monsieur.*"

"His address?" Dupre furrowed his brow.

It seemed that the task of removing an obstinate spot from the glass had rendered Julien deaf.

"He just lives round the corner," piped up Danielle, who was busy pouring cold milk into tiny white jugs.

Dupre looked at her and smiled gratefully. When he turned back, Julien was glaring at her.

"I have a better idea," said Dupre, thinking that as soon as they left to go get Michel, Julien would call ahead to alert his brother. "Please call your brother and tell him to come here right now. Tell him it's an emergency."

Julien finally looked up from the glass in his hand. "What is this all about?" he demanded. "What do you want with him?"

Dupre pursed his lips and then decided to hurry this along. "He is a witness to a crime, and it's important that we speak to him."

"And what if I don't want to call him?" asked Julien, thrusting his bulky chest out.

The policeman stared him down. "Listen, Monsieur Briancon. I don't have time for games. I know that you owed Madame Markovic a great deal of money," he said, adopting the judge's tactic and looking for any sign of name recognition.

Julien stiffened and then looked convincingly taken aback. "Wait a moment, who is this Madame Markovic?"

Dupre was satisfied that he had no idea who he had been dealing with. But what about his brother? "That is the real name of your tenant. A very dangerous woman and a wanted war criminal."

Julien swayed backwards and put his hand to his forehead, eyes wide with alarm. Danielle let out a small gasp as she stared at them both open-mouthed.

"So, you and your brother had a good reason to kill her. Not to mention the fact that I think you ransacked her offices to try to locate the promissory note you signed. Perhaps I should arrest you too and close this place down."

He glanced around the restaurant. The place was packed, as might be expected on a holiday. When he looked back, Julien's demeanor instantly changed. From what Danielle had told him last time he was here, Julien was essentially straight. He could imagine the war going on inside Julien's head. Did he give his criminal brother up, or go down in flames with him?

"All right!" said Julien, resigned. "All right!"

With obvious reluctance, he took out his cell phone and dialed.

"Put it on speaker," Dupre ordered. He didn't want any passwords or codes to pass between them. It took several rings before a gruff, sleepy voice answered.

"You need to come to the restaurant," Julien said.

"What for?"

"EMERGENCY," mouthed Dupre to Julien.

"I need your help now," said Julien. "So don't give me any of your shit. It's important."

They heard grumbling at the end of the line before a gruff agreement. Julien hung up and looked at Dupre, defeated.

"I suppose a coffee would be out of the question?" asked Dupre.

Julien snorted. Ten minutes later a disheveled, sleepy-eyed Michel wandered into the restaurant and stopped when he saw the detectives. He shot an evil look at his brother.

"Monsieur Briancon," said Dupre. "Thanks for stopping by. Now, if you'll come with us, we need to ask you a few questions."

Despite his relief at making concrete progress, it was a miserable ride back to the police station. Gaston caught up on his emails while Dupre chafed over the potential loss of his evening plans. Michel glared out the window in the back. The smell of Michel's body odor, doubtless the result of not showering after a late-night drinking session, forced Dupre and Gaston to continuously wind their windows up and down, alternating between banishing the smell and keeping the air-conditioned air in. It made for a most uncomfortable journey, but in the end, Dupre's concern for his dinner plans had been for nothing.

When they reached the station, Briancon clammed up, demanding a lawyer. With a prayer of thanks, Dupre was most happy to oblige. He didn't think Michel would find anyone on Quartorze Juillet, and he was right. Briancon was locked up for the night, while Nash also stewed in a cell down the corridor. He was, thank God, free.

"Be in bright and early," warned Jacques as Dupre made his way out of the station with Arielle.

"Bien sûr, mon Capitaine!" smiled Dupre. *"Bonne fête nationale."*

He almost skipped with relief as they hit the street. "I'll pick you up before seven," he said to Arielle. He had to get home and shower and change. He shuddered when he thought of the state he had been in last time he ate there. He would make an extra effort this evening.

Arielle did a double take as he pulled up in his sleek black Citroën hybrid crossover. He jumped out to open her door.

"Louis," smiled Arielle, feigning amazement. "I nearly didn't recognize you! And what's with this car?"

Dupre blushed. "This is my weekend car."

She whistled. "Some weekend car. You have a lot of explaining to do. And pressed pants, a dress shirt…" She reached out and turned his lapel out so she could see the tailor. "…and an Yves Saint Laurent jacket. *Tellement chic!*" She breathed in his aftershave. "And Dior, if I'm not mistaken."

Dupre smiled deprecatingly. "You have a good nose." He waved his hand at her elegant blue cocktail dress and the diamond drop earrings. "You see, I had to at least try to compete."

But her comments had given him confidence, something he sorely needed tonight. And, he admitted to himself, he wanted to stick it to that supercilious maître d'.

"Ah," said Gustav when they arrived, eyeing Dupre suspiciously as he presented himself. "You have a reservation?"

"I do," said Dupre.

The maître d's eyes fell on Arielle. His face seemed to say, *Are you really with this policeman?* Finally, with a sardonic pout, he said in a reluctant tone, "This way."

He swept into the restaurant like a stiff breeze, leaving them trailing in his wake.

To his utter disappointment, Dupre found that they were not assigned Madeleine, but a young, quiet waiter who was polite and professional. On any other evening that would have been fine. But this evening that was not what he was here for. Dupre's eyes searched the restaurant anxiously for the object of his affection.

"Is everything okay?" asked Arielle, watching his eyes flit around.

"Fine," said Dupre, gathering himself and turning his attention to his beautiful dinner companion. He noted that more than a few male diners were appraising her admiringly.

To start, he ordered the tuna tartare and Arielle ordered the langoustines two ways, with courgette flower emulsion. He ordered a bottle of his favorite white wine, Château de Fontcreuse, and delayed their entrees. Dupre wanted to kill some time. He still hadn't seen Madeleine. That suited Arielle just fine. It allowed her to badger Dupre into divulging his wealthy background based on minor French nobility.

"Zut! So your family is big in textiles," Arielle enthused, her face alight with excitement. Before Dupre could answer, her eyes popped wide as she added, "Are you a count or something?"

Dupre's face scrunched as if in pain, his voice reluctant. "I guess you could say that, but it's *vicomte.*"

Arielle giggled. "Vicomte Dupre. Who would have thought."

"Look, Arielle, this goes no further. I mean it. I get enough shit at work as it is."

She held out a mollifying palm to him. "Don't worry, Louis. I can keep a secret." She paused for a beat. "So why a policeman?"

"Ah, I am afraid I am a disappointment to my family. The corporate lifestyle was not for me. My sister now runs the company with my father. Far better than I could have. She has two children and is everything my parents wanted." His face fell in an expression of regret.

Arielle reached across the table and placed a hand over his. "Well, we are all grateful you have eschewed a life of nobility to help us tame the criminal element in society."

He nodded and then, neatly turning the tables, said, "And you, Arielle, why are you with us? With such marvelous credentials you could be in Paris where you would get much more recognition… and money."

She shrugged. "I don't like Parisians."

He chuckled. "*Ni moi.*"

Her face got serious suddenly. She winced, and to Dupre, it was apparent she was recalling a painful memory. "My older sister died of a drug overdose when she was a student in Avignon. I wanted to make sure bastards like Markovic and the Brise were put behind bars where they could do no more harm."

That sobered him up. So that was why she had such a reaction when she discovered Borrell's true identity. Then Arielle tossed her head and changed the subject herself. "Now, why are we here?"

Their starters arrived, and Dupre bent his head to his plate, grateful for the reprieve. But Arielle was not to be put off.

"Okay, so which one is she?" she asked, looking around the tables.

"Who?"

Arielle clucked. "The mysterious woman we are here to meet."

Dupre grimaced uncomfortably, rubbing at the back of his neck.

"Come on, Louis. Don't keep me in suspense."

She glanced around the room again. "Is she that attractive woman sitting by herself in the corner?"

Dupre himself was searching the room.

"Ah, *non,*" uttered Arielle as she saw a middle-aged man join the woman in question and give her a peck on the cheek. "I see she has a ring, and here comes her husband now."

Dupre exhaled a deep sigh. "She is not here," he murmured disconsolately. It would be just his luck if she had the evening off. He hadn't thought to check.

At that moment Madeleine appeared behind Arielle carrying a large platter of food. His face must have lit up like a beacon because Arielle turned and followed his gaze.

"Is it the waitress?" she said, raising an eyebrow.

Dupre colored.

"*Oh, mon dieu!*" said Arielle. "It is the waitress!"

"Ssssshhh," said Dupre.

As if she'd heard her own name, Madeleine looked over. When she saw Dupre, she put the platter down, checked with the dinner guests at the table, and made her way over to them.

"Monsieur Dupre," she said, coolly appraising Arielle.

"Bonsoir, Madeleine," nodded Dupre. "Lovely to see you."

"I see you dressed for the occasion," she said, "this time."

Her eyes flicked between Dupre and Arielle without any of the warmth and good humor he had previously experienced.

"This is my colleague, Arielle," Dupre hastily offered.

"Pleased to meet you," Madeleine said in an exaggerated, professional way, but her eyes indicated quite the opposite.

Dupre was baffled, particularly when Madeleine said in a short, tight voice, "Well, enjoy your meal," before turning abruptly and walking away.

"You should ask her out," Arielle whispered. "She likes you."

"She does?" said Dupre. "It would not seem so." He rubbed disconsolately at his neatly cropped stubble. "Perhaps I made a mistake."

"Are you kidding? Did you see how jealous she was?" Her eyes crinkled with amusement.

"Jealous?" Dupre expostulated. This thought ricocheted around inside his head like a pinball, and he cupped a hand to his mouth.

"*Certainement*," said Arielle. "And she needs to know I am not your date. Everybody needs to know that this is not a date." Doubtless she was thinking of the *merde* that would come their way if news of this outing reached police headquarters.

It had never occurred to Dupre that anyone could think that Arielle was his date. She was way too pretty, youthful and vibrant, like a favorite niece. Surely Madeleine must see that. He blew out his cheeks in frustration. If Arielle was right, he would have to set Madeleine straight and quickly.

When their entrées arrived, he turned his attention to the side of pork with sausage bonbons. Sadly, he found he had lost his appetite.

"*Ah, Louis,*" Arielle said, raising her glass toward him, "*bon courage.*"

Dupre gave her a glum smile before clinking glasses. "Happy Quatorze Juillet," he said in a voice laced with irony.

"Look, there she is now, and she doesn't seem busy. Go get her."

She shooed him away from the table. Dupre summoned all his inner fortitude, rose, and walked over to where Madeleine was standing to one side surveying her tables.

"Madeleine," Dupre began. "Could I have a word with you in private?'

The waitress studied him for a moment before inclining her head to a quiet corner of the patio.

When Dupre rejoined Arielle, his face was wreathed in smiles and there was a jaunty bounce in his step.

"She said yes," he gushed.

"What?" Arielle looked alarmed. "You proposed to her?"

"No, no," he chuckled. "She said she would go on a date with me."

"*Superbe!*" Arielle said. "Then it truly is a happy Quatorze Juillet." And they both raised their glasses high into the air.

29

Max was overwhelmed by a feeling of déjà vu, only this time it was Jeremy Nash, not Hassan, on the other side of the steel-topped table, and he was in the first chair with Helene Blanc sitting slightly behind him and off to one side. He had come straight from dropping Luke at camp and was feeling irritated and put upon. But he also felt guilty that Nash was here, solely at Max's instigation, to answer for a crime he now felt, more than ever, that the Englishman did not commit. He watched Jeremy's hooded eyes drift admiringly up the shapely legs of Maître Blanc, a predatory expression on his face. The man disgusted Max, and he made no attempt to hide the fact.

"So why were you searching Madame Borrell's apartment?" Max asked curtly.

Jeremy's attention switched to him, and he looked petulant. "I already told the police I wasn't in that apartment."

"Look, anything you say to us is protected. But we need to know the truth."

Jeremy sat back and crossed his arms. "Same answer."

Max exchanged a glance with the French lawyer. She raised her eyes to the ceiling and shook her head. "How do you explain the blood found on her balcony, which has now been confirmed as yours?"

"Do I have to keep repeating myself?"

Only Max's lips smiled. "No, you don't. And I don't need to waste my time." He pushed back his chair and started to rise.

"Okay, okay. I already told those morons that I cut my hand and flapped it about. A spot of blood must have flown over onto her balcony."

"Wow, how unfortunate for you." Max half turned to the French lawyer. "Isn't that unfortunate, Maître Blanc?"

Her lip twisted in a mocking smile. *"Oui, certainement. Très dommage."*

"Maître Blanc agrees it was most unfortunate."

"I got that," Nash spat.

Max ducked his head below the table. As he thought, Jeremy was wearing brown loafers, not the sort of footwear to climb balconies in. He straightened up, folded his arms across the table and gazed at Nash. He counted to ten and then said blithely, "It is particularly unfortunate because someone stepped in that blood, and from the timing, it seems very unlikely that it was the victim. The police are now going through your apartment, checking the bottom of your shoes for a matching trace."

Jeremy went white. He ran the tip of his tongue over his thin lips, and after a moment, he made a suggestion.

"Well, what if I stepped on some blood on my own balcony?"

Max nodded as if he thought this was an actual possibility. "Oh, they are looking for traces of blood on your balcony too. I sure hope you didn't clean too well and they find some. From the state of your kitchen and the rest of the apartment, they didn't seem to think you were big on cleaning."

He paused as he watched fear and desperation flicker across Nash's face. Then he decided to take a risk.

"And then there's the sweat they found in her apartment. You know they can get DNA from sweat, right?"

Jeremy ran a hand wildly through his hair and gabbled, "They didn't say anything about sweat."

"Well, they wouldn't show you their whole hand, would they?"

Jeremy crumpled as he buried his face in his hands. His muffled voice leaked out. "Oh God, Oh God!"

Max had him. "Why don't you just tell us what happened?" Then he added in a kindly voice. "I don't think you killed Madame Borrell, but we cannot help you unless you tell us the truth. As they say, the whole truth and nothing but the truth."

Jeremy raised a face drained of all color, his eyes aghast. "No, I didn't kill that bloody woman." The statement seemed to give him some renewed strength. "But I'm beginning to wish I had!"

Helene Blanc leaned forward and said in a soothing voice. "So, Monsieur Nash, why don't you tell us what happened?"

Jeremy looked at Max, and he nodded.

"Oh, alright then. Yes, I was in her apartment. Hassan told me when she went out, and I hopped across to her balcony."

Max whistled, thinking he wouldn't like to make that leap, balcony to balcony.

"I like to rock climb, all right?" said Nash. "I'm rather good at it."

Helene Blanc interjected. "Why would the concierge tell you when Madame Borrell went out?"

Jeremy scowled. "He owed me," he said darkly.

"Because?" Max prodded.

"Let's just say he got me into this mess in the first place."

"How so?"

Jeremy let out a capitulating breath. "He worked for Borrell and arranged some adult entertainment for me."

"Hookers?" Max said.

"Salopes," Helene said.

"Yes, alright, prostitutes," spat Jeremy.

"And?"

He sighed deeply. "They filmed us secretly, and then we got demands from Borrell."

"Us?" asked Maître Blanc.

"I'm not saying who I was with. Just a friend."

Max pursed his lips for a moment. "And what did they want?"

"It doesn't matter. Let's just say that I preferred to recover the SD card she waved in my face, gloating bitch!"

"So that is what you were looking for in her home and at her office?"

Jeremy scowled. "That's why I searched her apartment. I didn't even know she had an office until Hassan told me, and by the time I got there, the police were already swarming all over the place."

"Did you find what you were looking for in her apartment?" Max asked.

Jeremy let out another deep sigh. "No. Then I heard Hassan's voice in the corridor outside. He was talking loudly with Borrell, trying to warn me that she was coming back. So, I flew out the patio doors and cut myself on the railing in my haste."

He paused to gauge the effect his words were having. "I didn't kill her."

Maître Blanc had been taking notes, and now she tapped her pen pensively on her lips. "I'm not sure the police will see this account as anything but a very solid motive."

Nash squinted at Max belligerently. "Look, you're supposed to be this hotshot lawyer. I need you to get me out of here. I've already wasted enough time, and I had plans for Bastille Day."

"I haven't agreed to represent you yet, Jeremy. You asked for me, and I came to try to help. The rest is up to Maître Blanc... if she will have you."

"One last thing," the French lawyer said. "What time did this take place?"

Jeremy's face scrunched in thought. "Around six. I thought she had gone to play tennis." He barked out a humorless laugh. "But according to Hassan, she got halfway there and discovered she had left her favorite racquet in the apartment after it had been re-strung." He threw out his hands. "Unbelievable."

Nash had his head in his hands as Max and Helene Blanc made their way outside to the hallway. "Sweat? I didn't hear that they had found sweat?" she whispered when they were firmly out of earshot.

Max grinned. "They didn't, but it was worth a shot."

She looked amused. "And it worked. Interesting approach! Well, what now?"

"I think it is time for another talk with our concierge," Max said grimly.

As they walked down the corridor, a dapper and whistling Dupre came along.

"Ah," the lieutenant said. "Just in time. The captain and judge would like a word."

Max ran his eyes up and down Dupre, appraising him with a smile. "Dupre," he said. "A good night last night, eh? You look very refreshed!"

"Ah," said Dupre, "a perfect night." He tapped the side of his nose.

In the captain's office, an impassive Claire Lejuene sat waiting for them with Jacques, wearing his usual irascible expression.

"So?" Jacques demanded.

"He is ready to talk," said the Maître.

"Has he told you about the video?"

"You know?" said the Maître.

"Yes, we have recovered it from the victim's computer. It does not paint him in a very good light."

Claire Lejeuene's lip curled in revulsion. "The worst possible light."

The Maître looked surprised. "Really? For having sex with a prostitute? I'm surprised he even thought it worth worrying about. Half the politicians in France..." she stopped abruptly as she caught the judge's eye.

An ominous quietness gathered in the room as they all looked at each other for a long moment. From the grim smile of satisfaction on the captain's face, Max could tell something bad was coming.

The judge seemed to be trying to clear something unpleasant from her throat. "I'm sorry to say the video shows Nash with two young girls. Very underage girls."

Max's face scrunched in disgust. "He failed to mention that."

"Well, I think we can go ahead and charge him with the murder now," said Claire. "We have this evidence, and we know for sure that he was in the apartment. Obviously searching for this video."

The Maître nodded. "Very well," she said. "But what evidence of Borrell's murder? You can place him at the scene at some point in time, and you have a motive, but what evidence of murder?"

Jacques blinked at the lawyer. "What more do we need? We have motive and opportunity."

Max found himself fighting an internal battle of whether or not to leave Nash the pedophile to his fate. Reluctantly he shook his head and spoke up. "You only have one problem. The timing doesn't track. I'm fairly sure we can prove Nash was in the apartment at six p.m." He paused, collecting his thoughts. "And she played tennis after that, right?"

Claire eyed him in surprise and then held up a hand to Jacques, who was about to explode. "And how do you know this?"

"Let's just say we may have found a witness to the break-in."

"Who is this witness?" demanded Jacques.

Max exchanged a glance with Helene Blanc. "I'm afraid we can't tell you that until we have spoken to them." He shot Claire an apologetic glance.

Jacques surveyed Max with narrowed eyes, his distaste evident in the slow spread of his tongue across his front teeth. "You are going to obstruct justice?"

Helene Blanc jumped in. "*Capitaine*," she said sharply. "Let's not make this personal. You know we are under no obligation to share anything our client may have told us, or what we subsequently discover."

Claire Lejeune cast Max a disappointed glance.

"Look" said Max. "As soon as we have confirmed what we believe is true, I will be happy to share it with you."

The Maître peered down her nose at him. "As long as it doesn't breach attorney-client privilege, of course."

"Of course," said the judge, sardonically.

It seemed that the captain needed the last word. "So, he was there at six," he sneered. "Who's to say he didn't go back later?"

Max pinched his bottom lip, lost in thought, then roused himself. "That's possible, but from what we know, unlikely."

"And you certainly can't *prove* he went back later," Maître Blanc added, giving Jacques a tight smile.

30

Claire caught up to Max as he exited the police station. "We have to talk," she said.

Max craned his head around her to survey the street.

"What do you want to talk about?" he asked. He hoped she wasn't going to press him on the witness issue.

Claire shook her head. "Let's go upstairs."

He grinned reflexively. "I thought you'd never ask."

She punched him in the arm.

"So?" he invited, as they entered her office.

"It's about Claude."

Hoping to head off an unnecessary confession, he cut in. "Well, I am a little hurt to find out about you and Claude. I thought you were making a play for me." His eyes crinkled.

She tossed her head. "You wish. Besides, if that was the case, why would I get Sam here?" She put her fingertips to her lips, tapped a few times and then poked him in the chest. "You didn't actually think… "

"No," Max interjected hastily. "Of course not." He couldn't tell if she was being serious. "Honestly. I was kidding. You have been more than kind to an old classmate and his son, and I know you have been trying to cheer me up."

"Well, alright then." She peered at him with her head cocked on one side in a very fetching manner, a bemused smile on her lips. "You know you have been cheering me up as well. I can't think why we weren't friends back at Uni. Anyway…"

Before she could get back to her confession, he said, "I like Claude. I liked him instantly, even in the pink spandex."

She giggled. "Yes, that can be a little hard to take, but he's a good guy."

"He certainly seems so. Luke likes him, and you know what they say about children and animals." He paused and examined her face. "As long as you're happy."

She gave an answering wry smile and flick of one eyebrow.

"So is that it? That's all you wanted to talk about? I thought it was something important."

She laughed and then stopped short as a dark thought intruded. "Well, I guess we should get down to business. Why on earth would you want to represent Nash?"

Max sighed. His conscience simply would not let him railroad the guy. "He's pathetic. But he's British, for which I feel some slight allegiance. And I just don't think he did it."

Claire eyed him askance. "Why ever not?"

"Just a hunch. I mean, look at him."

Claire eyed him sharply. "What do you know?"

Max held his gaze steady. "I just don't believe he could have stuck a knife in someone and ripped it up through her body with such venom. And what would his motive be for such a vicious attack?"

She shuddered. "To get the video back, of course."

"Recovering the video would hardly justify such a brutal murder. In fact, how would that help him recover the video?"

Claire heaved a sigh. "My gut tells me you're right, but he is our best suspect, so Jacques will never release him. God knows he has motive—and I'm sure that video will not warm the jury towards him. And we can place him at the scene. It's a slam dunk conviction."

"Eight hours before the murder took place, and you don't have a murder weapon."

"Come on! It was most likely a heavy-bladed kitchen knife, just like the one found in his dishwasher—clean, of course."

"But why would he leave it in the dishwasher for two days to arouse suspicion? He could have just cleaned it and put it back in the drawer. Every apartment has a heavy kitchen knife. Could he have used his to cut cheese the day after the murder?"

Claire rubbed the nape of her neck. "Yes, he could have. We cannot definitively tie the knife to the murder, but it is certainly suggestive. As for timing, Jacques may be right. Not having found what he was looking for earlier, Nash went back. I think a jury will see it that way. No, I'm afraid without more, I'm going to have to charge him with the murder."

Max's shoulders slumped in resignation. "Can I see the police file? I hate doing it, but I suppose I have to try and help him."

"Sure," she replied. "I just want to get to the truth. Speaking of which…" She smiled sweetly at him. "Sam?"

He sighed. "In some ways she made things better, and in some ways worse."

"Give it time. She's a good friend. Luke seemed to like her."

"*Chérie,*" he said, giving her a quick peck on the cheek, "*c'est un coup bas.*"

She winked. "Just observing the facts as any good judge should do. Come on, let's see if we can find that police file."

Half an hour later they were still sitting in Claire's office. Max read through a sheaf of papers while Claire dealt with her email and returned a few calls. When she finished, she sat back and stared expectantly at him. "So, defense counsel?"

"Well, your honor. Let's review the case against Jeremy Nash."

She inclined her head. "Go on."

"So, Nash has admitted that he went into her apartment to look for evidence that would incriminate him and a friend in prostitution." He steepled his fingers under his chin. "By the way, has he said who this friend is?"

Claire shook her head. "He is still refusing to name them."

Max blew out a breath and nodded. "Okay, so he went into her apartment. He says at six p.m. when he knew she wouldn't be there. You have established that she played tennis that evening, so that makes sense, whereas trying to search her apartment after midnight when she most certainly would be at home makes no sense. If he had found the video, he would have left. If he didn't, he would either give up or go back another time when she was out. She might have had a gun."

"Well, perhaps he didn't find what he was looking for and waited for her to come home and then attacked her in an attempt to recover the video. And things got out of hand."

Max shook his head and skimmed a photograph across the desk at her. "Look at where the body was found. Slumped just outside the bedroom door, facing the entry. It's as if she came out of the bedroom and was stabbed and slid down the door frame. And look how she's dressed."

Claire examined the picture in her hand. "Oh, I see. She's wearing silk pajamas."

"Yes, and she is not wearing shoes. There is no way she came in from the street like that."

Claire's frown deepened. "So, she went into the bedroom and changed."

He smiled the smile of a lawyer about to wreck the prosecution's case. "So, your premise is that having searched the apartment and not finding what he was looking for, Nash waited eight hours until she came home at two in the morning. He didn't confront her straight away but hid somewhere while she went into the bedroom and changed, waiting till she came out and then stabbed her once, with extreme malevolence."

He skimmed another photograph across to her. "No other marks on her but the weal across her wrist. Wouldn't he have tortured her to get her to hand over the video before killing her?"

"Not if she gave him the video straight away and then he killed her."

"So where did he get the knife? Why would he bring a knife if he went to search an empty apartment?"

"As you said, maybe he was hiding in the kitchen, heard her coming and grabbed one of her knives."

"It wasn't one of her knives you found in his dishwasher, though, was it? I noticed that she has a very nice set of Shun. His was your average rental apartment knife. And a bloody knife wasn't found at the scene. If I remember correctly, I don't think any of hers was missing, so the killer didn't take one of hers with him. But you can check."

"Right," she said thoughtfully. They looked at each other for a long moment.

"Well, he still could have taken a knife with him, just in case?" Claire suggested somewhat lamely.

"But you don't have the bloody dagger. What about the gun? Where does that figure in your theory? Then there's the blood. This would have been quite messy. He would have been covered, yet he escaped across the balcony leaving only a drop of his own blood behind. Was any of her blood found in his apartment? Shower drain? Bloody clothes? Apparently not."

"True," she admitted. "Perhaps he scratched himself getting in and left by the door."

Max shook his head. "Still the same problem. Surely there would be some trail of blood out of the apartment." He paused as a startling thought occurred to him, and he filed it away, keeping his face impassive. "Remember, he appeared on his balcony moments after the scream and he looked quite normal to me—no sign of any blood. And then there is the issue of where Borrell spent all that time," he went on relentlessly. "What was she doing from after tennis until she arrived home at two in the morning? Have you tracked her movements? Perhaps through her phone?"

Claire huffed. "Alright, alright, you win, damn you. I said my gut told me he didn't do it. But however unlikely, it is still possible that not finding what he was searching for, he returned in the early hours of the morning when he thought she would be asleep. She woke and surprised him. He tried to get her to tell him where it was at knifepoint, she resisted, and he stabbed her. That's what Jacques will say."

"I'm sorry, but if this was the States, I could drive a truck through the holes in your case, and I would have picked your theories apart in front of a jury. All you have is his admission that he entered Borrell's apartment sometime in the early evening when, incidentally, I think I can prove that Borrell was out, to search for something. Far from being a motive, killing her was against his interests."

She folded her arms as she considered his words, her mouth gathered in a stubborn *moue*.

"And I'll tell you another thing," he said as he remembered something from the autopsy report that again gave him a sinking feeling in the pit of his stomach. The pieces were all falling into place. "Your ME says the wound was most likely inflicted by a right-handed person. Nash is left-handed."

"So, what do you want me to do?" she sounded exasperated. "Release him? Jacques will have a fit. He's determined to nail Nash and will probably file a formal complaint. The way things are with Vincent right now, I'm not sure what he or his friends at the Ministry might do with me. I think Vincent would like an excuse to keep me at home being a housewife."

Max realized what she said was true, and he had no wish to jeopardize her career. Jacques would need someone to pin the murder on. "I'm betting that between the Russian mob and the Brise de Sang, she has pissed off someone. Dupre told me that mob killings are almost never solved."

She grimaced. "That may be so, but I don't think that will satisfy Jacques when he has such an enticing suspect in hand. But while we are at it, I may as well tell you, since we apparently owe this to you, that the victim's real name was Biljana Markovic. She is a wanted Serbian war criminal with ties to a Serbian crime gang, Senjicari." She paused, watching him. "You don't seem surprised."

"I'm not. I guessed she was Serbian, and it was easy to figure out why she would be in hiding here. I looked up wanted war criminals online and quickly found a picture of her." He shrugged to express how simple it had been.

Claire looked up at the ceiling, muttering something under her breath. "I can see how you got your reputation. Well, I'm not going to tell anyone how easily you found the answer. Jacques is not even happy that you were the one to point Dupre in the right direction."

That brought a smile of satisfaction to his face. "Serves him right. I bet he's not happy at all. His list of suspects is growing by the hour and makes Nash's conviction even less likely." As he said this, he was uncomfortably aware that this development had only brought the search closer to the real culprit.

31

After leaving the station, Max made his way back to the Old Gendarmerie. He hoped that Nash would agree to be represented by Maître Blanc and that she would take the case. After hearing about the video, he wasn't sure he could stomach representing such a pervert.

Hassan was out by the pool. He looked uncomfortable when Max approached.

"Sit," Max commanded, pointing to the patio table under a yellow umbrella.

Hassan hesitated.

"Sit!"

Hassan reluctantly sat. "But I have work..." His voice tailed off when he saw the expression on Max's face.

"I believe I know who killed Madame Borrell," Max said curtly. "And I believe that you had something to do with it."

"Monsieur?" The young man feigned a look of surprised confusion.

Max waved his hand dismissively. "I also know about the video and that you helped Monsieur Nash break into the apartment earlier. You are in this up to your neck. You are a good actor, Hassan. One of the best I've seen. You had me and Maître Blanc fooled, but it won't work anymore."

Hassan hunched over, his dark eyes suddenly shrewd and calculating—not at all the scared young man he had previously seemed.

Max glanced around and lowered his voice.

"Right now, the police have Nash in custody. They are charging him with the murder. When they find out you helped him, and he's bound to talk, they will be coming for you. Accessory to murder. *Vous comprenez?*"

Hassan licked his lips and his façade flickered, his shoulders sagging. His voice wobbled. *"Oui. Je comprends."*

"So, we must make them think the murder is on either the Russian mafia or the Brise de Sang."

Hassan looked surprised and relieved at the same time.

"And you are going to help me."

The concierge's face fell.

"Now, tell me everything you know about Madame Borrell and her business dealings."

"But I already… "

Max waved away the excuses. "You can start with the video. The police are going to ask you about it."

Hassan's leg jiggled up and down like he needed the toilet. "I did not know this, Monsieur Dempsey. I swear. But she obtained some girls for him… and filmed him with them. He thought it was me, but I swear I knew nothing. I just introduced him to Madame Borrell." He paused. "He told me that a very powerful friend in Avignon was also filmed."

Max nodded. So that was the friend Nash meant. Some bigwig trying to cover his arse. However, this news didn't help Nash. It only confirmed his motive and put him in an even worse light.

"Where did Borrell get the girls?"

"The Brise de Sang. When Monsieur threatened me with his powerful friend, I told him they couldn't be as powerful as the Brise de Sang, and he looked very scared."

"I'll bet. Do you know who this friend was?"

"Non, monsieur."

"How did you know Madame Borrell could get him girls?"

The concierge looked down at his feet. "I knew she had connections to the Brise de Sang."

"Tell me about those connections."

"I'm sorry, but I don't know anything else. You should ask one of the brothers at the restaurant where she has her office. From something she said, I'm sure one of them is connected."

Max fell silent while he considered how to proceed.

"Yes, I heard about them, and I understand that the police now have a Michel Briancon in custody," he finally continued.

"Yes, him," Hassan said excitedly. "He is the one who brought the girls, I think."

"Well, that's good," said Max. "A definite connection. Right."

Max stood up and beckoned Hassan into the apartment complex. They took the lift together in silence, Hassan seemingly resigned to his fate.

Max rapped loudly on the door next to his own apartment. It was answered by a surprised-looking Hans.

"Ah, Max! Hassan? Is everything all right?"

Max's face scrunched. "Not really. Is Angela in? I need you both to come with me. Hassan here has something he wants to show us."

Hans eyed them quizzically. "Really? And what's that?" he said. "Have you got a new floor polisher?" he chuckled.

Max gave a wan smile.

From within the apartment, Angela called. "Who's that, Hans?"

She made her way to the door and, like Hans, looked surprised to see the two. "Are we having a party?" she smiled. She was dressed for the pool.

"We need to show you something in Madame Borrell's apartment," said Max.

For a brief moment, dismay flickered on Angela's face. "Madame Borrell!" she said, a slight hitch in her voice. "Whatever for?"

"You'll see when we get there," said Max.

Hans and Angela swapped a puzzled look before Angela grabbed a kaftan, and they closed their apartment door behind them.

Hassan let them into Borrell's apartment with his master key.

"Should we be going in here?" asked Hans. "Isn't it a crime scene?"

"It's okay. The judge is a friend, and she has given her permission," Max said.

A little white lie didn't matter at this stage.

The apartment was eerily quiet with the buzzing police presence gone. It felt less sinister, but for Max, it still felt oppressively gloomy. He reflexively compared it to the home he had shared with Emma, the comfortable living room, the cooked-in kitchen, the inviting dining room, and most of all, the loving bedroom, a warm and welcoming atmosphere. This was the sadly expensive but sterile habitation of a person without warmth or love.

"So, this was where she died," Max said, turning to look at Hans and Angela and then Hassan and pointing to the pool of blood on the carpet, now a rusty brown. With no family that they knew of, Max wondered who would now come in to clean up the place and take away Markovic's belongings. Perhaps all of it would be forfeited to the State anyway as proceeds of a criminal enterprise.

"Tell me about it," said Max, turning to Angela.

His eyes bored into hers. Angela put her hand to her chest and stepped back.

"About what?"

"About how you killed Madame Borrell," Max replied, "or should I say Biljana Markovic?"

At the sound of the victim's real name, Angela gasped. An ominous silence hung in the air.

"I don't know what you're talking about," she said quietly after she had gathered herself, but her voice was trembling.

"Oh, I think you do," said Max.

Hans spoke up angrily and stepped toward Max. "Max! How dare you accuse my wife. What is this madness?"

Angela put a restraining hand on her husband's arm. Hassan stared down, shuffling his feet.

"Hans, stop the act," cried Max. "I've figured most of it out. I just want to be sure I fully understand it."

Angela looked at Hans, and they both looked at Hassan.

Max stood and waited. He knew it would come out. He

knew she would break. And then, there it was—an explosion of tears from Angela and a cry like a trapped animal. She turned onto Hans' shoulder, who wrapped his arms around her as she began to rack with sobs.

For Max, it had all come together on a canoe in the middle of the Gorge du Gardon in one soul-crushing moment. In the shadow of the spectacular aqueduct, he'd looked down at his hands, biting back a cry of rage and anguish at the unfairness of life. Since Emma's accident, they had left everything and everyone behind, and until that sickening moment, he had not realized how much the Dutch couple's friendship had meant to him and, more cruelly, to Luke. He had not been able to stomach confronting Angela then in front of Luke. He needed time to think, and he needed to be sure. It had overshadowed his Bastille Day celebrations and weighed on him like a thundercloud as he had wrestled with what to do. That he needed to confront the couple had been in no doubt. It was a matter of when, how, and what happened afterward. With the news that Hassan had been involved, both with Nash and the terrible videos and now, as he understood it, the crime scene, bringing the three together would allow them to address the fallout.

"How did you know?" Hans asked, his face a picture of despair.

"*Jebi Ga,*" said Max. "I play soccer at home with a guy who uses that expression a lot. *Fuck it!* But you see, he is Croatian, not Dutch. That's what Angela said when she tipped into the water out of the canoe. *Jebi Ga.*"

"*Jebi Ga,*" Angela muttered into Hans' shoulder with a false laugh. "My mother always said my mouth would get me into trouble."

"And there were other clues too—the *Krafne* you served us up for dessert. Luke liked them so much that he made me look up where we could get more. And there it was: Croatia. And you said you grew up around red wine." Max smiled disconsolately. "Not much red wine produced in Germany, but quite a lot in Croatia. I'm guessing your parents owned a winery."

Angela nodded miserably.

"And then I realized I hadn't seen you that night. I thought it strange at the time that the gunshot and the scream didn't bring you out. Even if you do sleep naked."

Angela had turned to face him and was nervously plucking at her kaftan with her left hand. Now she blushed.

"Someone as curious as you would have thrown something on. You said Hans sleeps like a bear in winter, meaning you are more likely to be woken and get up, like the night Luke screamed. You said you heard the shot. But there are still some things I haven't figured out. What happened with the gunshot? Why was there no bullet found?"

Angela shrugged, turning away from Hans. Her shoulders slumped in what might have been remorse or relief at her secret being found out.

"When I entered her apartment, I expected her to be asleep. I couldn't have known that... that some *supak* had already broken into the place earlier."

"Arsehole," translated Hans.

"Anyway, because of him, Markovic was on her guard. I must have made a sound as I crossed the living room because as I approached the bedroom where I expected to catch her sleeping, I heard the rustle of her gown as she came to investigate. I stepped to one side as she came through the bedroom doorway."

"She had a gun," Max said, thinking ahead to whether he could mount a self-defense plea.

She nodded. "I had brought only a knife."

Angela's eyes glinted with malice. "I knew just how to do it to inflict the most pain. It was she who taught me on my own father and brothers."

Hans writhed in agitation, his face a picture of misery. "Of course, I wanted to go with her, but she wouldn't let me."

She reached over and squeezed his hand. "It was a personal thing that I had to do myself, and if anything went wrong, I did not want you to be involved. And it did go wrong. I reacted first, hitting her wrist with the hilt of the knife. She dropped the gun and it fired when it hit the floor. It was an old gun, from the Second World War. A lot of the partisans used surplus old weapons. My father had one, an unstable gun very likely to go off if dropped." She smiled viciously. "She probably kept it as a memento of her ugly deeds. Anyway, the patio doors were open, and the bullet must have disappeared into the night. That noise was not part of the plan; I held my knife to her throat and waited to see what would happen. And while we waited, I told her who I was and watched the fear flood her face. She begged for her life, said she was just following orders." Her lip curled in contempt. "Then she tried to grab my hand, but I am much stronger now than when she last saw me. I was suddenly consumed with rage."

Angela's eyes shone, her stare unfocused, like she was watching something play inside her head.

"So, I stabbed the Bitch of Brdo where it would cause the most pain, and she screamed." Angela grimaced, an expression of regret. "I had not expected her to make so much noise when I killed her. This was a problem, so I called Hans on my phone."

Hans grimaced. "I put her on speaker and covered my phone with a dish towel so that if anyone heard her voice, it would sound like she was just talking in the bedroom."

Angela continued, "I could watch you both from Markovic's apartment. The rest you know."

Max nodded appreciatively. "Ingenious. No wonder I thought her voice was muffled by sleep. And your performance, Hans—brilliant. You gave nothing away. And since then, you have gone on as though nothing happened." He was starting to feel angry and betrayed. He and Luke had dined with this pair the day after and discussed the murder.

"As far as I was concerned, nothing had happened," Angela said. "It was an act that belonged in another place in another lifetime." She held his eyes. "It wasn't me. It was someone who died a long time ago and came back just for one evening."

"Well, you fooled me," he said somewhat bitterly. "You should both be on stage." He was conscious that it wasn't the murder but the betrayal that bothered him. At least Angela had the grace to look ashamed.

He took a deep, calming breath. He still had one or two issues to clear up.

"What about the blood? Must have been messy?"

Angela's nose wrinkled. "Yes, I had her blood on my clothes and hands. But I just stood there until I was sure she was dead and all the fuss had died down. Then I walked out of the apartment through the front door down to the pool and took a quiet swim."

"And Hassan gave you the key so you could let yourself into her apartment, and early the following morning, he cleaned up any blood trail you may have left behind," Max said.

Hassan stood listening, chipping at the ground with the toe of his shoe, looking as if he wished he could dig a hole through the floor that would swallow him up.

"I saw you, Hassan, remember. The following morning, coming out of the elevator with a mop and buffing machine. I thought at the time it was an early start for you." He massaged his furrowed brow. "I made the connection to you later when the police said there were no traces of blood in the corridors." He searched their faces one by one. "If I hadn't noticed that no one came out onto the balcony that night, she wouldn't have been discovered for days, perhaps weeks, by which time I'm guessing you would have been gone."

"That was the plan," said Angela. She reached out and touched his sleeve. "You are too clever, my friend."

"Sorry."

How odd to be apologizing to a murderer.

"In case the chlorine didn't do a thorough job, Hans and I went out early the next morning to dispose of my clothes somewhere where they would not be found. We were coming back when you met us the following morning," explained Angela.

Max surveyed the couple, whom he had considered close friends, with a heavy heart. "Again, I am truly sorry things have worked out this way."

"Don't you want to know why I did it?" she asked.

"Oh, I know who Markovic is, so I think I can guess, but why don't you tell me."

Angela contemplated him defiantly. "Max, what would you do if you found the driver of the car that killed your wife?"

"I can't. He died in the car crash."

"But what if he hadn't? He was drunk. So, what if he lived and you could meet him face to face?"

Max had imagined that scenario a hundred times or more. He had even wished that the drunken bastard had survived so he could have had the satisfaction not just of killing him with his bare hands but much worse. His eyes narrowed at the renewed thought.

"I would want to kill him," he said grimly.

"Yes," said Angela softly. "And he didn't cause that accident deliberately, in hatred, because he enjoyed it. He didn't rape Emma first and make you watch like they did to my mother."

Max shuddered. He simply could not adequately imagine that kind of horror.

"Then they shot her in the head and gutted my father and two older brothers. I watched them die slowly in agony." Tears were coursing down Angela's cheeks. "I was only eight years old. That sick bitch was in charge of the unit. She stood and watched while her comrades… " Her voice tailed off, and Hans enfolded her protectively in his bear-like arms again.

"They would have killed Angela as well," he choked out. "But Markovic thought it was amusing to leave her alive. They…"

His voice broke. It was a long moment before he collected himself. Max blinked at the moisture in his eyes. He couldn't even look at Angela.

"They injured her inside. So she could never have more Croatian bastards, they said."

He sobbed, squeezing Angela even tighter.

"Oh, Angela," Max cried, feeling his own tears streaming now.

Angela gave him an ephemeral smile. "I couldn't believe it when I saw her in the lobby one morning." Her tone was bitter. "She had changed. Elegant clothes. But I would recognize her anywhere. She, of course, did not recognize me. And in that moment, I knew I would kill her for what she did. I could not allow her to live out her days as a rich woman in hiding."

"But why not go to the police?" asked Max.

"Hah!" She scowled. "Do you know what sentence the last female war criminal got? Eight years for genocide, death, rape and torture. I was not going to let her get off that easily. Particularly as she was continuing her disgusting actions here."

Max nodded. "The Brise de Sang."

Angela shook her head. "I don't know about them. But Hassan told us what she was doing to him. Prostituting him. Terrorizing him with threats to get him fired, and worse. Trafficking women. She deserved what she got."

"So, that is how, why, Hassan became involved."

Hassan nodded.

"But how did you come to know about them?" Max asked Angela.

"I saw how Hassan looked at her when her back was turned. Believe me when I say I can recognize hatred when I see it. Then I saw them together in Cassis. Hans was playing golf. I wondered why Hassan would be with her there and followed them to her building. I waited a long time sitting in the café downstairs. Eventually Hassan came down looking so miserable. I stopped him, and we talked. He told me everything, and when I told him who she really was, he felt disgusted and unclean. I took a chance and told him I was going to kill her, and he agreed to help."

In a flash of understanding, Max knew just how Hassan had played him. All along, he had known about the planned murder. He smiled grimly to himself. He wasn't often fooled.

"I always knew he was holding something back," said Max.

"Well, he could hardly turn me in without telling them that he helped. And I had saved him from his life of shame," said Angela.

Hassan tilted his head towards her in an expression of gratitude.

"So, what now?" Hans asked. "I love her and cannot see her go to jail."

"I understand," Max replied. "I would feel the same way."

"If I go to prison," spat Angela, "then it will have been worth it for the look on her face as she begged for mercy before I stuck her in the gut and then ripped upwards."

Her face contorted in a fierce grimace, and her left arm performed a reflexive upwards motion, hand clenched around an imaginary knife.

"She must have died in agony, with plenty of time to remember what she did to my family."

Max stood, hung his head and closed his eyes, drifting. His senses, which had been so focused on Angela, now picked up the odors and sounds of his surroundings, and with them came a modicum of calm. This couple were his and Luke's friends. He could not see Angela go to jail. He had answered his own question—did anyone deserve to be killed?

"Well, I'm not the police," he finally said, giving voice to his thoughts. "I have no obligation to report any of this to the authorities."

He gazed from Angela to Hans whose face looked overcome with relief.

"Thank you, my friend," Hans murmured.

At that moment, Max's phone rang. He glanced at the screen and saw that it was Claire. He answered, turning away from the three, not for privacy, but out of habit. "Hey Claire, what's up?"

A pause.

"I see. All right. Okay. Well, yes, I can come back if that's what he really wants. But I don't want to represent him. Can't Helene Blanc handle it?"

"Okay." He sighed. "As a favor to you."

When he hung up, Max told the three that Jeremy Nash was being charged with the murder of Borrell and various offenses related to his pedophile acts and was insisting that Max be added to his legal representation, alongside Helene Blanc.

"Pedophilia?" exclaimed Angela and Hans in unison.

Max explained, watching their faces assume expressions of disgust.

"Another disgusting human being who deserves what he gets," said Angela. "You are not going to represent him, are you?"

Her tone and face left Max in no doubt that he would fall sharply in her estimation if he did.

"He almost got me killed," Angela added. "If it wasn't for him, Markovic would not have been waiting for me."

Hans grasped his wife's hands. "If his blood was found at the scene," he said, glancing at Max, "we should be home clear, *n'est-ce pas?*"

Max gave him a look of admonishment. "I don't like the man either, Hans. Doubtless, Jeremy Nash is an offensive shit of a human being, but that doesn't warrant a prison sentence for a murder he didn't commit."

Reluctantly, Angela nodded, but Hans did not agree. "I don't care if he is innocent. Better he goes to jail than my wife who has never hurt anyone." He scowled. "Except Markovic."

"Of course I won't help him with the pedophilia charges, but now I know the truth, and because I put him in this situation, I must do what I can with respect to the murder charges."

Hans stared hard at him.

"Are you going to tell them what you know?" Hans asked, an edge to his voice.

Max shook his head. "Like I said, I'm not the police, and I have no obligation to tell them anything."

Angela stepped toward Max and squeezed his hand. "I'm sorry for dragging you into this."

She looked over to Hassan. "And you too, Hassan."

Frowning, Max said, "Look, even if I convince them not to pursue Nash for the murder, they have several other viable suspects. They now know that Borrell was a Serbian war criminal. So, I'm willing to bet that they are also looking at the Balkans connection and the Corsican mafia side of things. But if none of their suspects pans out, they still might look elsewhere. Right now, she is not looking very hard at anyone else. But the investigating magistrate's no fool, and neither is that police lieutenant, Dupre." He gazed pointedly at them all. "If I can figure it out …" He left that thought hanging.

"So, what should we do?" Angela asked.

"I think it would be better if you weren't here," said Max, rubbing at his tired eyes. "I assume you didn't already leave because you didn't want to draw attention to yourselves, but you only have a week or so left of your holiday now. Perhaps it would be best if your office called, Hans, and there was an emergency that called you back early?"

Hans nodded. "I shall go and make immediate arrangements."

Now, how to get Jeremy out of trouble without dropping Angela in it.

"I shall miss you," Angela whispered in a low voice. "And Luke."

Max inhaled deeply and let it out slowly, his shoulders slumped. He couldn't help himself, and when Angela came to him he wrapped his arms around her tightly. How terrible that it had all come to this.

After Angela had followed her husband, Max had a thought. "One last thing," he said to Hassan. "The police told me they got the video of Nash from the cloud. But it must have been uploaded from the SD card Nash mentioned seeing. If I were Borrell I would keep a hard copy backup. That was what he was searching for. The police didn't find it at her offices, so it is, quite possibly, hidden here."

They stood in the middle of Borrell's salon, scanning the room. An SD card was small. She wouldn't have necessarily expected a break-in to her apartment, but she was so security conscious that she must have hidden it somewhere—somewhere the police had not discovered yet. He tried to put himself in the mind of the dead woman—a monster but an educated monster and a proud partisan. He was used to putting himself in the shoes of a witness.

As he surveyed the room, his eyes fell first on the sideboard. He opened the drawer of CDs and went through all the Serbian discs looking for an empty case. Nothing but music. Where else? His attention turned to the bookcase, and there it was. He was sure. It would be just the sort of ironic hiding place that would have appealed to a professor of languages. He strode quickly across and drew Dostoyevsky's Crime and Punishment from a middle shelf. He opened the cover, and there, in a hollow cut out of the pages, was a cache of SD cards.

"*Voilà*," he whispered. "Doubtless her insurance against a problem with the cloud."

Silently they left the apartment, each deep in their own thoughts, a handful of SD cards clutched in Max's hand.

32

As he entered his apartment, Max was still trying to wrap his head around all that had gone on. How did an escape from all they were suffering at home, a refuge in his favorite vacation destination, breathtaking Provence, turn out like this? A murder on their doorstep and the now agonizing dilemma of what, if anything, he should do about it, given his, and Luke's, close relationship with the perpetrator. Could he really represent Nash, a pompous Englishman he despised, not just for his sick perversions—and as perversions went, they were the lowest of the low—but for putting him in this position? Nash was not the murderer, but it would be so easy to let him go down for it. Not for the first time, he imagined a conversation with Emma. It happened a lot, where he let his thoughts and worries run free, and felt like she were there, right beside him, answering him.

What should I do? he thought. *What would you do, Emma? Am I doing the right thing in letting a murderer go? Even if she has been a Godsend for Luke and a true friend to me?*

He knew that Luke would be destroyed if he knew the truth. To lose his mother and then the second mother figure that had come into his life in such a short time. Did Markovic deserve to die? She certainly deserved to be punished. Would Angela commit any more murders? No. He didn't think so.

Follow your heart, he heard Emma say. *Not your head.* Ha! he thought. Emma knew well that, as a lawyer, he had difficulty overriding his cool, logical head. In the end there was no other decision. He could not let someone be convicted for a crime they did not commit, even a piece of filth like Nash. Ironically, it would probably be better for Nash if he went to prison for murder rather than pedophilia. Prisons were not kind to pedophiles.

He steeled himself. He would have to see this video of Nash before he went any further. Fortunately Borrell, or Markovic, had been compulsively organized, and the SD cards were all dated. He only needed the most recent one, dated the week before the murder after Nash had arrived. He cued it up on his laptop and sat back, prepared to be revolted. It was worse than he could have imagined, and he was about to turn it off halfway through, on the point of retching, when something even more horrifying happened. Another man stepped into the frame and took over. He was middle-aged, lean and naked, but it was the face that made Max gasp and close his eyes at the awfulness of what he was witnessing. He had seen that face before, on the mantel above a fireplace in the house of a woman he deeply cared about.

He stopped the video, his head drooping to his hands resting on the table. *Merde to the nth degree.* This just kept getting worse. How could he tell her? Had the police seen this? Did she already know? Not when he last saw her, he was sure.

With a sinking feeling, he dialed Claire's number. "I need to see you. Now."

"You've spoken to your witness?" she said eagerly. "What?"

Max's voice was grim. "There's something I have to show you. Can you come here?"

The was brief hesitation. "You sound serious. Can it wait until this evening? I'm kind of in the middle of something."

"I think you're going to want to see this as soon as."

There was a long pause during which Max imagined her mental wheels turning. "Okay," she said finally, "I'm on my way."

When Claire arrived at the apartment, Max first confirmed that Hassan could place Nash in the apartment at six. He was having a difficult time broaching the true reason for his call. The fact that she was standing before him with eager anticipation on her face convinced him that she had not seen the video. And her beautiful, friendly face made his heart melt for her. How he wished it was not he who was breaking the news to her.

"That's what you brought me all the way here to say?" she said incredulously. "I thought you had something to show me that couldn't wait."

"I do." He faltered. "You see, I had Hassan let me into the victim's apartment."

She looked at him reproachfully.

"I know. I'm sorry, but I had this idea. Anyway, we found a cache of SD cards with what I assume to be blackmail videos."

"So, you found some videos. They're probably the originals for what was uploaded to the cloud."

He searched her face. "Have you looked at those videos?"

"Just snatches. I didn't have the stomach for it." Then, misinterpreting where he was going, she quickly added, "But enough to recognize Nash in one of them."

"But you didn't watch the whole of that video?"

"No. Should I? It was repugnant."

Max took a deep breath. "Yes, there is something on that video you need to see. You'd better take a look." He pressed play and turned his laptop towards her, the sickening sounds coming clearly through the speakers making his gorge rise again. Claire looked first shocked and then horrified. She covered her face with her hand as she forced herself to watch for a full minute before she stopped the video and lurched to her feet. "Oh, my God. I think I'm going to be sick."

Max walked her out onto the patio where they stood taking deep breaths of the clean air. When she had finally regained some composure Claire turned to him with fury on her tear-stained face.

"That bastard." She gulped again. "Well, this certainly explains a lot." She was shaking with rage. "I don't care who he is. I'm going to put him away for this."

Then she collapsed into Max's arms just as the doorbell rang.

He deposited her into a chair and opened the door to find Claude standing there.

"Well, *mon ami,* I came as quick as I could. What has happened? Is everyone alright?"

"It's Claire."

The doctor started, lurching forward into the apartment. "Where is she?"

Max detained him. "She is physically okay, but she has had a bad shock. She is going to need a friend. I didn't know who else to call."

"You called the right person," Claude said. "Where is she?"

Max showed him to the patio where Claire was curled up on the chaise longue in the tightest ball possible.

Max made another call and left Claire in Claude's capable and loving hands.

Half an hour later he entered the Café des Artistes down the block from the police station. Dupre was already there nursing a glass of wine. As Max sat down opposite him, the policeman indicated the carafe with a questioning gesture.

"Thanks," said Max. "I think I need one. This has been a terrible day."

The policeman looked curious but did not press him. Max took a deep draught and sat back trying to decompress. Apart from the day Emma died, this must surely be the worst day of his life. After a long interval during which he just watched Max, Dupre finally said, "Well, Monsieur Dempsey, what new and startling insight do you have for me?"

Max sucked in a deep breath and steeled himself. He had been doing that a lot lately. "Have you examined all the videos you found on the cloud?" he asked.

Dupre looked surprised. "No, not yet. I was going to start on them tomorrow morning." He coughed. "They are best looked at in the cold light of morning, *n'est-ce pas.*"

"That's for sure. But I suggest you hold off until you speak to Judge Lejeune."

"Oh?" The lieutenant looked askance at Max. *"Pourquoi?"*

"Can I just say it's a matter of personal importance to her? I hope you can take me at my word."

Dupre appraised him from under a lowered brow. "Monsieur Dempsey. I do not share my captain's view of you. You have been most helpful, and it is clear to me that you have been reluctantly dragged into something you would prefer not to be involved in. So, I will do as you ask."

"Thank you, Lieutenant."

"Louis," Dupre said and held out his hand.

"Max."

They shook.

"Will you represent that scum, Nash?" Dupre asked.

"Ah," replied Max. "I had hoped that would not be necessary, at least with respect to the murder. I certainly won't help him concerning the other matters."

"*Bon.* But I sense you have something to tell me about the murder."

His gaze was piercing, and for a weird moment, Max had the feeling that Dupre could read his secrets.

"Just that Nash didn't do it, so you will not be able to prove it at trial." He paused and took another deep draft of wine.

"I mean, look at him. He's a pathetic bully and a coward. His kind take advantage of those weaker than him."

Dupre nodded thoughtfully. "I agree. I have seen many murderers in my time, and he doesn't fit any profile I have seen, but there is always a first."

"How are you doing with the Serbian and Russian angle?"

Dupre rubbed his jawline. "Ah! We are still working, but…" He rubbed his beard thoughtfully.

"What about BRDO?"

"Her office?" Dupre's face showed surprise.

"No, the town in Serbia. That is where she is from."

The detective's head tilted sideways as he appraised Max. "You are full of interesting and unexpected insights into this case," he said with a wry smile. "I am not even going to ask how you know that."

Max tried to look innocent. "Perhaps the connection will help."

"I'll look into it."

33

Sitting on the back patio of Marrakech in Apt, Max watched Zoya bustle from table to table. On their first trip to the restaurant, he had not even been aware of a patio. Now, it was their weekly treat, and Zoya reserved the best table in the flower-filled courtyard every Friday night for him and Luke. They were never allowed to pay: a thank you for helping Hassan. The sounds of a bubbling fountain rippled from the back wall of the garden, overlaid with subdued guitar-like music coming from a rabab musician inside.

On one side of him sat Luke and Yousef, who could sometimes sit and join them. The boys had become firm friends and Max loved to hear them chattering and laughing in French. Soon, camp would be over. Luke was in the running to be named Star Player of the Year, and at last, Max felt, deep inside, that bringing him to Provence and focusing him on football had been palliative for his grief and something of a foundation for a new start. It had proved the right thing to do. Luke had grown in confidence. His language and football skills had dramatically improved. And he had found his niche in the local cuisine. But Moroccan was still his favorite, and under Yousef's influence, Luke had begun to try new things.

Tonight was different. Their usual small table had been replaced with a long family trestle. On the other side of Max sat Claire. As ever, she was glamourous in her understated elegance, her hair set in a shiny, voluminous pile. Only the shadows under her eyes and a hollowing under her cheekbones betrayed the difficulties that she had endured over the past few weeks. The discovery of the video and the arrest of her husband in Paris had made headline news. The fact that Claire was the judge in a case where her high-profile politician husband was implicated made the scandal even more juicy.

She had, of course, recused herself from any further investigation. Vincent had shamed her and damaged her reputation. He may have destroyed her new career. And still, she found it hard to believe that he, like Nash, could be involved in such a deviant practice. It seemed possible that she would never get over the shock. But if she was going to get through the present ordeal and past the devastation of her husband's betrayal, it would be Claude who helped that happen.

He sat beside her now, holding her hand. He was the rock she could cling to for her future happiness. She had already filed for divorce, and, not surprisingly, Helene Blanc was going to represent her. Max almost felt sorry for Vincent. He would not relish being on the wrong side of Maître Blanc.

Once Claire had stepped back from the case, a new magistrate had been appointed to oversee the entire investigation—a dour Parisian investigator anxious to get out of Provence and back to city life. He had brought everything to a quick conclusion based on the good work that had come before. With Max's assistance, Helene had convinced him of the unlikelihood of convicting Jeremy Nash for the murder of Biljana Markovic. Being a savvy political operator who understood the ramifications of a failed prosecution, he dropped the murder charges, content to pursue Nash on other matters. Given the video evidence, Max was sure Nash would cut a deal to avoid a very long prison sentence.

Vincent, too, had a trial date set, but with his affluence and power, Max and Claire feared that he would somehow escape the charges, or get off with a slap on the wrist. Nevertheless, with his position as a former French minister and Claire's role as a British *juge d'instruction*, it was apparent that an international media circus was just around the corner.

Claire was planning to leave France when the case came to court, possibly to stay with Samantha in London. Max felt that was wise, although he was sorry to lose his friend, even temporarily. He was desolated for her and for her children. He well remembered the invasive and distressing press coverage of Emma's death and the detrimental effect it had on Luke—his main reason for escaping to France.

His thoughts turned momentarily inward to that kiss. Emma was irreplaceable, and her profound absence followed him everywhere, but he knew she would want him to move on, for Luke's sake as well as his own. He had never dreamed he would find anyone else, but Sam was not like finding someone new. They had history, and perhaps their time had finally come.

He wished she was sitting there tonight, breathing in the honeysuckle-like fragrance of the bougainvillea that draped the trellis surrounding the patio. Both he and Claire could use another friend.

At the far end of the table sat another foursome. Wearing a crisp pink polo and tailored golf shorts in contrast to his usual conservative business attire, Capitaine Jacques sat swirling a crystal tumbler of bourbon, cooling and diluting it with clinking cubes of ice. He seemed relaxed and even happy.

"What's with the captain?" Max murmured in Claire's ear. "He looks like he's actually enjoying himself. And he was even genial to me on arrival."

"Ah," Claire whispered back. "There is a rumor that the powers that be are very happy with the way things have turned out. He is widely believed to have brought to justice a large segment of the Brise de Sang and to have shut down a major transcontinental drug and human trafficking operation. A transfer back to Paris is very much on the cards."

"That could be good for the lieutenant, I suppose."

They gazed at Dupre, who sat opposite his boss, joking and laughing with Madeleine. Neatly groomed in his clean white shirt and pressed khakis, he bore little resemblance to the sloppy detective Max had first met. Madeleine was exerting her influence, and it seemed that good things were in store for Dupre.

And then there was Arielle, looking radiant in her usual effortless way and deep in conversation about gaming with Luke and Yousef, who stared into her pretty face with rapt attention. Dickens was tethered to Luke's chair to keep him from greeting every customer in the place, but many stopped by to stroke the excited puppy.

They were all celebrating. In exchange for partial immunity, Michel Briancon had revealed the secrets they needed to bring down the local chapter of the Brise de Sang. He had identified the Brise's man inside the Gendarmes. While shocking, Jacques had been thrilled that Armand de Silva was not a policeman in his command and secretly pleased by the discomfort it caused his macho gendarme rival, Commandant Fournier. Arielle's work in the cloud and the Brdo connection suggested by Max had provided enough information on the Serbian gang at the other end of the trafficking pipeline to shut that operation down. The Serbian police were very grateful.

The cloud also revealed that Markovic had steadfastly refused to sell out her real estate holdings to certain Russian interests. It was widely believed that this was what had got her killed. They did not expect to ever bring an individual to justice for her murder. Months of evidence gathering and preparing the various cases for trial still lay ahead, but as it stood, the magistrate from Paris had concluded his investigation. For once, Jacques did not argue.

Claire took a sip of her wine. "And what about you two? Now that your time here is coming to an end?"

Max thought of Yousef and his parents, of the friendships Luke had formed. He thought of the apartment where they lived, of the new couple who had come to stay next door. They were Parisian and paid little to no attention to Max and Luke—something Max could easily live with. He thought of Beatrice, who still smiled at him at the co-op, of Madame Hojberg, who still swam naked every morning, and of Sophie Duclos, who still jostled to serve him his morning croissants. He thought of football and cycling with Claude.

"Well," said Max, looking at Luke, who was using bread to mop up the sauce on his plate. "We were supposed to return to the States for school in September. But Luke has settled so well here, and I still have a book to finish. And ..." he paused for dramatic effect, "just this morning we received an invitation for Luke to try out for the Marseille Academy."

"What!" Luke spluttered, spraying flecks of bread across the table. "You didn't tell me that."

"I think Mr. Cantona may have had something to do with that!" Max said, giving his son a wink.

"Yes!" crowed Luke, punching the air.

Claire beamed. "That's awesome. Well done, Luke."

"Bravo," declared Dupre from the other end of the table.

Arielle grinned mischievously. "You know Louis here played for Marseille, Luke."

"Mais non," Dupre's shoulders sagged. "I cannot believe you told everyone that."

Madeleine stared at him in astonishment. Then she narrowed her eyes and said in a severe voice. "And what else are you keeping from me, Louis Dupre?"

She whacked him on the arm. The laughter around the table drowned out his response.

"So anyway," said Max, "in answer to your question, we are looking into the possibility of extending our stay."

"We are?" said Luke. "Cool. And Pop-Pop and Grandma will come visit if we stay, right? Now that Pop-Pop's feeling so much better."

"Yes, said Max. "I've already invited them to come over for the wine harvest next month."

"You know," Claire said, almost as an afterthought, "France is so much closer to England. You know Sam hates spending Christmas on her own in London." She watched Max's face fall. "Too soon?"

He gave her a sad smile. "I think it will always be too soon, but it's always good to see an old friend. However, Luke and I already have plans this Christmas."

"You have?" said Claire.

"The Netherlands!" said Luke through a mouthful of bread. "We're going to visit our friends Hans and Angela. I can't wait!"

Momentarily Max's thoughts turned inwards. Christmas with a murderer? But Luke was so psyched to visit them. How could he have explained to Luke his refusal to accept Angela's imploring offer? His paramount concern was Luke's happiness and so he pushed aside his own misgivings. Besides, who was he to judge? He knew in his darkest moments that given the opportunity... He caught Claire eyeing him askance, as if she could read his thoughts. Or was she wondering if he was just avoiding Sam? A small part of him admitted that perhaps he was. He shrugged, giving her his best attempt at an expression of innocence. "Yes. I hear they do a hell of a Christmas in Holland."

Graeme Chambers is a UK/US lawyer who lives in Chadds Ford, Pennsylvania with his wife (very much alive and well) and youngest son. He returns to Provence whenever possible.